Praise for the first Gilded Age Mystery

Still Life with Murder

"What a thoroughly charming book! A beautiful combination of entertaining characters, minute historical research, and a powerful evocation of time and place. I'm very glad there will be more to come."

—*New York Times* bestselling author Barbara Hambly

"Utterly absorbing. Vividly alive characters in a setting so clearly portrayed that one could step right into it."

—Roberta Gellis

"*Still Life with Murder* is a skillfully written story of intrigue and murder. Nell Sweeney is a winning heroine gifted with common sense, grit and an underlying poignancy. Readers will speed through this tale and be clamoring for more."

—Earlene Fowler,
bestselling author of *Steps to the Altar* and *Sunshine and Shadow*

"P. B. Ryan captures an authentic flavor of post–Civil War Boston as she explores that city's dark underbelly and the lingering after-effects of the war. The atmosphere is that of *The Alienist*, but feisty Irish nursemaid Nell Sweeney is a more likeable protagonist. I look forward to seeing her in action again."

—Rhys Bowen

"P. B. Ryan makes a stunning debut with *Still Life with Murder* bringing nineteenth-century Boston alive, and populating it with a vivid and memorable cast of characters. The fascinating heroine, Nell Sweeney, immediately engages the reader and I couldn't put the book down until I discovered the truth along with her. I can't wait for the next installment."

—Victoria Thompson,
author of *Murder on Mulberry Street*

Prime Crime Titles by P. B. Ryan

STILL LIFE WITH MURDER

MURDER IN A MILL TOWN

MURDER IN A MILL TOWN

P. B. RYAN

BERKLEY PRIME CRIME, NEW YORK

MURDER IN A MILL TOWN

A Berkley Prime Crime Book / published by arrangement with the author

PRINTING HISTORY
Berkley Prime Crime edition / July 2004

Cover design by Rita Frangie.
Cover illustration by Mary Ann Lasher.
Interior text design by Kristin del Rosario.

For information address: The Berkley Publishing Group,
a division of Penguin Group (USA) Inc.,
375 Hudson Street, New York, New York 10014.

ISBN: 0-425-19715-8

Berkley Prime Crime Books are published by
The Berkley Publishing Group,
a division of Penguin Group (USA) Inc.,
375 Hudson Street, New York, New York 10014.

PRINTED IN THE UNITED STATES OF AMERICA

10 9 8 7 6 5 4 3 2 1

For my daughter Leigh,
a constant source of
joy and inspiration.

Heaven and hell suppose two distinct species of men,
the good and the bad. But the greatest part
of mankind float betwixt vice and virtue.

—DAVID HUME

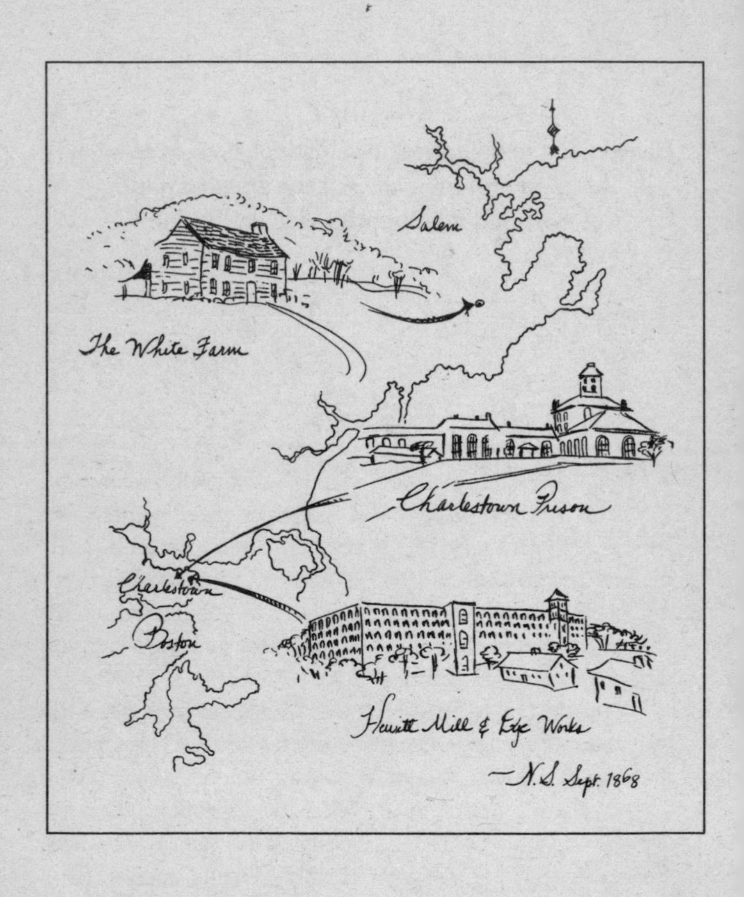

Salem
The White Farm
Charlestown Prison
Charlestown
Boston
Hewitt Mill & Edge Works
—N.S. Sept. 1868

Chapter 1

September 1868: Boston

"WE quarreled last March," said Nell Sweeney in a manfully deep, working-class English accent—or rather her best attempt at one—embellished with just the slightest quaver of lunacy. Reaching up to prevent her colossal papier-mâché top hat from sliding off her head, she added, "Just before he went mad, you know. It was at the great—"

"Point! Point!" Gracie Hewitt sprang up from her little gilt chair at the head of the nursery tea table. "You s'posed to point at the March Hare with your spoon."

"Oh, yes." How could Nell have forgotten, after the scores of times she'd been obliged to read aloud—and, more recently, perform—Gracie's favorite scenes from *Alice's Adventures in Wonderland.* She lifted the dainty silver spoon from its place next to her miniature gold-rimmed, bone-china teacup. "Have a seat, then, like a proper young lady, and I shall continue."

The little girl sat back down, fluffing up her white pinafore. A copy of that worn by Alice in Mr. Tenniel's illustrations, it was Gracie's first sewing project, crafted with Nell's guidance but entirely by her own plump little four-year-old hands. The stitches were wide-spaced and irregular, the tucking disastrous, the hem puckered. Gracie, bless her heart, wore it with as much unalloyed pleasure as if it were from the House of Worth.

"We quarreled last March—just before *he* went mad, you know." Nell aimed her teaspoon across the table at Albert, the lovingly tattered stuffed rabbit who'd been cast as the March Hare in this morning's production. She stole a glance at the book, wedged open by the teapot, to confirm the wording of the next bit. "It was at the great concert given by the Queen of Hearts, and I had to sing"—she cleared her voice dramatically—" 'Twinkle, twinkle, little bat. How I wonder what you're at.' You know the song, perhaps?"

"I've heard something like it." Not only had Gracie committed her lines to memory, but she spoke them with a subtle, and remarkably credible, upper-crust British inflection—a spot-on imitation of her beloved "Nana," Viola Hewitt. The effect was uncanny, putting Nell in mind not so much of Viola, but of Viola's eldest son, William. Same inky hair, same watchful eyes and knowing little smile . . . And when she spoke with that accent—milder than that of Will, who'd been brought up and educated in England, but close enough—it sent shivers up Nell's spine.

I'll be seeing you, Nell, he'd told her that day in Mount Auburn Cemetery just before he'd turned and walked away into the cold morning sunshine. That was five months ago—and of course she hadn't seen him. The circumstances that had thrown them together for those few weeks last winter had been extraordinary. She couldn't imagine a situation in which their paths were likely to cross again. Dr. William Hewitt, his medical degree notwithstanding, was a professional gambler and dope fiend. For all Nell knew, he'd dissolved like a wisp of opium smoke into the back alleys of Shanghai, never to be seen again.

That prospect filled her with a curious fusion of despair and relief. She should be glad to be quit of him, adept as he was at scratching open her deeply buried past. She should thank God he was gone and pray that he never returned.

She should.

"Miseeney!" Little hands slapped impatiently at the damask tablecloth as Gracie bobbed up and down in her seat. "You got to finish the song, so I can say my line." Her favorite line, she meant. "I said, 'I've heard something like it.' Now you say—"

"Yes, I know." Resuming her Mad Hatter voice, Nell said, "It goes on, you know, in this way. 'Up above the world you fly, Like a tea-tray—"

A knock on the nursery door made them both start: two loud raps, bony knuckles striking oak with staccato force—*once! twice!*—followed by a reverberating silence.

Gracie pulled a face. Even she recognized the distinctive door-knock of Mrs. Mott, the aging housekeeper who governed the Hewitts' Tremont Street mansion with despotic zeal—although her visits to the third-floor nursery were blessedly few and far between.

Nell reached up to remove her Mad Hatter headgear, hesitated, and merely tilted it to a rakish angle, causing Gracie to gasp in delighted anticipation of Mrs. Mott's reaction to such deviltry. It was a ridiculously tall hat with a flared crown in the continental style, very similar to that in the Tenniel illustrations, right down to the price tag reading *In this Style 10/6*. Nell and Gracie had made it together one blissfully rainy afternoon, out of flour paste, rabbit wire, blue and yellow paint, and a torn-up copy of the *Daily Advertiser*.

Nell opened the door with a flourish, gripping the hat's brim to keep it from falling off. "Mrs. Mott. What a rare pleasure. Do come in."

The black-clad housekeeper stood unmoving in the doorway, her mouth as pale and tight as an old knife scar as she took in Nell's headwear. Looking away with an ostentatious lack of expression, she said, "Your presence is required in the Red Room." *Your presence is required*, not *Mrs. Hewitt asks if you wouldn't please join her in the Red Room,* which Nell was quite sure was how her employer had worded it.

"I'll be down shortly."

"Immediately, if you please." The wording nettled Nell, implying as it did that Mrs. Mott had the right to issue her orders. As Gracie's governess—and Viola's de facto companion—Nell was neither servant nor gentlewoman, but that most rare and singular of creatures, a respectable working woman. She answered not to Mrs. Mott, like the rank-and-file household staff, but to Viola Hewitt, who accorded her a refreshing autonomy in the exercise of her duties.

Mrs. Mott surveyed the nursery as she did every room she entered, with a mechanically smooth swivel of her head reminiscent of a hawk scanning the terrain in search of something on which to pounce. It was a large room, decorated by Gracie's indulgent Nana to resemble a sitting room at Versailles, with an ornately carved, cherub-adorned ceiling, etched mirrors in gilt frames, and acres of gleaming floral damask in shades of ivory, shell pink, and sea green. Nell knew precisely what the grim old lady was thinking as she took in this frothy opulence: All this for a housemaid's unwanted bastard.

When Viola Hewitt made the decision four years ago to rear the newborn Gracie as her own, she'd had to fend off disapproval on every front. No one, however, had been more appalled than Evelyn Mott. The third generation of her family to serve the Hewitts, she prostrated herself at the altar of good breeding and its ancillary virtue, proper comportment. She suffered no deviations from propriety on the part of her household staff, and had become, by all accounts, apoplectic upon discovering that the maid Annie MacIntyre was with child; for, although Annie was married, her husband had been at war when Gracie was conceived. Viola's intervention, much resented by Mrs. Mott, had saved Annie's reputation and livelihood; she worked for the Astors in New York now, as did her husband. More important, it had kept Gracie from ending up in the county poorhouse, where, as Nell knew all too well, she would have been lucky to survive to her first birthday.

Mrs. Mott concluded her inspection by peering through her diminutive spectacles at the little girl whose existence so tainted her carefully regulated domain. Did she know who had actually fathered Gracie? The child's resemblance to Will grew stronger day by day—especially now that she was beginning to sprout so; she was as tall as some of the six- and seven-year-olds with whom she played every afternoon in the Common and Public Gardens. Mrs. Mott must at least suspect the truth, that Viola had adopted Gracie in part because the child had been fathered by her own son. Not that this would lessen the housekeeper's distaste for the little interloper. Quite the opposite, given how Mrs. Mott felt about Will.

"You should instruct the child not to stare at her elders," said Mrs. Mott. Before Nell could point out, probably unwisely, that Gracie was only staring *back*, the housekeeper said, "And you might dress her in something presentable before bringing her down. Mrs. Hewitt has callers."

Gracie, frowning in confusion, inspected her lovingly ill-made pinafore. With any luck, she wouldn't understand the comment—and wouldn't make Nell explain.

Nell didn't bother asking what she was supposed to have done with Gracie other than bring her down, since it was her job to look after her, and she wasn't about to leave her unattended. Miss Edna Parrish, the octogenarian nursemaid who'd cared for both Viola and her four boys, often helped with Gracie when Nell had other business to attend to, but she preferred to devote her mornings to needlework and her Bible.

"Who are the callers?" Nell asked.

"A male and a female. Common types, rather ill turned out. Irish, from the sound of them. It occurred to me they might be relations of yours—your parents, perhaps."

"My parents are deceased." Her mother was, at any rate, and her father may as well be. "I've no one else."

"Don't you?" Mrs. Mott said knowingly.

That caught Nell off guard. She groped for a response, thinking, *Don't let her know about Duncan. Anything but that.*

The housekeeper let a few long seconds pass, as if hoping Nell would fill in the silence with some intriguing disclosure, but Nell had learned that little trick, and kept mum.

"I thought Mrs. Hewitt had mentioned a brother," Mrs. Mott said. "Or did I mishear?"

Nell let out her pent-up breath as silently as she could. "Yes. I mean, no, you didn't mishear. I have a brother,

Jamie. James. Or had—I haven't seen him in years. Why would you think the visitors are related to me? There are thousands of Irish in Boston."

"I daresay." Mrs. Mott's nose twitched, as if she'd just caught a whiff of something putrid. "But not many who'd have the cheek to walk right up to the front door of a house like this, instead of round the back. Fewer still who'd manage to get themselves served tea in the Red Room." Turning, she said, "Don't dawdle."

"What does that mean—pwesentable?" Gracie asked after the housekeeper had left. "Does it mean like a pwesent?"

"Something like that," Nell hedged. "I think she meant you ought to wear a fancier frock. But your pinafore is so very pretty, and Nana loves it. Best you stay as you are, I think."

That seemed to please Gracie, who stood and let Nell tidy her plaited hair so she'd look pretty for Viola. Buffing her right shoe against her stockinged left leg, the child said, "Doesn't Mrs. Mott know my name?"

"Yes." Nell licked her fingertips to smooth down the stubborn little stray tendrils.

"Then why does she always call me 'The Child'?"

For the same reason she called Nell "The Sweeney Girl," and Gabrielle Bouchard, Mrs. Hewitt's nurse, "The Negress." To ignore a person's name was to ignore—or deny—her very humanity. "She's old," Nell told Gracie as she retied her blue hair ribbon. "Old people forget things."

"You're old, and you don't forget things."

"I'm twenty-six. Mrs. Mott is. . ." Twice as old? Three times? "Much older."

"No, no!" Gracie protested when Nell started to take off the ridiculous hat. "We not done."

"Buttercup, Nana is downstairs waiting for—"

"Just til my line," Gracie pleaded, reseating herself at the table.

"Oh, all right. Let's see . . ." Adjusting her hat, she sat down and sang, "Up above the world you fly, like a tea-tray in the sky."

Gracie lifted the Dormouse, played by a little mouse-shaped cast-iron doorstop on the chair next to her, and made it move around a bit while making yawning sounds. In a squeaky mouse voice, she said, "Twinkle, twinkle, twinkle, twinkle . . ."

"Well, I'd hardly finished the first verse," Nell continued, "when the Queen jumped up and bawled out, 'He's murdering the time! Off with his head!' "

Here came Gracie's favorite line, delivered with a sniffy dispassion that would have done the most venerable Brahmin matron proud: "How dweadfully savage."

VIOLA'S private withdrawing room in the Hewitt home—an imposing mansion on Tremont Street's "Colonnade Row" section, facing Boston Common—was an Oriental-inspired haven furnished with exotic antiques and silken hangings in shades of vermilion, magenta, and cinnabar. The south wall was dominated by an immense seventeenth-century Japanese screen depicting a hawk in the snow against a sky of brilliantly burnished gold leaf. Before this wall, on the majestically carved Japanese chair that Nell called the "Lion Chair" and Gracie the "Thwone," sat Viola Lindleigh Hewitt.

A tall, angular lady with lightly silvered black hair, Viola was the kind of female often described as "handsome." She had on her bronze silk day dress this morning—sans crinoline, as always—ornamented with two armloads of bone and ivory bracelets. From the ease with which she reclined in the regal chair, one would never guess that her legs were all but useless, having withered away following a bout of infantile paralysis ten years ago. The only hint as to her infirmity would be the two ivory-handled folding canes hooked to the back of the chair.

"Nana!" Gracie squealed as Nell led her into the room. She launched herself—and the horde of dolls she'd hauled along to play with—onto Viola's lap for the warm hug she knew she could always count on.

Across the room sat a middle-aged couple, their humble attire a striking contrast to the lush velvet couch on which they sat. What Nell could see of the woman's hair beneath her shabby bonnet was like wiry steel that had been left out in the rain to rust. Her nose was ruddy, her eyes red-rimmed. In her hand she clutched a damp lavender handkerchief that Nell recognized as Viola's.

The woman nudged the man, causing the tea in his cup to slosh onto the saucer. He shot her a look. She glanced at Nell and jerked her chin upward, whereupon he hauled himself to his feet, ducking his head in an unpracticed attempt at a bow. Black Irish he was, with pockmarked cheeks and outsized ears. Nell acknowledged the gesture with a nod and a reassuring smile. He glanced at his wife—there was no mistaking that this was a married couple—who motioned him back down.

"What a darlin' little girl," praised the woman. There was just a whisper of Ireland in her voice, an age-softened but unmistakable lilt. "Your granddaughter, ma'am?"

"I adopted her, actually," Viola replied in her pleasantly sandy, British-accented voice. A deliberately misleading answer, of course, since Gracie really was her granddaughter. "Always did want a little girl—four sons will do that to you—and then, just when I'd accepted that I'd never have one, along came Gracie. One of the happiest days of my life."

"Ah." The woman's uncertain smile betrayed her surprise that a lady of Viola Hewitt's position would adopt a child; bloodlines meant everything in Boston society.

Easing the child down from her lap and turning her to face her callers, Viola said, "Gracie, this is Mr. and Mrs. Fallon."

"How do you do?" said the child, who'd only recently overcome her shyness with strangers.

Mrs. Fallon displayed a mouthful of crooked teeth. "Why, ain't you a regular little doll. Knows her manners, she does."

"Thanks to Miss Sweeney." Viola gestured Nell into the armchair next to her. As she took her seat, Nell noticed Mrs. Fallon appraising her over the rim of her teacup. Nell's wardrobe, chosen and paid for by Viola, tended toward understated refinement, epitomized by today's fashionably sleek dove gray dress, the sole adornment for which was Nell's omnipresent gold pendant watch. Her auburn mane had been twisted this morning into a fat chignon secured by a pair of pearl-tipped hair picks—a gift from Viola for her birthday last month.

Mrs. Fallon looked as if she didn't know quite what to make of a girl with an Irish surname who dressed so elegantly and held a position traditionally held by patrician young women from good families—meaning rich and Protestant—who'd found themselves in reduced circumstances. It was a look Nell was accustomed to; she'd learned to find it amusing.

"Mrs. Fallon," Viola said as Gracie settled down at her

feet, fiddling with her dolls, "why don't you tell Nell what you've just told me."

The Fallons stared at Nell, clearly as baffled as she as to why Viola had summoned her. "It's our girl," Mrs. Fallon said. "Our daughter, Bridie. Well, Bridget, really, but we call her Bridie."

"*Her* daughter," Mr. Fallon interjected, with a nod toward his wife; his brogue was stronger than hers. "My stepdaughter."

In a low, strained voice, Mrs. Fallon said, "What godly difference does that make, Liam?"

He raised his hands in a placating gesture. "Just settin' things straight."

"*My* daughter, then. She turned up missing three days ago—Sunday it was. The coppers think she run off with her fella, but I know her better than that. She wouldn't never just up and leave like that—never."

Her husband cocked a skeptical eyebrow. Nell glanced at Gracie to see how much of this she was absorbing, but she seemed to be intent on trying to force a miniature baby bottle into the mouth of her favorite doll.

Mrs. Fallon slid a hard glance in her husband's direction before continuing. "The cops, they won't do nothin', so we went to Mr. Harry, thinking they'd be sure to help if he told 'em to, but he said it wasn't none of his concern."

Harry? Nell aimed a quizzical look at Viola. Harry Hewitt was the second eldest of her three remaining sons. The youngest, Martin, the last to still live at home, was pursuing his Masters in Divinity at Harvard University. Next oldest was the late Robbie, who died four years ago at the notorious Andersonville prison camp in Georgia. Viola's eldest, Will, the black sheep, had been missing since his own stint at Andersonville, except for those brief weeks last winter when he resurfaced with a murder charge hanging over his head.

That left Harry, the wildly profligate middle son, to help run—if only nominally—his father's two hugely lucrative businesses: Hewitt Shipping, and Hewitt Mill and Dye Works. Harry served as general manager of the latter, an enormous textile factory just across the river to the north in Charlestown. In fact, he was more or less a figurehead; Nell would have been surprised if he knew any more about dying and weaving than she did. His father, August Hewitt, governed the more complex and demanding shipping concern.

"Mr. and Mrs. Fallon live in Charlestown, and Bridie works at the mill," Viola explained. "That was why they thought Harry might be able to help."

Able? Probably. Willing? Harry Hewitt only cared about Harry Hewitt. By his own admission, there was little in life he deemed worthy of effort aside from the pursuit of simple animal gratification. *Once one has absorbed that essential truth,* he told her last winter, when they were still on speaking terms, *it's actually quite liberating. The rules that keep others on a short leash don't exist for you—as they shouldn't, because they're arbitrary and suffocating, most of them. Everything becomes possible. Nothing is taboo.*

"We went to Mr. Harry's office at the mill," Mrs. Fallon said, "but like I said, he didn't see where it was none of his business. He said if the cops thought she run off with Virgil, she probably did."

Nell said, "Virgil . . . ?"

"Hines." Mrs. Fallon grimaced. "A handsome enough brute, but a right bad egg. Got out of prison last May, and by the end of the month, him and my Bridie was stuck together like they'd been glued. Can't imagine what she seen in him."

"The state prison in Charlestown?" Nell asked.

Mrs. Fallon nodded. Her husband said, "It's just down the road from the mill there."

"Why do you ask?" Viola wanted to know.

Because that's where Duncan is. Nell smoothed her skirts, hearing Duncan's most recent letter to her, the one that came last Friday when she was wearing this same dress, crackle in her pocket. "No particular reason."

"Don't see how you can call him handsome," said Mr. Hines, "what with them stars on his forehead."

"Stars?" Nell asked.

"He was in the Navy during the war," Mrs. Fallon explained. "Got one of them, what do you call 'em, where they prick a pitcher into your skin."

"A tattoo," Viola said. "Seamen like to get them."

"Yes, I know, on their arms," Nell said. "But the *forehead*?"

Mrs. Fallon shrugged. "Like I says, I got no idea what she seen in him."

"How old is she?" Nell asked.

"Twenty-one."

"And she lives with you?"

Mrs. Fallon said "Yes," Mr. Fallon "No."

Nell cocked her head, as if to ask, *Which is it?*

Darting a look at her husband, Mrs. Fallon said, "She did live in Boston for a while—the North End—but she's been back home all summer."

"Because of Mr. Hines?" Nell asked. "To be near him?"

"I reckon," Mrs. Fallon answered after a short pause.

Nell said, "I assume, Mrs. Fallon, that if the police believe your daughter ran off with Mr. Hines, that he's gone, too."

"No one's seen him round Charlestown the past few days," Mrs. Fallon replied, "but that don't mean Bridie run off with him—least, not of her own accord. She's a good girl, she is. Deep down."

That met with a dubious little grunt from Liam Fallon. Ignoring it—or too distressed to notice—his wife said, "My Bridie, she's got the prettiest red hair you ever seen—shines like heaven itself when the sun hits it just right. Big green eyes, pink cheeks . . . If something's happened to her . . ." She lowered her head, dabbing her face with the wadded-up handkerchief, her shoulders shaking.

Her husband plucked a tea sandwich from the stack on the table in front of him and pried it open, critically examining its contents.

Just as Nell was about to rise from her chair to go comfort the poor woman, Gracie said, "Why you cwyin'?" She crossed to Mrs. Fallon, baby doll in tow. "It's all wight," she soothed. "Don't cwy. Here, you want to hold Hortense?"

She offered the doll to the weeping woman, who accepted it in that instinctively maternal way some women had, automatically supporting its little head as she held it to her shoulder. "This is just how my Bridie felt," she said tremulously, "when she was little like this, all heavy and soft. My other babes, they was all sickly. Wasn't none of 'em lived very long. But that Bridie, she was as hale and hearty as they come."

"Good girl," Nell mouthed to Gracie as the child settled back down with her other dolls.

"When the Fallons realized Harry wasn't going to help

them," Viola told Nell, "they decided to go to Mr. Hewitt himself."

"We went down to that building near India Wharf where he has his office," Mrs. Fallon said as she patted the doll's back, "but he wouldn't see us. Sent some fella out to swat us away. Fella said if Mr. Harry didn't think there was nothin' to be done, then there was nothin' to be done. I asked him what Mr. Hewitt would do if it was *his* child that disappeared, but he said I was bein' . . . somethin' . . ."

"Important," her husband offered through a mouthful of food.

"Impertinent?" Viola ventured.

"That's it. He walked us out of the building and told us not to come back."

"How dweadfully savage," Gracie said.

All eyes turned to her.

"Come here, buttercup." Gracie climbed onto the lap of her governess, who whispered into her ear, "It *is* dreadfully savage, but you must remember not to speak when the adults are having a conversation."

"Mrs. Fallon thought if she came here," Viola said, "and appealed to me as a mother, that she might find a more sympathetic ear."

And, clearly, she had.

"Have you asked your daughter's friends and associates if they know where she might be?" Nell inquired.

Mrs. Fallon nodded as she stroked the doll's back. "I musta talked to everyone in Charlestown, or tried to. Some of 'em, like them girls she worked with at the mill, they wouldn't give me the time of day. Others, they'd talk, but there wasn't much they could tell me. One day Bridie's there, the next day she ain't. She just up and disappeared.

Went off to work Saturday mornin' and just never come home."

"Saturday?" Nell said. "I thought you said she disappeared Sunday."

"Ah." Spots of pink blossomed on Mrs. Fallon's cheeks. "Fact is, she, uh, well . . ."

"She didn't never come home on Saturday nights," her husband said. "That Virgil, he'd meet her at work and them two would head off somewheres to . . . well . . ."

"I see," Nell said. "But she usually returns the following day?"

"Every Sunday evenin' by six o'clock," Mrs. Fallon said, "on account of that's when Virgil has to have Ollie Fuller's cart back to him."

"Ollie's a coal dealer up in Charlestown," her husband explained, "but he don't work on the Sabbath, so he lets Virgil rent his cart from sundown on Saturday to sundown on Sunday."

"Where do they go in the cart?" Nell asked.

Mrs. Fallon shook her head. "She didn't like to talk to me about it. She knew how I felt. Father Dunne at Immaculate Conception keeps askin' why she ain't in church on Sundays. What am I supposed to tell him?"

"I still say Jimmy might know somethin' about all this," Mr. Fallon told his wife. "If you really want to find her, you'll ask—"

"I said I'd do the talkin'," she muttered. "Didn't I say I'd do the talkin'?"

"Jimmy?" Nell asked.

"He isn't important," Mrs. Fallon answered quickly.

"He's Bridie's husband," Mr. Fallon said.

Chapter 2

MRS. Fallon glared at her husband, her blush deepening to a livid, blotchy stain.

"Ah," said Viola.

"Curiouser and curiouser," Gracie said.

Oh, dear. Nell and Viola exchanged a look.

"I should think Gracie would be happier playing somewhere else right now," Viola said. "Perhaps we can ask Miss Parrish to—"

"No!" Gracie wrapped her arms around Nell's neck and clung tightly. "Don't want Miss Pawish. Want Miseeney."

"Speaking of naps," Nell said, "isn't it about time Hortense went down for hers?"

"No, no, not yet," Gracie protested. She usually tucked the doll into her cradle when their midmorning snack was delivered to the nursery.

"Close enough." Setting the little girl on her feet, Nell

said, "I wonder if Mrs. Fallon would like to help you put her down."

Mrs. Fallon, still cuddling the doll as if she were her own baby Bridie, hesitated for a moment, then smiled. "Why, yes, I . . . I'd be happy to. More than happy," she added with a look of gratitude that gave Nell a pinch of guilt, seeing as this was really just a ruse to get her out of the room.

The novelty of sharing this task with someone new evidently appealed to Gracie, who promptly took Mrs. Fallon's hand and led her away.

"So," Nell said as Mr. Fallon sorted through the tray of sandwiches, "it would appear as though your stepdaughter has one too many men in her life."

He snorted in affirmation as he plucked a sandwich from the pile. "She was paintin' on the lip rouge when she was still in short skirts, that one. Weren't no better than she ought to be, right from the get-go."

Weren't? "Do you think she's dead?"

He chewed and swallowed, then started rummaging through the stack again. "A girl like that never comes to no good, that's all I'm sayin'."

"Tell me about her husband," Nell said. Viola followed the interrogation quietly, content to let Nell conduct it as she saw fit—clearly her purpose in having called her down. Often since last winter, when Nell had helped to clear Will of the murder charge against him, Viola had praised her governess's "penetrating mind."

"He's a deep-sea fisherman, gone for weeks, months at a time. They been hitched about a year. God knows what he was thinkin', marrying a jade like Bridie. She was the kind that needs a keeper." Stuffing the sandwich into his mouth, he added, "*Is* the kind," as an afterthought.

"Jimmy, is it?"

"Sullivan. Jimmy Sullivan. My wife thinks he walks on water, but he ain't no saint, let me tell you that. He's got a short fuse, that Jimmy Sullivan, and he's a bruiser. Makes a pretty penny fightin' other bruisers bare-knuckled when he's in town."

"Has he ever taken those fists to Bridie?" Nell asked.

"Once or twice, when she was beggin' for it—makin' eyes at other men, comin' home drunk . . . What man wouldn't, with baggage like that to keep in line? Even my wife told Bridie it was her own fault. Tried to make her stop slippin' around on Jimmy while he was off fishing. Said adultery was a sin, said she ought to know better."

"Did Jimmy know she was unfaithful?"

"He suspected, on account of the whispers, and seein' how she acted with other men. She always denied it, though, and a pretty wench has a way of makin' a man believe what she wants him to believe. But he was away more than he was home, and when the cat's away . . ."

"So there were other men besides Mr. Hines?"

"Oh, she gave it away pretty free, least til Virgil come along at the end of May. I never knew their names, them others, but all summer it's been 'Virgil this' and 'Virgil that.' "

"When did she move back home?"

"June. Jimmy come home a few days early and caught the two of 'em in the act. Gave Bridie a black eye, but he didn't lay a hand on Virgil. Told him he knew it was all Bridie's doin', that she was like a bitch in heat, and . . . Oh, sorry," he mumbled, looking back and forth between Nell and Viola.

"We're both quite unshockable," Viola said, with a little smile in Nell's direction.

"So he just let Mr. Hines go?" Nell asked.

Mr. Fallon nodded. "Said there wasn't a man alive could resist a hot little piece like Bridie when she was shovin' her . . . uh, self in his face, so Jimmy didn't blame Virgil one bit. Said Virgil'd get off without a beatin' long as he took Bridie out of there and kept her away for good. Told him if he was smart, he'd learn to keep her in line with his fists, 'cause it was all she understood."

"Did Mr. Hines take that advice, do you know?" Nell asked.

He shook his head. "She's been livin' with us since June, and I ain't seen no fresh bruises, but could be he's the type to just hold it all in til he can't take it no more."

Or the type to hit her where it wouldn't show, Nell thought.

"If them two run off together," Fallon continued, "and she makes a fool out of him like she done with Jimmy, no tellin' what might happen."

Reaching for another sandwich, he added, "Or already has."

"I feel sorry for her," Viola said after the Fallons had left.

"Mrs. Fallon?"

She nodded. "And Bridie, too. It's easy to label someone a fallen woman, and dismiss her as worthless, but these things are—"

"Complicated?" Nell finished with a smile. It was a familiar refrain from Viola, for whom life wasn't sketched in black and white, but rather painted up layer by layer from a palette of infinite hues and shades. And, too, hadn't Mr. Hewitt saved her from her own youthful indiscretion by marrying her after she became pregnant, by another man, with Will? Like Nell, Viola Hewitt knew all too well the many factors that could tempt a female into sin . . . just as she knew the repercussions, despite having been spared them herself.

Viola said, "I have a favor to ask of you."

Nell sighed.

"If I could look into this myself," Viola said, "I would. But with these pointless legs of mine . . ."

"Mrs. Hewitt—"

"You were such a help to me last winter, after Will was arrested. I know you can find out what became of Bridie. You've got a way about you. People trust you. They tell you things. And you're so savvy, so perceptive."

"I did a great deal of stumbling about and backtracking last winter," Nell said. "I drew more wrong conclusions than you know." *You infer too much,* Will used to say. *Far too many facile assumptions.* And he was right.

"Harry won't help," Viola said. "Mr. Hewitt won't help. That poor woman has no one to turn to but me. And I have no one to turn to but you."

"I've got Gracie to look after."

"She'll sleep til three or three-thirty, and then Miss Parrish can watch her."

"You mean you want me to do this right now? Today?"

"In a situation like this, time is of the essence. I'll have Brady drive you up to Charlestown in the brougham so you don't have to bother with a hackney. And I'll give you a letter introducing you and asking for cooperation and so forth. That might help smooth the way a bit." A classic Viola Hewitt understatement. She was one of the two or three most eminent ladies of Boston, a renowned philanthropist and the matriarch of one of its oldest families. Her name opened doors all over the city.

Nell studied the pattern on the Oriental carpet, reflecting on all Viola Hewitt had given her in the past four years, the most precious of which was Gracie. Looking up, she met Viola's benevolent gaze. "You know I can't refuse you anything."

"Thank you, my dear." Reaching across the space that separated them, she squeezed Nell's hand. "You're not just my legs, you know. You're the daughter I never had, even more so than Gracie. I don't know what I'd do without you."

Chapter 3

"THIS here's the weaving room," said the young mill girl who'd agreed to guide Nell to Bridie Sullivan's former workstation, hollering to be heard above the mechanical din that filled the Hewitt woolen factory.

To call such a cavernous space a room was like calling Boston Harbor a little inlet. High-ceilinged and about a hundred yards long, it occupied the entire third floor of this huge stone edifice. Hundreds of power looms whirred and clacked and rumbled as scores of young women—some of them little more than girls—trotted up and down the aisles, tending them. Midday sunshine flooded the vast white-washed space through banks of tall windows, their glass frosted lest the workers be distracted by the view of the stream that had powered this mill before Mr. Hewitt replaced water power with steam.

"Bridie, she worked on them machines over there, with

Ruth and Evie." The girl pointed to two young women struggling together to adjust the leather belt connecting a loom to the line shaft overhead. One was tall, sturdily buxom, and brown-haired; the other plain and petite, with sallow skin and thin cornsilk hair scraped back into a knot at her nape. Like the other mill girls, they wore aprons over their threadbare dresses, the skirts of which were hemmed short, displaying their shoeless feet and ankles.

"The tall one's Ruth," the girl yelled. "Ruth Watson. Little blonde is Evie Corbet."

"Do you think they'd talk to me?" Nell asked loudly.

"About Bridie?" The girl offered a doubtful little shrug. "If they do, they won't have nothin' nice to say, I'll tell you that. They never did take to her, and since she got herself sacked, them two been doin' the work of three."

"Sacked?" Nell asked. "Bridie was fired?"

"Sure, why do you think she ain't here no more?"

Nell wondered if Bridie's mother knew she'd lost her job, and decided she did. Mrs. Fallon hadn't wanted to tell Nell about Bridie's being married, probably because it would mark her as an adulteress. Most likely she'd wanted to withhold all unflattering information about her daughter, at least until Viola had agreed to help her.

"You might want to wait til Ruth and Evie ain't workin' to talk to 'em," the girl advised. "Foreman'll get mad. Maybe during the noon dinner break. It's comin' up presently."

Nell thanked the girl, pressed a half-dime into her hand, and went outside to wait.

HEWITT Mill and Dye Works was housed in a complex of buildings laid out at drearily precise right angles, ruining an otherwise bucolic setting. Anchoring the arrangement was the woolen factory, a colossal stone box surmounted by a disproportionately puny cupola. It was like a village unto itself, this compound, with its own store, its own church, and rows of brickboarding houses in which the mill girls lived.

Trees had been planted in soldier-straight lines punctuated by the occasional stone bench. Seating herself on the bench least likely to be seen from Harry Hewitt's office window beneath the cupola, Nell peeled off her black crocheted gloves, withdrew her little leatherbound sketchbook and mechanical pencil out of the chatelaine hanging from her belt and executed a swift drawing of the woolen factory.

At precisely twelve noon, a bell within the cupola started clanging. Within seconds, mill employees were streaming through the front door into the welcoming sunshine. Most of the females headed for the company boardinghouses, where their dinner presumably awaited them. A few lingered in the courtyard to chat with each other or flirt with the men.

Nell caught sight of Bridie's former co-workers, Ruth and Evie, talking to two other mill girls and a strapping young black-haired fellow. He whispered something to the tall brown-haired girl, Ruth, who looked around, then motioned for the others to follow her. Her little blonde friend hesitated a moment before giving in to their cajoling, and the furtive little group disappeared between two buildings.

Nell followed them through a patch of woods to a secluded stretch of riverbank, where the girls were lounging on the grass by the water, watching the young man roll a cigarette. He was coatless, his collarless shirt open, sleeves pushed up. All of the girls, except for Evie, had their skirts rucked up almost to their knees, an indiscretion that would have ruined them utterly and forever had they been Boston society daughters.

"You plannin' on sharin' that, Otis?" asked a pretty, plump young woman as she unbuttoned her snug collar.

Otis smiled at her as he ran his tongue along the cigarette paper and rubbed it down. "Sure, Mary, I'll give you a taste if you like." Leaning over, he slid the cigarette between her lips, withdrew a box of matches, and lit it. "I get a kiss for every puff, though."

That met with a flurry of giggles that tapered off as the girls noticed Nell walking toward them. They hastily tucked their legs beneath their skirts; Mary hid the cigarette behind her back. Nell had seen women smoking only twice before—an actress and a prostitute. It still struck her as bizarre.

"Good afternoon," Nell said as she joined them.

They exchanged looks. "Afternoon," Otis muttered.

"Is that cigarette smoke I smell?" Nell asked.

Mary was clearly trying to maintain a neutral expression, but her eyes betrayed her dread. Sanctimonious August Hewitt had established strict rules of conduct for the young women employed in his mill; smoking was no doubt cause for censure, if not outright dismissal.

"*I* was smoking," said the young man as he reached behind Mary to take the cigarette back. "She was just holding it for me while I took my boots off." Never mind that those boots—he was the only one wearing them—were still on his feet.

"I was only asking," Nell said, "because I came back here to have a smoke myself, but I seem to have left my cigarettes at home. I don't suppose you could spare one?"

They scrutinized her openly, from her smart little hat to

the toes of her black satin boots, no doubt wondering what a lady of her supposed station was doing sneaking cigarettes.

"I'm not trying to get you in trouble, if that's what you're thinking," Nell said. "I don't work for Mr. Harry, or anything like that."

Ruth said, "What're you doin' here, then?"

Nell withdrew her sketchbook and opened it to the drawing of the factory. They passed it around with considerable interest, peering over one another's shoulders for a better view.

"You an artist?" Otis asked.

"Course she is." Ruth pointed to the drawing. "You think just anybody could do this? Looks just like a photograph."

Not quite, but close enough; Nell was a fanatic for detail even in her quick sketches. Viola, an accomplished painter who'd studied in Paris when she was young, was always encouraging Nell to be looser, less strictly representational, but deliberate sloppiness went very much against her grain when she was capable of such exactitude.

Flipping through the sketchbook, Otis said, "You draw people good, too. Real good."

Nell thanked him. "Say, have you ever had your portrait done?"

"Me?" He snorted as he handed back the little book. "Naw."

"How about I give you a sketch of yourself, and in return you give me a cigarette?" she asked.

"Really? You want to draw *me?*"

The girls chortled suggestively as Nell lowered herself onto the grass, praying her dress didn't stain. She opened her sketchbook to a blank page and rummaged through her chatelaine for her pencil.

"That Otis," Ruth said. "He's a regular ladykiller."

"It ain't like that," Otis protested. "She's an *artist*."

The girls teased him good-naturedly as he settled into the pose suggested by Nell—reclining with an easy-to-draw three-quarter profile, his face dappled by sunlight filtering through the trees overhead. A warm breeze flickered the leaves, which still wore their deep, late summer green; the nearby stream burbled soothingly.

"Are all of you from around here?" Nell asked as she sketched.

"Otis is," Mary said through a ripple of smoke as she passed the cigarette to Ruth. "And Evie there." She nodded to the blonde girl. "I'm from New Hampshire. My folks are dairy farmers."

Ruth, it turned out, hailed from Vermont; the other girl, Cora, from northwestern Massachusetts. All had been brought up on farms. Most were sending the money they earned, or most of it, back home to their folks. Mary was working so that one brother could go to college and the other could start a lumber business. Only Cora was keeping her earnings for herself; to Nell's surprise, she was saving to send herself to Mount Holyoke Seminary.

Otis rolled Nell a cigarette when she tore out the finished sketch and gave it to him. She tucked it into her chatelaine "for later." All the girls except for quiet little Evie were begging to be drawn. Mindful of the brevity of their dinner hour—or rather, half-hour—Nell posed them together for a group portrait.

"Do your folks ever worry about you?" she asked as she blocked out the composition with light pencil strokes. "I mean, you're all fairly young, and most of you are far from home."

"Nah, they keep a tight rein on us here," Ruth said.

"Too damned tight," Cora grumbled, the coarse language prompting giggles from everyone but Evie, who let out a scandalized little gasp. "Just 'cause we work for them, they think they own us. They tell us when to go to bed and when to get up in the morning, who we can talk to, and about what."

"If we step off company property after work," Mary said, "we get chewed out but good, and a black mark goes on our record."

Ruth said, "The house mothers, they follow your every move and report the bad stuff to Mr. Harry so's he can decide what to do about you."

Cora rolled her eyes. "Talk about the pot calling the kettle black."

"The gall," Mary said, "a hound like that, with his ways, passin' judgment on us."

"Try not to move, Mary," Nell said as she swiftly sketched in the girls' features. "Have you ever known him to actually fire anyone for disobeying the rules?"

Ruth said, "Well, there was this one girl, Bridie Sullivan . . ."

Nell managed not to smile.

"Her and Evie and me, we all worked together on the same bank of looms—just since June, which was when Bridie started working here. She got herself sacked a few days ago, but there ain't no question she had it comin'."

"Evie?" Everyone turned to find another young man—huge and hulking, with overgrown white-blond hair—emerging from the woods that separated the river from the mill. "Evie, what you doin' here? You're s'posed to be at dinner."

Evie sighed. Speaking for the first time, she said, "It was too nice out."

"I went to your house, lookin' for you," he said, his

pout very much at odds with his bulk and that thick-chested voice. "Mrs. Hathaway, she's writin' you up for skippin' dinner. You din't ought to skip dinner."

"Sorry, Luther. Here." Evie patted the ground next to her. "You sit right here with me til it's time to go back."

The others greeted Luther familiarly as he lumbered over to Evie and sat cross-legged. Evie finger-combed his hair as he gazed, open-mouthed, at Nell. "What you doin'?"

"Don't stare, Luther," Evie said. "She's drawin' a pitcher. Of Mary and Ruthie and Cora."

"Can I see?"

"It's not done yet, but here," Nell said as she turned the sketchbook to show him.

He grinned in childish delight at the unfinished sketch. "Looks just like 'em!"

"Luther is Evie's brother," Otis told Nell. "Been workin' here since they was little."

"What kind of work do children do?" Nell asked as she returned to her drawing. "Those machines are all so big and complicated."

"I was a doffer," Evie said. "I took the full bobbins off the spinning frames and put the empty ones on—just fifteen minutes out of every hour. The rest of the time, I got to play. Luther ran errands for the men in the spinning room."

"He still does, don't you, fella?" Leaning over, Otis gave Luther a playful sock on the arm. "Don't know what us mule spinners would do without ol' Luther."

Rubbing his arm, Luther told Nell, "I'm strong as an ox. Ain't nobody can carry as much as me, nobody."

"He's a hard worker, our Luther," Otis said. "We give him sweets when he does good."

"I don't do it for the sweets," Luther said, seeming genuinely insulted. "I get money, just like you."

"What is it they pay you again?" Otis asked with a conspiratorial wink at Nell. "Two dollars a week? Ain't that what you were makin' when you were nine?"

"Don't ride him, Otis," Evie said. "You know how he gets when people laugh at him."

"I get two dollars and fifty cents." Luther glowered at Otis. "You don't know everything."

Wanting to defuse the suddenly tense atmosphere and refocus the conversation on her reason for being here, Nell said, "What did you mean before, Ruth—that this Bridie Sullivan had it coming to her when she got fired?"

"Bridie's gone," Luther said.

His sister said, "Hush, Luther. Everybody knows that."

"She was a bad girl."

"Luther, just be—"

"Why do you say that?" Nell asked with feigned nonchalance as she continued to draw, glancing back and forth between her three subjects and her sketchbook.

Evie answered for him. "He's just saying that 'cause it's what everyone else says."

"We knew what she was from the get-go," Ruth said. "Very first day she come to the mill, I says to Evie, 'this one's trouble.' All laced up tight, with that mountain of red hair. Thought she was better than us, bein' as she'd lived in Boston and all."

"When all she really was," Mary interjected, "was cheap Irish trash."

Nell continued sketching, her expression carefully neutral. It was only those from the old country who recognized her Irishness without hearing her name. There followed a flurry of complaints about no-account foreigners taking over their jobs at the mill, but soon enough attention returned to Bridie Sullivan. Nell heard all about Bridie's face paint and flirty ways, her suspiciously fine clothing and hair combs and boots—the latter being a particular sore point. Evie, she noticed, had fallen silent again.

"Never did go to church with us," Mary said, "and she'd raise holy hell about havin' the church tithes taken out of her pay."

"On account of she's a Catlic," Ruth added.

"The church is Protestant," Cora explained. "Congregationalist. And she didn't even live here—she lived with her folks. If you ask me, she had a point."

"Evie and Luther are Catlics," Ruth said. "They go to their own church on Sundays, but they don't get all het up about the tithes."

"They should." Cora said.

Evie shrugged and plucked at a blade of grass. Her brother just looked confused.

Ruth said, "You're a spooler, Cora. You never did have to work with that Bridie Sullivan, otherwise you wouldn't be makin' excuses for her."

Redirecting the conversation yet again, Nell asked them how Bridie had come by all her fine trappings.

"Men give 'em to her," Ruth said. "For, you know, makin' free with herself. That's the kind she was."

"She had this sweetheart, Virgil," Cora said. "Good looking fella."

" 'Cept for them stars," Ruth said with a shudder.

"I liked them stars," Mary said. "Made you wonder about him."

Ruth laughed. "I'll say they did."

"If he'd been ugly to start with, I might have felt different about the stars," Cora said, "but he was so well-built, you know, with shoulders out to there. Dark hair but real fair skin, and the biggest blue eyes you ever saw. The other girls used to try and catch his eye sometimes, til they found out he'd just got out of the calaboose."

"What was he in for?" Nell asked.

"Nobody was on good enough terms with Bridie to ask," Cora replied.

"He wasn't the only one she was dallyin' with," Ruth said. "Everything in trousers came sniffin' around sooner or later, and they didn't usually leave disappointed, if you know what I mean—so long as they made it worth her while."

Mary said, "The really fancy stuff—the bonnets and car bobs, and most of them dresses—it was Mr. Harry give her them."

"Harry Hewitt?" Nell asked, looking up. "Were he and Bridie . . . did they . . . ?"

"Every chance they got," Ruth said. "He'd have that little lickfinger Carlisle come pull her off her shift and bring her up to his office. She'd come back with her hair done different, and this *look* on her face."

"He pulled her off her *shift*?" Cora asked. "Evie, is that true?"

Evie, sitting next to her brother with her arms around her updrawn legs, her gaze on the patch of grass at her feet, answered with a shrug.

Ruth nudged Cora with her shoulder and said in a low voice, "Don't be askin' her about Bridie and Mr. Harry."

"Oh yeah, I forgot."

Nell must have looked confused, because Otis grinned and said, "Evie's sweet on Mr. Harry, has been ever since she was this high. Ain't that right, Evie?"

"Leave her be," Ruth said, while Evie tightened her arms around her legs and looked away.

"Yeah, you leave her be," Luther echoed, his neck reddening.

"Aw, come on, Evie knows the score," Otis said as he set about rolling another cigarette. "Mr. Harry, he don't want nothin' to do with her. All's he wants is a Bridie Sullivan, or one of them others, to lift her skirts for him up in that fancy office of his."

"Others?" Nell asked.

"Bridie ain't hardly the only one," Otis said. "There's always at least half a dozen of the girls at his beck and call. 'Harry's Harem,' we call 'em. He's got a window on his office door with some of those what do you call 'em . . . venetian blinds on it. Whenever the blinds are drawn, you can bet everybody knows just what's goin' on in there."

"Bridie's the main one, though," Mary said. "Or was. You shoulda seen him when she was around. Couldn't take his eyes off her. It's like she'd put a spell on him."

Ruth said, "Evie, don't listen to them. They don't know what they're talkin' about."

Otis made a sound of disgust. "You ain't doin' Evie no favor, tellin' her that. For cryin' out loud. Harry Hewitt ain't lookin' for no mill girl to fall in love with and take home to Mama, 'specially some mousy little hayseed like—"

"You shut your mouth," Luther demanded. "Just shut your mouth."

"I ain't sayin' nothing Evie don't already know," Otis said. "Why don't you tell your sister not to get all moony over a rich pretty boy that ain't never gonna look twice at the likes of her? Here she is, all wrung out over Mr. Harry and eaten up with jealousy over Bridie Sullivan, when—"

"Evie!" Luther called out as his sister bolted up and raced off into the woods. Rising to his feet, his face blood-flushed now, he turned to face Otis. "You made Evie feel bad."

"Luther," Cora said quickly, "go after your sister. Go on," she urged, pointing to the woods.

Luther hesitated, looming over Otis with his big hands contracting into fists as if of their own accord. Still grinning, Otis struck a match and lit his cigarette, but his hands, Nell noticed, were just ever so slightly unsteady.

"Evie needs you, Luther," Cora urged. "She might be crying."

Luther looked toward the woods, then back at Otis, his jaw set, rage sparking in his eyes. When he turned and ran off after his sister, everyone, Nell included, slumped in relief.

"That Luther, he's like a big kid most of the time," Ruth told Nell. "But when he gets riled, he don't know his own strength. He beat a man bloody last year—almost killed him—for talkin' lewd to Evie."

"Otis," Cora said, "what were you thinking, baiting him that way?"

"Me and him are friends," Otis said through a stream of smoke. "He'd never hurt me."

"Don't you be so sure," Ruth muttered.

"You done with that pitcher yet?" Mary asked Nell. "I'm achin' all over from holding myself so still."

"Just about," Nell said as she added some unnecessary shading. "You know, something doesn't make sense here. If Bridie was . . . well, if she and Mr. Harry were . . . you know . . . then why did he fire her?"

"Seems he didn't like to share," Otis said, to appreciative laughter from the mill girls.

"He found out about Virgil, then?" Nell asked.

Otis nodded as he drew on his cigarette. "Happened last

Friday, when they rung the evening bell at six-thirty. Mr. Harry, he's standing out in the courtyard, talkin' to some fella. These ones"—he indicated his female companions—"they're all whispering and giggling, on account of this fella's looks. I swear, I thought they was gonna swoon dead away. They can't resist a fella that dresses like he's got a few shiners in his pocket."

The girls exchanged dreamy smiles and little moans of yearning.

"It wasn't his clothes, you bonehead," Cora said. "That fella had a face like on one of those Roman statues, and you're just jealous 'cause girls don't look at you that way."

Pointedly ignoring her, Otis said, "So, the bell rings, and everybody come pourin' outa the wool building, as usual. That Virgil, he was waiting for Bridie to get off work, only always before he kind of hung back where he wouldn't attract too much notice. That evening he was waiting right up by the front door."

"Was he often waiting for her when her shift ended?" Nell asked.

"Three, four times a week," Otis said, "but always on Friday and Saturday. I don't know what they did on Fridays, but—"

"Don't you?" Ruth snorted with laughter; her friends followed suit.

"On Saturdays they left town," Otis said. "I was talkin' to one of the other spinners a few weeks ago—fella name of Nate. Nate had finally worked up the nerve to ask Bridie to go walkin' with him after work one Saturday, only to have her tell him she couldn't, on account of her fella was meetin' her to take her to the White House."

Nell frowned, wondering if she'd heard right.

"Not *the* White House," Otis said. "That's just what she

called it—maybe 'cause it's white, I don't know. She said it was an old farm nobody worked no more, but the farmhouse was still there, and that's where her and Virgil went to be alone."

"So he was waiting right up by the front door that Friday evening . . ." Nell prompted.

"Right, and soon as he sees Bridie, he grabs her, kisses her—but good—with everybody standing around watching, including Mr. Harry. You should've seen him. Hoppin' mad, you could tell, but holding it in till he went all purple-like."

"Why do you suppose he was so upset?" Nell asked. "I mean, it's not as if they were real sweethearts or anything. From what you say, he had plenty of other girls willing to . . . give him what he wanted."

"I know, it don't make a whole lot of sense," Ruth said. "But I'll tell you what, he was fit to be tied. Went stormin' back inside. Bridie and Virgil took off, but then a few minutes later, us all are headin' back here for a smoke, when we hear her voice. Her and Virgil are havin' a little set-to in the woods there. She was mad as a wet cat that he went and kissed her like that, in front of Mr. Harry."

"She mentioned Mr. Harry by name?" Nell asked.

Otis grinned. "Yeah, seems he knew about Mr. Harry, but Mr. Harry didn't know about him."

"Until that kiss," Mary said. "Bridie was all het up over it, tellin' Virgil he went and ruined everything. Said, 'We won't get so much as a nickel five-cent piece out of him now.' "

Nell looked up from her sketchbook. "She said that? Are you sure?"

"Oh, yeah." Otis flung his cigarette butt into the stream. "She musta decided she wanted more than just trinkets outa him. Mostly what we heard from Virgil was just him tryin' to shush her. He talked some, but we couldn't make it out real good. Didn't have no trouble hearin' *her*, though. Them Irish girls, they can get riled up good."

"Was Evie with you?" Nell asked.

"Yep."

"When did Bridie get fired?"

"Next day," Ruth said. "Saturday. We was waitin' on the dinner bell, so it was near to noon. That flunky of Mr. Harry's—Carlisle—he come down to fetch Bridie upstairs. She struts off with that *smile* of hers, like she's somethin' special 'cause she spreads her legs for the likes of him. I seen her take her rouge pot outa her apron pocket as she heads into the stairwell. Ten minutes later, she's back, red as a beet, with her eyes all swollen. Me and Evie, we asked her what happened, but she wouldn't even look at us. Never said a word, just took off her apron and grabbed her shawl out of her cubby and left. That was the last I seen of her."

Mary squirmed, rubbed her arm. "You done yet?"

From the direction of the mill came the pealing of the bell summoning them back from their dinner break.

"Yes, I suppose I am," Nell said.

Chapter 4

"READY to go back, then?" asked Brady from the driver's seat of the Hewitts' glossy black brougham as Nell approached, buttoning on her gloves.

"Not quite. I need to speak to Mr. Harry before I go."

"Take your time, miss," he said in his raspy brogue. "I'm not mindin' all this heavenly sunshine, I'll tell you that." A jovial Irishman of middle years, Brady was one of the few Hewitt retainers with whom Nell enjoyed genuinely cordial relations.

"The thing of it is . . . I was wondering if you wouldn't mind coming upstairs with me."

"To see Mr. Harry?" he asked in a tone of puzzled amusement.

"Yes."

Brady's smile dissolved as he got it: Nell didn't want to be alone with Harry Hewitt. He opened his mouth as if to ask why, but changed his mind, to Nell's relief. She liked

Brady. She didn't want to have to concoct some specious rationale for dragging him along, but she would, rather than tell him the truth. Viola Hewitt had already lost one son to Andersonville and another to the lulling embrace of Morphia. It would kill her if she were to find out what had transpired between Harry and Nell last May—to be forced to confront the beast lurking beneath her son's urbane façade.

HARRY Hewitt met Nell's eyes through the glass-paned door of his opulent, sun-washed office as she waited with Brady in the secretary's anteroom.

His burnished gold hair oiled just enough to impart the perfect patrician sheen, Harry sat perched with a cigar and a glass of whiskey on a corner of his marble-topped desk. He was nattily attired as always, in a slate-colored morning coat and paisley cravat, which he wore drawn through a signet ring so that it hung straight down his chest, rather than bow-tied—a fashion introduced by the eccentrically elegant Mr. Dickens during his reading tour last year and emulated by no one in Boston, to Nell's knowledge, aside from Harry. He was groomed to a high polish, the only flaw in his appearance being a small scar on his left eyelid—its provenance known only to Harry and Nell—which caused that lid to droop ever so slightly.

On a coat tree in the corner there hung a cashmere overcoat, one of those awful new homburg hats, a silver-handled walking stick, and a long, pearl-gray gentleman's scarf of heavy silk twill embroidered with Harry's distinctive, vine-framed double-H monogram. About a dozen others, in a rainbow of hues, were hung on pegs on the wall. Harry's scarves had become, along with his unique vests and cravats, something of a sartorial signature. In Boston, one said "Harry Hewitt" the way the rest of the world said "Beau Brummel."

Harry's secretary, the balding and bespectacled Carlisle, was announcing Nell's request for an audience and holding out Viola's folded letter with *To Whom it May Concern* written on the front in the violet ink of which she was so fond. Harry barely glanced at the letter. His gaze shifted from Nell to Brady, and back again. A corner of his mouth quirked knowingly. Too late, Nell realized her mistake in bringing along a protector. She'd learned long ago not to let dangerous men sense her fear, but such hard-won wisdom was difficult to retain, given how tame and privileged her life had become.

Carlisle continued to offer the letter, but Harry made no move to take it. He raised his glass to Nell, his eyes hard, his smile grim, and tossed back its contents in one gulp, then shook his head to Carlisle and waved him away.

"I'm sorry, miss," said Carlisle when he rejoined them, "but Mr. Hewitt is terribly busy this afternoon, so I'm afraid he won't be able to—"

"Tell him I'll catch up with him sooner or later." Nell snatched the letter from his hand and left.

"HOME now, miss?" Brady asked as he handed Nell into the big black brougham.

She settled into the front-facing seat, arranging the folds of her skirts, feeling the contours of the two letters in her pocket: Viola's and Duncan's.

"Miss?"

"Yes. Home."

He shut the door, climbed up into his seat, lifted the reins.

"No," she said through the open window.

"Miss?"

She drew in a breath, let it out slowly. "Take me to the state prison, please."

There came a moment's disbelieving silence. "The state—"

"It's about a mile that way, I believe." She pointed down the road.

"Whatever you say, miss." He snapped the reins.

Nell reached into her pocket, pulled out Duncan's letter, unfolded it. The paper was coarse, cheap, brownish, the penmanship immature but painstakingly inked, with no cross-outs and surprisingly few misspellings—remarkable, considering that he'd had almost no formal schooling as a child, and could barely write his name when she'd known him. Nell suspected that this letter, like the seven others he'd sent her over the past four months, had been copied and perhaps re-copied in an effort to get it just right.

Sept. 2nd 1868, Charlestown Prison

My Darling Girl (for I will never stop thinking of you that way),

Oftentimes I wonder if you even open these letters, since you have never written one back to me. But I will keep on writing them in the earnist hope that some day you will find it in your heart to write back to me.

I do not expeckt you to forgive me for how I hurt you but I beg you to believe that I have changed. I was a diffrent man then. I was angrey and I did not even no why. Father Beals says 8 years in this place have humbled me, and it is a good thing I got bagged because humilty is good for the soul and I believe that is true. I believe I am closer to Jesus because I am in this place. Did you ever think you woud hear me talk about Jesus?

He is a Piscopal chaplan Father Beals but he is a good man, as good as any of our preists I say. Any way he is all we have here so he will have to do. And I reckon it is not his falt he was born Piscopal.

I have missed you so much these past 8 years. I do not no any fancy way to say it. I just miss you. I do not no how I will make it threw the rest of my time here without seeing you. That is some thing I cannot bear to think about.

It is no surprise to me that you do not want to write to me after what I did to you the last time we were to gether. I do not blame you one bit. I am more sorry than I can say but you no that if you have been reading my letters. You also no that I need to say it to you're face like a man, the new man I am now not the old angrey one. Please Nell come visit me here just once. I will not keep you long. It will be so good just to rest my eyes upon your face once more. And tell you how sorry I am.

I no you must want me to stop writing to you, that is why you do not write back. Nell, I swear to God that I will stop writing to you if you only will come see me once and let me say how sorry I am. Just once for a few minutes so I can say what I would have said long ago were I a better man.

I never thought I was the kind of man to beg but I am humble now and I am begging you. Please come to me Nell. Just once.

I remain, truly and devotedly,

Your faithfull and loving Duncan

Nell touched a finger to the little scar near her left eyebrow, feeling the half-inch ridge even through the knotted threads of her glove. A knife scar, the least of those Duncan had dealt her the last time she'd seen him.

"You want to leave?" he'd growled as he kicked her to the floor, then kept kicking her, pausing only to unbutton his trousers. "You can leave when I'm done with you." He pummeled her as she thrashed, tore her basque open from collar to peplum, yanked at her stays. *He's scratching me,* she thought . . . on her face, her chest . . .

Then she saw the flash of a blade, the droplets of blood spattering his face, and she realized she might very well be dead before this was over—or wish she was.

Now, eight years later, Nell was still quite alive, and Duncan was serving a thirty-year prison sentence—but not for what he'd done to her. His conviction was for the crimes of armed robbery and aggravated assault, committed the day before his attack on her.

His first letter, dated May 15th, had left her stunned and shaken. Why, after all these years, had he decided to reestablish contact with her? And how on earth had he found out that she had moved to Boston and was living at 148 Tremont Street? How did he know she was a governess, and that she worked for the Hewitts?

The tone of the letter—so sincere, so penitent—did little to comfort her. Hadn't he always known how to act and what to say to make her forget, or overlook, what he really was? Uneducated he might be. Unintelligent? Hardly. Oh, he could play dumb when it suited him, but a stupid man could never have taken such effortless command of Nell's heart and soul, could never have talked her into the things he talked her into, could never have made her love him beyond all reason.

As contrite and affectionate as his first letter was, Nell had felt not the slightest temptation to answer it. He'd gotten his claws around her once; she wasn't about to step into his cage and let him try it again. The second letter, which arrived three weeks later, unnerved her even more than the first. *If you coud find it in your heart to come visit me, I could say these things out loud like a man instead of just scraching them onto this paper like a coward. Please, Nell . . .*

Please, Nell . . . Please, Nell . . . Please . . .

That had been his tormented refrain over the past four months. Come see me once, just once, and then you'll never have to hear from me again.

She got into the habit of listening for the postman so that she could be the first to sort through the newly arrived mail stacked on the Hewitts' monumental, mirrored hall-stand. God forbid one of the family—or Mrs. Mott!—were to notice a letter addressed to her with *Massachusetts State Prison* printed on the back.

She thought she'd have a reprieve when she left Boston in mid-July to spend six weeks with the Hewitts at Falconwood, their Cape Cod summer home, as she did every year. A week after arriving there, she was appalled to receive a letter from Duncan bearing Falconwood's address. It was as if he was an all-seeing, all-knowing god . . . or wanted her to think of him that way.

The carriage rattled to a halt outside a tall iron gate manned by two uniformed guards. Nell showed them Viola's letter and explained that she was here to see the warden. They waved the coach through that gate, directing Brady to a courtyard anchored by a fort-like building that bore an uncanny resemblance to the Hewitt wool factory. It was the prison's administrative building, where, according to the guards, the warden's office was located. To the left was another large building, even more forbidding in appearance, with iron bars on the windows; to the right, two big barnlike structures from which came a cacophony of hammering and clanging.

"You want me to go in with you?" Brady asked as he helped her down from the coach.

She shook her head. "No, I'm fine."

"You sure, miss?"

No. "Yes. Of course I'm sure."

Chapter 5

"VIRGIL Hines?" The warden, a florid, jowly fellow named Clarence Whitcomb, leaned back heavily in his chair, which groaned under his weight. "Not what you'd call a model prisoner, certainly, but not as irredeemable as some. Of rather . . . limited intellect, I should say, but not altogether dim. Likeable, in his way. Rather, er, glib in temperament—more talkative than most. You'd hear him laughing when he ought not to have. Silence is highly prized here."

"Is it?" asked Nell from across what seemed like an acre of polished walnut. With the heavy curtains drawn and only a single desk lamp to dispel the gloom in the oak-paneled office, it might have been midnight rather than the midst of a sunny afternoon.

"Silence gives them an opportunity to reflect and repent," Whitcomb said. "Reflection, hard work, prayer, and instruction—those are the cornerstones of prisoner life here. They're a grossly undisciplined breed when they come to us. Our objective is not so much punitive as restorative. By inculcating in these men a sense of order, we're preparing them to reenter an orderly world."

Nell almost laughed out loud at the notion of the world being "orderly." Schooling her expression, she said, "An ambitious goal."

"But one which we pride ourselves on attaining." Mr. Whitcomb lifted Viola's open letter from the desk in front of him, rubbing the thick vellum between his thumb and fingertips as if assessing its quality. "Mrs. Hewitt is trying to locate him, you say?"

Nell nodded. "He disappeared Sunday, along with a young woman from this area named Bridie Sullivan. It's really Miss Sullivan we're trying to locate—her mother is beside herself—but we suspect that if we find Mr. Hines, we'll find her."

"Seems reasonable."

"Was he the type of man to . . . do harm to a female, do you think?" Nell asked.

"There's nothing in his history to suggest it," Whitcomb said. "No arrests for, er, such crimes as such a character flaw would suggest."

"What did he do to get sent here?"

"Stole a lady's reticule from a coat peg in a tea shop. He was a sneak thief—strictly crimes of opportunity. He'd take whatever was lying about unattended, pick the occasional pocket, do a little confidence work . . ."

"Confidence?"

"Swindles, humbugs—small time, of course. It takes real brains to carry out a complicated bunco scheme. Never used a weapon that I know of. He was sentenced to three years, but only served one. You're familiar with the concept of parole, yes?"

"Oh, yes." Some thirty years ago, the Commonwealth of Massachusetts instituted a novel new form of clemency—still, to Nell's knowledge, the only one of its kind in the nation. After serving one-third of his term, an inmate was eligible to be released into society, under supervision and with the threat of revocation should he revert to his former habits. Nell's disapproval of the parole system stemmed from entirely selfish motives. God help society—but most of all, her—should Duncan ever reenter it! In theory, parole was only granted to the most harmless and well-behaved of prisoners. Nell prayed—literally, and at regular intervals—that the Massachusetts Board of Parole would be savvy enough to keep Duncan under lock and key for the full thirty years of his term.

"Mr. Hines was released in May?" she asked.

"That's right. I don't recall the date offhand, but it was early in the month, I believe. It's no surprise to me that he found a lady friend so quickly. He wasn't a bad looking fellow—if a bit on the scrawny side when he first came here. I put him to work in the stone shops, and that turned him into a man right quick. Nothing builds muscle like stone-cutting."

"I wondered what was going on in those buildings," she said.

"We take shelves of granite from a local quarry and split them into paving stones and building blocks. Fine work the men do, and for a competitive price. I'm proud to say we've got contracts from as far away as . . ." Whitcomb's gaze strayed toward the open door behind her. "Ah, Father Beals."

Nell turned to find a man standing in the doorway. Were it not for his garb—a plain black coat and trousers, with one of those new Anglican clerical collars—she would never have guessed that this was the "Piscopal chaplan" mentioned in Duncan's letter. He wasn't nearly as old as she had envisioned, mid-thirties by her guess, with longish brown hair worn with a side part, so that a great swath of it fell over his forehead. He had striking eyes, dark and sweetly mournful, in contrast to his otherwise fair coloring.

"I beg your pardon, Mr. Whitcomb," Beals said, stepping back. "I didn't realize you were with—"

"Not at all." The warden waved him into the office. "Come on in, old man, and let me introduce you."

The priest entered with a slightly awkward gait—not a true limp, just a bit of asymmetry, as if one leg weren't doing quite its fair share of the work.

"Miss Nell Sweeney, this is the Reverend Adam Beals, our chaplain. Father Beals is the fellow you should be talking to, Miss Sweeney. You're lucky to have caught him in, though. He's only here Sundays and Wednesdays."

"Pleased to make your acquaintance, Miss . . ." Father Beals paused in mid-bow, looked up at her with recognition in his eyes. ". . . Sweeney."

"Father." Nell inclined her head and looked away quickly, knowing he'd connected her with Duncan, who must have mentioned her, and praying he didn't bring it up in front of the warden. *Please, St. Dismas, please please please let him keep his mouth shut.* Of all the ghosts of her disreputable past, Duncan was potentially the most devastating.

"Have a seat, Father." Whitcomb gestured Beals into the leather chair next to Nell's and handed him Viola's letter, grunting with the effort of leaning across the table. "You knew Virgil Hines fairly well, as I recall. Seems he and a young lady disappeared from this area recently. Miss Sweeney is looking into the matter for her employer, Mrs. August Hewitt, at the request of the young lady's mother."

Beals frowned in concentration as he read the letter.

"Did Mr. Hines happen to tell you what he planned to do after his release?" Nell asked.

"Yes, of course," the priest said. "I always discuss a parolee's intentions with him, so that I can share them with his parole officer. In Virgil's case, he knew exactly what he wanted to do, which is why I'm somewhat mystified that he chose to remain in the Charlestown area. He was from Salem originally. Always said he'd go back there the instant he was released. His plan was to use his stone-cutting experience to find a job in the Cape Ann quarries so that he could save enough money to buy a farm he's had his eye on."

"Really?"

"That was what he told me. All the men in his family had been fishermen for generations. He loved being at sea—he enlisted in the Navy during the war—but he said it was too brutal a life, fishing, that you had to be away from your family too much."

"I understand he came out of the Navy with quite an unusual tattoo."

"He served aboard the U.S.S. Kearsage when they sank the Alabama in June of sixty-four. The crew and officers all got stars on their foreheads to commemorate the victory."

"All of them?"

"Most, anyway. I was gratified that he'd chosen farming over picking pockets and snatching purses. It's an honorable calling—I told him so. I gave him a writing box when he was released, so that he could write and let me know how things had turned out."

"Has he?" Nell asked.

"Not yet, no," he said as he brushed a fleck of lint off the arm of his chair, "but I'm sure he will, once he's settled."

"It's a thoughtful gift," Nell said.

"Our Father Beals is one of those reformer types," Whitcomb confided with an indulgent smile. "A champion of the common man, don't you know."

"They're lucky to have you," Nell said.

The priest looked down with a diffident half-smile, absently finger-combing the hair that hung over his forehead. "I'm only the interim chaplain here, Miss Sweeney—just until they find a permanent replacement for old Father Bannister, God rest his soul. That's why I'm only here two days a week. I'm actually assigned to Emmanuel Church on Newbury Street in Boston. I've been helping out here about eight months so far, but I must tell you they've been the most gratifying eight months of my career."

"The prisoners love him," Whitcomb told her.

"Enough to be absolutely truthful with you?" Nell asked the priest. "What I mean is, would Mr. Hines have admitted it, do you think, if his plans had actually been . . . less than honorable?"

Reverend Beals smiled. It was a pleasant smile that didn't completely conceal the fact that he was sizing her up, but with a subtlety appropriate to his vocation. "Some of them tell me everything. You wouldn't believe the things I've heard, and the things I've talked men out of. Others, they hold their cards a bit closer to the vest."

"Which type was Mr. Hines?" Nell asked.

"The more candid type—very much so. He loved to talk, and our conversations gave him an opportunity to do that.

Despite his criminal past, he always struck me as somewhat guileless. Yes, I believe that he sincerely intended to return to Salem and become a farmer—eventually."

"Did he ever talk about women?" Nell asked.

Beals chuckled. "What twenty-four-year-old man doesn't talk about women? He was no innocent where women were concerned—he'd had sweethearts—but he was no lothario either. He seemed almost . . . worshipful of them. If you want to know whether I think he was capable of abducting this girl against her will, or worse, the answer is no."

But of course he would take that stand. *A champion of the common man, don't you know.*

"Is there anything else we can assist you with, Miss Sweeney?" Whitcomb slid his watch from his vest pocket and flipped it open.

Never slow to take a hint, Nell said, "No, you've been most helpful, both of you." She rose; the two men followed suit. "Good to meet you, Warden . . . Father."

"I'll show you the way out," the priest offered, gesturing her through the door.

"I admire your approach to these prisoners, Father," Nell said as he escorted her down the hall, "your willingness to look beyond their crimes to the men themselves."

"There but for the grace of God go you or I."

Ah, but Nell had, in fact, gone there, back when God's grace hadn't shone quite as brightly in her life as it had these past few years. She wondered if Duncan had shared the sordid details of her past with this Father Beals. Suddenly she felt as if she were walking down this corridor stark naked.

"They're not monsters, these prisoners." Beals walked beside her with his hands clasped behind his back, his gaze on the stone floor ahead of them. His right leg was the weak one, she saw, but not by much, and it looked like a condition he'd learned to live with rather than a recent injury.

"Monsters don't exist," the priest continued. "Only men whose souls are in a state of arrested development. The problem is in the way they were reared—or rather, not reared. Most of them had little in the way of decent family life or religious instruction when they were growing up. They were street arabs, most of them, simply thrown out into the world to fend for themselves at an appallingly early age . . ." He turned to look at her. "Like Duncan."

She stopped walking; so did he.

Silence engulfed them for one painfully long moment. He was looking at her; she was looking at the stone-block floor.

"My wife had hair your color," he said.

She looked up sharply.

He looked away, smoothing his hair as before; a nervous habit, it would seem. "You do know that Episcopal priests can marry," he said.

"I . . . yes, I suppose I did know that."

"She passed away. A boating accident."

"I'm terribly sorry."

"It was eight years ago," he said, as if that should mitigate the tragedy.

"She must have been quite young—and you, as well."

He nodded, clearly ill at ease. "The thing is, I know something of men and women—the bonds that can form between them, how transcendent love can be . . . and how excruciating. I know about passion, about loneliness . . . especially loneliness."

I have missed you so much these past 8 years. I do not no any fancy way to say it. I just miss you.

"I doubt you know the whole story, Father," she said.

"I believe I do," he said gently, his gaze lighting on the scar near her eyebrow.

"Then you understand why I have no desire to visit him."

"You're only human. Humans are naturally self-protective. Of course I understand."

"But . . . ?"

"But he's changed."

She looked down, shook her head. "Father . . ."

"Do you know why he learned to read and write?"

She looked up.

"They're voluntary classes. A local schoolmarm comes in twice a week. He's been taking those classes for years. Do you know why?" When she didn't answer, he said, "So he could write to you."

She stared at him.

"He won't attend my Sunday services—says the pope wouldn't approve. But I host voluntary Bible study on Wednesday afternoons, and he hasn't missed a single session. Often he stays afterward to talk. He tells me what's on his mind, asks for advice . . . Sometimes we pray together."

Still she said nothing.

"Don't tell me you think it's impossible for a man to change," he said.

"Of course it's possible. But Duncan, he's . . ."

"Monsters don't exist, remember? He's just a man. A flawed man, by his own admission, but a man who's worked very hard at becoming better."

She studied the floor. *Nell, I swear to God that I will stop writing to you if you only will come see me once.*

"We have a room for visits," Beals said. "No one is ever

in there this time of day. Duncan is cutting stone right now, but I could—"

"I won't be alone with him," she said.

A second passed. The priest smiled. "I'll wait right outside the door. I'll hear you if you call me."

Chapter 6

"NELL?" Duncan stood in the doorway of the small, simply furnished visiting room, staring at her as if she were a visitation of the Holy Mother. Even in his sleeveless undershirt and striped prison-issue trousers, stone dust matting his honey-brown hair and coating the sweat that sheened him head to toe, he was shockingly handsome.

Deadly handsome.

Handsome as the Devil, as Bridie's mother would say.

Father Beals, standing behind Duncan, caught Nell's eye and said, "I'll be waiting right outside."

She nodded. Duncan entered the room, automatically ducking his head the way tall men did, and Father Beals closed the door behind him.

For a long moment, they just stared at each other.

"I can't believe it," Duncan said in that roughly soft voice of his, that voice that always reminded her of a lion's purr. "I didn't think you'd ever come. And now you have, and look at me." He swatted at his trousers, raising a cloud of dust that glittered in the bands of sunlight from the single barred window. "But look at *you*," he said softly, almost reverently. "My God, Nell, you look . . ."

He took her in with an expression of awe—the chic little hat, the sleek princess-skirted dress, her gloved hands tightly clasped, her eyes, her mouth . . .

"You look . . ." *Like a lady.* That was what she thought he was going to say. Instead, he said, "Like an angel."

Nell felt the absurd urge to thank him for the compliment, but her throat didn't seem to be working.

He took a step toward her.

She backed up into the scarred old wooden table that occupied the middle of the room, four chairs tucked in around it.

Duncan hesitated, lowered his head, rubbed the back of his neck. "Will you sit with me?" Crossing warily to the head of the table, he pulled out a chair for her, then circled around to the other end and pulled out one for himself.

Nell sat, smoothed her skirts, folded her hands on the table.

Duncan sat opposite her, tugged a grimy handkerchief out of his pants pocket, and wiped the dust off his face. "I woulda shaved if I knew you were comin'," he said as he rasped the cloth over his prickly jaw.

"I—" Nell's voice snagged in her throat; she cleared it. "I probably shouldn't have come."

"Don't say that," he implored, reaching across the table.

She shrank back.

His jaw clenched; his hand curled up. "God, please don't say that. You don't know how I've wanted this. You don't know what it means to me, being able to see you again, to see you looking so . . ." His expression sobered. "To know that I didn't . . . that what I did to you, how I treated you, didn't . . . destroy you."

"I almost died."

He closed his eyes.

She said, "The baby did die."

His throat moved as he swallowed. "I'm sorry, Nell." He looked at her, his eyes gleaming, voice hoarse. "I'm more sorry than I can tell you. I was . . ." He shook his head. "I was gonna say I was drunk. But really I was just . . ." He sat back, expelled a ragged sigh. "I was just so mad at you for wanting to leave me, 'specially with the law after me 'cause of the Ripley thing. It was like you were turning your back on me just when I needed you most. I didn't understand that it was all my fault, that you'd taken as much as you could take."

She nodded distractedly. "Yes. Well . . . I appreciate that, Duncan. Father Beals tells me you've changed, and I hope, for your sake, that it's true."

"It is true," he said with quiet fervor. "Don't doubt it for a second."

"I'm glad," she said, although she was far from convinced. Duncan had always been a consummate actor. "I hope you meant it when you promised not to write to me anymore if I came to see you. My position with the Hewitts means a great deal to me. The little girl I care for, Gracie, I love her as much as if she were my very own. Mrs. Hewitt doesn't know about . . . how I was before. About you . . . about any of it. A governess is expected to be completely above reproach. If she were to find out—"

"I done you enough damage. Don't worry. I won't send you any more letters." He smiled. "You talk like a book, almost. Not hoity-toity exactly, but . . . different from before."

"I *am* different, and I have a whole new life. But I'll lose it—and I'll lose Gracie—if my old life ever becomes known. I've only ever told two people about it, two people I could trust completely, and even then I didn't tell them all of it, just—"

"Who?"

"Who did I tell? Well, Dr. Greaves. He was the doctor who treated me after . . ."

Duncan looked down, nodded.

"He was very good to me, very kind. He let me assist him in his work, and he taught me all about medicine and, well, lots of things. History, French, writing, comportment . . . I lived in his house in East Falmouth for four years. The cook and housekeeper and I all had little dormer rooms upstairs." Although she rarely slept in hers, once she started sharing Dr. Greaves's bed, but Duncan didn't need to know that.

"Who's the other one?" he asked. "You said there were two you talked to."

Something in his tone made her reluctant to bring Will into this. "Why do you care, Duncan? Why should it matter to you?"

He lifted his shoulders. "Just curious. I used to be the one you trusted, the one you told stuff to. Well, me and your brother."

It was true. At one time, Duncan and Jamie were the center of Nell's world, the bedrock beneath her feet. Now Duncan was locked up in here, and Jamie, if he was still alive, was probably locked up somewhere else.

"Everything changes," she said. "Take you, talking about Jesus."

"Yeah," he said a little sheepishly. "That's Father Beals's doing."

"I must say, I'm a bit worried about what you may have said to him. You seem to have talked to him quite a bit."

Duncan nodded. "He's a good man, for a Piscopal. He started me thinkin' about God, and what's gonna happen to my eternal soul after I kick the bucket."

"Does Father Beals know about me? About . . . ?"

He grinned. "About Cornelia Cutpurse, you mean?" It had been her nickname among the thieves, whores, and cardsharps of the Upper Cape, into whose dark and lively world Duncan had introduced her at sixteen. She'd been proud of that name, and of the nimble fingers and ghostly stealth that had inspired it. "Yeah, he knows."

She rubbed her forehead, the air leaving her lungs in a moan.

"He's got this way of makin' you feel . . . I don't know, like you can tell him things," Duncan said. "Like he'll understand, and not just cast judgment. Talking to him, it's like goin' to confession, only better, 'cause he talks back instead of just telling you how many Hail Marys you owe. You were like that, back when we were together. I could never keep anything from you."

"You told him everything?" she asked, deeply dismayed. "About you and me?"

"Yeah, but see, it don't matter. You got nothin' to worry about from him, Nell. He don't even know the Hewitts, and if he did, he wouldn't tell 'em nothin'. Tell you who you *should* be worried about, though." Duncan leaned forward on his elbows, the sunlight turning his eyes a scalding, lucent blue. "The son."

She stared at him. "The . . . ?"

"I know he's the other one, the one you think you can trust. I know you're sweet on him, but he's—"

"Wait a minute . . ."

"He ain't what he seems. You think you know him, that he's a gentleman just 'cause he's a Hewitt, and he knows how to dress and act, and all the rest of it, but if you knew how he really is, what he does when you ain't around . . ."

"Wait a minute!" How could he know about Will? How could he know about any of it? "Where do you get your information?" she demanded. "How do you know where I live, who I work for, who I associate with? How did you know I went to the Cape with the Hewitts over the summer?"

He shook the handkerchief out, scrubbed it over his hands. "That ain't important."

"Of course it's important. You've been locked up in here for eight years. How are you finding these things out?"

"Just 'cause you're in jail don't have to mean you're completely cut off from the world, not if you're smart."

"You're wrong about me being sweet on him," she said.

"Look, I know about you two, all right? I know everything. But what *you* don't know is, men like that, one woman is never good enough for 'em, and there's no getting serious about some sweet little thing from the old country, no matter how pretty she is or what kind of airs she puts on. That type, they only want a woman like you for one thing."

"You don't know everything, Duncan." It had never been like that between her and Will. Nor would it . . . could it . . . ever be that way.

"I know enough."

"Believe what you will." It hardly mattered, at this point. He'd promised not to write to her anymore. With any luck, he'd keep that promise, and she'd never have to deal with him again. "I don't think we have anything more to say to each other," she said as she rose from her chair. "Except goodbye."

"I know where you can find Virgil Hines."

She stilled, sat back down.

"I got a pretty good idea, anyway," he said.

She waited him out.

"When Father Beals came and got me, he told me you were here because of Virgil. He said Virgil and some girl went missing a few days ago."

"Did you know Mr. Hines?"

" 'Mr. Hines?' " Duncan snorted with laughter. "Damn, you *have* gone all highfalutin on me, haven't you?"

Nell regarded him in expectant silence.

"I didn't know him well," Duncan said, idly dragging the now-filthy handkerchief over his upper chest, "but I knew him. There's only about three-hundred of us here, all told, so everybody knows everybody else. He had a big mouth, that Virgil. Liked to talk about a little farm north of here that's not being worked anymore on account of all the rocks, and nobody lives there. He used to hide out there from the law after he done something stupid, which I take it was pretty often. A nice enough fella, but not the swiftest upstairs."

"Where is this farm? Did he say?"

"South of Salem."

Salem was about ten or fifteen miles to the north. "He wasn't any more specific than that?"

"He was, actually." Duncan lazed back in his chair, smiling in that cocky way she'd once known so well. "Like I said, he was a talker."

Nell gave him a look that said, *Go on,* but she knew Duncan well enough to suspect that it wasn't going to be quite that easy.

"You know, I really need to be getting cleaned up for Bible study," he said as he wadded up the handkerchief and stuffed it back in his pocket. "I don't like to show up all covered with—"

"You bastard," she said tightly.

He burst out laughing. "*That's* my Nell!"

"I'm not your Nell, Duncan. I stopped being your Nell eight years ago."

"And it was all my fault, and I'll have to live with that for the rest of my life. You're mad at me, and you got a right to be. But you can never stop being mine, not entirely."

"Actually, yes, I can. And I have." She stood and pushed her chair back. "Goodbye, Duncan."

"Don't you want to know where the farm is?" he asked as he rose.

"Do you intend to tell me?"

"Sure. Next time."

"Next . . . ?" *Of course.*

"I've got to wash up now," he said as he crossed to the door, "but come see me again and we'll talk some more."

"You told me if I came to see you once—just once—you'd leave me alone."

"I told you I'd stop writing to you. I never said I wouldn't try to win you back."

"Win . . ." On a gust of incredulous laughter, she asked, "Are you *serious?* Even if I were fool enough to want anything more to do with you, would you honestly expect me to wait another twenty-two years for you?"

"It won't be that long. I'll be out on hocus pocus in two years—maybe sooner, with good behavior counted in."

"Good behavior? *You?*"

"Father Beals wrote somethin' up saying he thought I should be released next year, and the warden signed off on it. It's up to the Parole Board, but if I keep my nose clean between now and then, Beals says there won't be any problem. He says he's gonna give me a writing box when I get out, so I can—"

"Oh, my God." The world seemed to wobble on its axis. Nell grabbed the table to steady herself. "I can't believe this. I don't believe this."

"You better get used to the idea, darlin', 'cause I'll be a free man before you know it, and then it'll be you and me again, just like before."

Her voice tremulous with outrage, Nell said, "Do you honestly think I'd let you near mc again, after what you did to me?"

"I'm a different man than I was back then," he said as he reached for the doorknob. "After I get out of here and you get to know me again, you'll see that's true."

"Never! I don't believe for a moment that you've changed, Duncan, not really—not inside, where it counts," she said as the door swung open. "You're still the same sly, devious son of a bitch you always were, and I'll be damned if I come back here and let you . . ."

Father Beals, waiting out in the hall, stood gaping at her, clearly astounded to hear such language come out of a lady's mouth.

Duncan burst out laughing. "Oh, Nell . . . Darlin' girl, I just can't tell you how good it is to see you again."

Chapter 7

IT'S about time, Nell thought when she saw the front door of number 10 Commonwealth Avenue swing open. Yellow gaslight fanned out onto the front stoop as the silhouette of a man emerged from Harry Hewitt's handsome bay-windowed brownstone and hurried down the steps.

It was a nearly moonless night, and Nell was a good hundred feet away, hidden behind one of the many plane trees that had been planted in two stately rows down the grassy esplanade separating the north and south sides of this unfinished boulevard; still, she could tell, to her dismay, that the figure walking swiftly toward nearby Arlington Street wasn't Harry. He was too short, too slight. Harry was tall—not as tall as his brother Will, but taller than average, and he moved with a distinctive masculine grace, like all the Hewitt men.

Nell recognized this man when he passed beneath a

streetlamp—about forty, with receding blond hair, quite well turned out in a black frock coat and gray trousers. He was Harry's valet and all-around manservant, Edwin Speck, whom he'd brought with him when he moved out of his parents' home last March in protest over his father's refusal to dismiss Nell for being an "insolent little bog-trotter who should learn to peel potatoes and keep her damned mouth shut." That August Hewitt would have sacked Nell in a heartbeat had his wife not threatened to leave him over it did little to placate Harry. Mr. Hewitt's friend Leo Thorpe held the deed to the Back Bay town house in which his son Jack used to live, so Harry offered to rent it; he never spent another night under his parents' roof.

Nell held her pendant watch close to her face, squinting to read it in the dark: almost ten o'clock. She'd been lurking here, waiting for Harry to head out for his nightly debauchery, for over an hour.

She tugged her shawl more snugly around herself, rubbed her arms. It had been an unusually warm day for September, prompting her to wear her favorite summer dress one last time, but the temperature had been plummeting since nightfall, and she was starting to shiver.

Last night she'd conducted a similar, if briefer, vigil. After returning from Charlestown, she'd fed Gracie her supper, tucked her in, and walked over here in the hope of following Harry to some public place where she could question him in relative safety; never again would she enter his home alone. Unfortunately, he never left the house. At half past nine, his valet walked down to the corner, as he was doing now, and hailed a hack heading south on Arlington. Forty minutes later, it pulled up in front of 10 Commonwealth. Speck got out and paid the driver as two giggling women emerged from the vehicle rather clumsily, not so much because they were unaided, but because they were clearly sotted. They were the frowziest of street-walkers, all rouge and bosom and swaying hips—and not even that pretty, although they oozed a frank carnality of a type most men found irresistible. The valet herded them, laughing and stumbling, through the iron gate, up the front steps, and into the house. A few minutes later, lamp-light shone through the windows of the second floor master bedroom. Dark forms moved behind the curtains, shifting, merging . . .

It would appear that both Harry's secretary and his valet counted pimping among their many and varied duties.

Frustrated but not defeated, Nell had returned to Colonnade Row determined to try again tonight. Now, as Edwin Speck flagged down yet another hack on Arlington, she was beginning to wonder if Harry Hewitt, spoiled and lazy as he was, no longer cared to go in search of his evening entertainment, but preferred to have it delivered directly to his doorstep.

Nell groaned as the hack pulled over to the curb. Except this time, instead of entering it, Speck merely said something to the driver, who steered his horses around the corner and down Commonwealth. As the hack pulled up in front of number 10 with the valet jogging alongside it, Harry Hewitt stepped out of his house, dapper as always in full evening dress beneath an open black great coat, including one of his signature garish waistcoats, this one of an Oriental-patterned crimson brocade.

Whispering a brief prayer of thanks, Nell watched Harry adjust the angle of his opera hat as he strode through the front gate, his long ivory scarf snapping smartly. His servant bowed as he held the gate open, then trotted to the hack to get the door, bowing a second time. "Good luck with the cards tonight, Mr. Hewitt."

Harry didn't so much as grunt a response. He settled into the seat, looking faintly bored, as Speck said to the driver, "He's going to Orlando Poole's."

"What's that?" the young driver asked. "A restaurant?"

"Christ," Harry growled from inside the hack. "Province Street. Corner of Bosworth."

Flicking his reins, the driver guided the coach in an about-face on the wide, granite-paved street and headed back toward Arlington.

Nell waited until Edwin Speck had reentered the house to walk up to the corner and wave down another hack.

"Orlando Poole's," she said as the driver handed her into the shabby brown Landau. "It's on Province and—"

"I know where it is," he said in a gruff, whiskey-scented Irish brogue. "Patrick Nulty's been drivin' this hack enough years that he don't need to be spoon-fed no addresses, thank you very much." He stared at her a moment, scratched the graying stubble on his chin. "I must say, though, you don't quite seem the type."

Before she could summon a response to that, he shook his head in evident bemusement, climbed up onto his box and snapped the reins.

THE Landau clattered to a stop on the narrow cobblestone lane, eerily dark save for a single ornamental lamp—oil, not gas—suspended from an iron arch over the stone steps that led from Province Street to Bosworth. Brick buildings loomed on either side, their ground-level shops well-shuttered, a scattered handful of upper windows faintly lit. It reminded Nell of the illustrations in Dr. Greaves's book about medieval London.

"Um . . . where exactly is Orlando Poole's?" Nell asked Patrick Nulty as he helped her out of the coach.

"Right there." He cocked his head toward a set of stone steps that led to a door partially below ground. "Ain't you never been to Poole's hell before?"

"I . . . no, but I . . ."

"You do know what kind of a place it is."

"It's a gaming hell," she said with feigned confidence. Retrieving her little purse out of her chatelaine, she asked, "How much do I owe you?"

"Five cents. You ain't goin' in there to pray over 'em, are you? They'll laugh you out of there so fast—"

"No, I just . . . The truth is, I need to talk to someone, and the only way I can do it is to go in there." Suspecting Nulty had undercharged her, perhaps because he liked her, or perhaps because he felt sorry for her, or perhaps because she was Irish—those from the old country always knew—she gave him a dime and said, "Keep the change."

He contemplated the coin as if it were the first time he'd ever seen Miss Liberty. "Tell you what. Business is slow on Thursday nights, and I could use a little break. Why don't I just wait right here so's I can take you back home when you're done with your business inside?"

"I actually don't live very far from here," she said. "Just three blocks that way—Tremont and West. I can walk."

His eyes betrayed his surprise that she hailed from Colonnade Row, but all he said, as he climbed back up into his box, was, "It ain't good for a lady to be wanderin' the city alone at night. I'll be right here. And if you happen to need a helpin' hand in the meantime, you'll know where to find me."

Nell thanked him, descended the stone steps and knocked on the door, which bore no street number or other identification of any kind. She was about to knock a second time when it swung inward, courtesy of a burly, plainly dressed colored man who looked from her to the hack, and back again. "Yes?"

"I, um . . . I'm looking for Orlando Poole's." Nell glanced behind this man to the hallway in which he stood, which was dimly lit and unfurnished.

"Sorry, miss," he said as he stepped back from the door. "There's no one here by that name."

"Um, wait," she pleaded as he shut the door in her face. She stared at it for a moment, then turned and climbed back up to the brick sidewalk, to find Nulty chuckling as he raised a flask to his mouth. "Why are you laughing?" she asked. "That was very embarrassing. You sent me to the wrong door."

"I sent you to the right door. But it's that fellow's job to make sure only the right sort gain admittance, and he must have decided you didn't qualify."

"Not because I'm . . . You don't suppose he could tell I'm Irish."

"Nah, it's the way you're dressed."

Nell opened her shawl and looked down at herself. Of all the coolly sophisticated frocks Viola had ordered for her over the past four years, this one was by far the prettiest, a confection of gauzy smoke-colored lawn over a matching silk underdress. Although demurely styled, with long, full sleeves and a prim collar of Brussels lace, the fabric of the outer dress was so sheer that her bare arms and the snug, low-cut underbodice were clearly visible beneath it. "This is the only dress I own that doesn't make me look as if I'm in half mourning."

Nulty winced. "I'm that sorry to hear it." Jamming the cork back into his whiskey flask, he said, "You look like the wife of one of them Beacon Hill nabobs when they head up to the North End to do charity work. Why do you think I asked if you meant to pray over 'em? That fella probably thought the same thing."

A trill of feminine laughter drew their attention to the stairway connecting Province Street to Bosworth. Two young couples in evening attire came into view beneath the oil lamp, their movements unsteady as they made their way down the stone steps. One of the ladies had let her cloak slip off her shoulders, undraping a blue satin gown that was terribly chic, and also quite daring in that it left her upper bosom and arms completely revealed.

One of the gentlemen paused at the bottom of the steps to light a cigar. It was the first time Nell had seen a man of his station smoking on the street—a violation both of etiquette and city law. This was the fast young set to whom Nell, cocooned in a world of Brahmin propriety and centuries-old tradition, was rarely exposed.

"Spence, old man," the other gentleman slurred, "can't you wait til we're in Poole's to light that damned thing?"

"You'll end up having to pay another fine," warned the lady in blue.

"There are no watchmen round here," he said as he spun the tip of the cigar slowly in the flame of his match.

"Here, take this." Nell handed her shawl up to Nulty, then unpinned her hat and gave him that as well. His eyes widened when she removed her lace collar and undid the top few buttons, pushing aside the tissue-thin fabric to uncover her upper chest. In an effort to liven up her tame chignon, she plucked at a few tendrils around her hairline, letting them frame her face in curls—a hairstyle not dissimilar to that of the lady in blue. Her two-button kid gloves could stay, she decided, but the chatelaine had to go. Before handing it up to Nulty, she withdrew from it the cigarette that Otis had given her at the Hewitt Mill two days ago.

The driver shook his head, grinning, as she turned to greet the two approaching couples. "I say, I don't suppose one of you could spare a light."

There was a moment's pause as the party regarded her curiously. Although cigarettes were making inroads among wealthy young mavericks—Will Hewitt smoked them—it was the rare female who indulged. Their eyes betrayed the nature of their speculations: Was she a wanton, a whore even, or one of their own? The ladies' gazes scanned her dress; the men's lingered on her bosom.

She must have passed muster, at least with the cigar smoker, who tipped his hat and bowed before stepping forward to strike a match. Knowing better than to try to inhale the smoke, Nell merely held it in her mouth for a moment before letting it out. "Many thanks."

"Don't mention it." He nodded and rejoined his group, who proceeded down the stairs that led to Orlando Poole's, with Nell casually bringing up the rear as if she were one of them.

"Good evening, Mr. Cabot, Mr. Amory," greeted the Negro as he held the door for them. "Ladies."

Nell shielded her face as she passed him by turning her head to blow out a stream of smoke. He led them down the dismal little hallway, the muffled babble of voices and music growing louder as they approached a second door at the end. Opening that door, he gestured them into an enormous room that blazed so brightly with light and people and noise that Nell felt a moment's reeling disorientation.

Like Alice entering Wonderland, she thought as she surveyed all this busy, smoke-hazed opulence: the crystal chandeliers, gilt-framed mirrors, and sumptuous furnishings; the pianist playing "Juanita" at a shimmering grand piano; the waiters weaving deftly to and fro, their drink trays held high over the heads of their elegant clientele. A heavily laden banquet table took up most the back wall, with tables for poker and faro to the left, beneath a dozen bright pendant lamps. It was primarily men, quite dashing in their white cravats and tail coats, in that section of the room. The ladies, all young, all sensuously stunning in the latest Paris fashions, had mostly gravitated to the other side, which was more soothingly lit and furnished in intimate little groupings of plush velvet chairs and couches around low marble tables.

Nell ventured warily into this dazzling bacchanalia, keeping to the sparsely occupied perimeter of the right-hand section to avoid being seen as she searched for Harry Hewitt among the men gathered around the gaming tables. The way the tables were set up, however, the dealers stood facing her, while all she could see of the players, for the most part, was their backs. Given their identical dress, the fog of cigar smoke enveloping them, and her distance from the gaming pit, it was a tedious business to sort through them one by one.

"Nell? Dear God, it *is* you." The voice, lazily deep and British-accented, was so familiar—and so startling—that Nell was seized with a sudden ache in her chest, as if her heart had contracted into a tight little knot.

Chapter 8

NELL turned to find none other than William Hewitt rising from one of the tufted velvet chairs, bearing an expression of utter incredulity.

"Dr. Hewitt." She couldn't help gaping at him, not only because it was so unexpected to encounter him here—to encounter him anywhere after all these months—but because of how he looked. When she'd first beheld him last winter in that bleak little police station holding cell, he'd appeared every inch the derelict: ill-clad and grimy, battered from an overzealous police interrogation, and reeling from opium sickness. The Will Hewitt standing before her tonight in white tie and swallowtail, his black hair gleaming, a dainty orchid in his lapel, was a different man entirely.

"Back to 'Dr. Hewitt,' are we, then?" he said. "The last time we saw each other, I thought we'd agreed on first names. I must say it's not very sporting of you to amend the terms of our acquaintance without me being there to plead my case."

"Where *have* you been?"

"No place quite as interesting as this one's just become." He glanced at her unbuttoned bodice, her coyly exposed arms . . . the cigarette. "You seem to have undergone quite a transformation in my absence."

He was teasing her; she saw it in his eyes. Still, like a fool, she said, "I just . . . I needed to get in here, and the only way was to look like . . . well . . ."

"I tried to tell you once that it was possible to look too respectable. You didn't believe me." Indicating her half-burned cigarette, he said, "Are you going to smoke that? I'm fresh out."

She handed it to him; he inspected it. "No lip rouge. You don't wear it?"

"Of course not."

He took a puff, his gaze lighting on her mouth as he blew out the smoke. "I always thought you must wear a bit, at least."

She looked away for a moment, discomfited by the directness of his gaze.

"What on earth possessed you to come here?" he asked. "This hardly seems the kind of place to lure a young lady as monstrously respectable as yourself."

"I followed your brother here."

"Harry?" Will looked toward the gaming pit on the other side of the vast room.

Nell tracked his gaze to a faro table, where four men, one of them evidently Harry, were placing their bets. "I need to talk to him," she said.

"We arranged to meet here. He made me wait over an

hour, then pulled out a roll of greenbacks and headed straight for the pit."

They'd arranged to meet? During Will's brief and turbulent sojourn in Boston last winter, he'd had no direct contact at all with Harry; they hadn't seen each other since Will's Christmas furlough from the Union Army in '63. Now Will was back in town, and out on a spree with his brother. Nell's mind reeled with questions, but all she said was, "I'm surprised you're not over there yourself."

"Oh, I wouldn't wager tuppence in this place. This is a skinning joint. They entice the carriage trade here with all these gaudy trappings, then gull them out of everything in their pockets. Harry refuses to believe it because they keep the Pernod flowing like water, and he never sees a bill."

"I need to speak to him," she said.

"He won't want to speak to you." Leaning over, Will snuffed his cigarette out in an ashtray on the little marble table in front of his chair. "He doesn't seem terribly fond of you since . . . the troubles last winter."

"I apologized for the things I said about him."

"You accused him of murder, Nell. That sort of thing tends to stick in a fellow's craw."

"It's just that he seemed so . . . guilty."

"He was born seeming guilty."

"Your cognac, sir." A waiter with a trayful of drinks placed a snifter and a linen napkin on the table.

"Who ordered that?" Will indicated an egg glass half-filled with acid-green liqueur among the whiskeys and champagne flutes on the waiter's tray. The absinthe sat on a gold-rimmed saucer next to an identical saucer bearing a small pitcher of ice water, a sugar cube, and a slotted spoon.

"It's for a gentleman over there," the waiter said, nodding toward the faro tables.

"Red waistcoat?" Will asked.

"That's right."

"Take it back."

"But . . ."

Will handed him a couple of coins. "Bring him a whiskey instead. If he argues with you, send him to me."

"Yes, sir."

"And the lady will have . . . ?" Will looked inquiringly toward Nell.

"Oh, no—nothing for me. I didn't come here to—"

"But you're here now, so you may as well sit with me and have . . . a cocktail? A sherry, perhaps. At least a cup of tea."

It had been a very long time, indeed, since Nell had sat in a public house and had a drink in the company of a man. A woman in her position enjoyed certain privileges denied to the unwed ladies in whose homes she served, such as the freedom to come and go unescorted, but socializing with men was strictly forbidden. The reason, of course, was that the governess was expected to remain unmarried so as to devote her full attention to her charge, the presumption being that marriage was the ultimate goal of any association with a man. Since Nell had no such designs on Will, and Will no designs of *any* kind on her—opiates having robbed him of all fleshly hungers save the craving for more opiates—what harm could there be in allowing herself this isolated indulgence? Except . . .

"I wouldn't want to be seen," she said.

"Sit with your back to the room. No one will take any notice of you in this dark little corner. They're all far too fascinated by themselves, in any event."

She seated herself opposite Will and let him order her a sherry; he asked for a tin of Bull Durhams for himself.

"It shouldn't surprise you," Will said as he cradled the snifter in his palm, swirling the cognac to warm it, "that Harry was unmoved by your apology. Contrition is a foreign notion to him. Never having been called upon to answer for his sins, he never really absorbed the whole concept of penitence and forgiveness. Any sorrow he feels as a result of his own hurtful acts has more to do with fear of repercussions than with guilt or shame."

"Not that repercussions have ever been an issue with him."

"No. Saint August would never think of allowing his own flesh and blood to twist in the wind that way. Not when Leo Thorpe is so adept at fixing things."

Leo Thorpe, attorney, city alderman, and August Hewitt's oldest and closest friend, had been sweeping Harry Hewitt's worst transgressions under the carpet since Harry's adolescence. The arrests for public inebriation and lewdness, the whores, the gambling, the pregnant mill girls, the drunken fistfights . . . All it ever took was Alderman Thorpe to grease the right palms, and it was as if none of it had ever happened.

"I'm surprised to find you and Harry in contact with each other," Nell said.

Will held his snifter to his nose for a moment to savor the cognac's aroma, but he didn't sip it. "I got back to town six days ago—Friday morning. Took a room at the Revere House, stuffed myself on oysters, and then I strolled on down to Colonnade Row. I sat on a bench just inside the Common, across from my parents' house, and waited for you to step outside."

She didn't bother asking him why he didn't just walk up to the front door and knock. Long estranged from his parents, especially his coldly judgmental father, it was little wonder he didn't care to face them.

"I was on my sixth cigarette," he said, "when I finally saw you come out. You weren't alone, though."

"Ah." Nell was beginning to understand. "Gracie."

"You were laughing, the two of you. You took her by the hand and ran across the street and into the park. She had a little toy sailboat with her."

"She likes to sail it in the Frog Pond."

"I hid until you'd passed."

"Will . . ."

"She's a pretty little thing."

"You should have—"

"No, Nell," he said gravely. "I shouldn't have."

"Wouldn't you like to finally meet her? I mean really meet her, face to face? You're her father."

"A father who makes his living playing cards and can't go four hours without a syringe full of morphine."

She'd wondered whether he was still addicted. "It's still just morphine, then?" she asked. "You haven't gone back to . . . ?"

"The pipe?" He shook his head. "No, I've managed to steer clear of all that. Opium . . . it's too seductive, too . . . mesmerizing. It consumes me, it becomes all I want, all I can think about. Morphine doesn't carry quite the same allure. I use it like medicine, twenty milligrams by injection six times a day—just enough to keep from going into withdrawal. And, of course, to keep the leg from aching too badly."

"It still troubles you, then?" Four years ago, a bullet had torn a chunk out of Will's right thigh. His limp was far worse when he was sober than when he was under the influence of the poppy.

"It's not too bad," he said, "so long as I don't let too much time pass between shots."

The waiter came with her sherry, the cigarettes, and a box of matches. Will clicked his glass against hers. "To the renewal of our acquaintance. May it remain both intriguing and agreeable."

The sherry was sticky-sweet and slick as satin. Nell felt it warm a path all the way down to her stomach.

"Do you mind?" Will asked as he opened the Bull Durham tin.

"Not at all."

Withdrawing a cigarette, he said, "While you and Gracie were conducting nautical maneuvers in the Frog Pond that afternoon, I procured a little runabout for the day and drove up to Charlestown to see Harry."

"You went to the mill? You didn't happen to be talking to Harry out in the courtyard when the dinner bell rang?"

He stilled, the lit match in one hand, the cigarette in the other. "Were you there?"

"No—not on Friday. I was there yesterday, and some of the mill workers mentioned having seen your brother talking to a man last Friday who . . . matched your description." *I swear, I thought they was gonna swoon dead away.*

"You should have seen Harry's face when his secretary announced me." Will lit the cigarette, blew a stream of smoke away from her. "We hadn't seen each other in, what—almost five years?"

"Why did you seek him out?" She almost said, *Why on earth?*

Will settled back in his chair, crossed his long legs,

studied the cognac in his glass. "I'd been thinking about him since last winter, when I came to realize how little he'd changed, and that I bear a certain measure of responsibility for his weakness of character."

"For not having steered him toward righteousness during his rakehell adolescence?" Nell asked. Will's self-flagellation over this issue was familiar territory. "Your mother told me there was little you could have done, with you two being six years apart in age, and Harry so resistant to accepting guidance."

"If anyone could have managed it, it would have been I. We were fundamentally alike, Harry and I, both drawn to sin like crows to carrion. I could have made him listen, forced him to change . . . if I hadn't been so utterly self-absorbed."

"You were in England most of that time," she reminded him. "I don't know what you think you could have accomplished during the few weeks each year you were home on holiday."

"And I suppose we'll never know. But there's no reason I can't try to make up for lost time now. This is the third evening Harry and I have spent together since I've been back."

"If your purpose in befriending him now is to mold him into an upright gentleman of strong morals and steady habits, I wish you the very best of luck. God knows you'll need it." She raised her glass in a mocking toast.

He smiled into her eyes. "I've missed you, Nell."

She looked down, took a sip of her sherry. "What have you been up to these past months?"

He shrugged. "The usual. Three or four different cities, a hundred different card games."

"Will you be in Boston very long?"

"I'm here for an ultra high stakes poker game that's to

take place at the Parker House on Monday. Did you miss *me?*"

"Oh, shit."

Nell looked up to find Harry hovering over them, a glass of whiskey in one hand, cigar in the other, regarding Nell with an expression of disgust.

Will said, "There's a lady present, old man."

"Is there?" Harry made a show of looking around. "All I see is some impudent little Irish bitch who managed to slither in here when no one was—"

"That's enough, Harry." Will rose to his feet, a hard thrust to his jaw.

Harry backed off a step, grinning. "Steady, now. No point in coming to blows over some cherry you're trying to pluck. She's a ripe one, I'll give you that, but a bit on the sour side, and damnably hard to pry off the stem. I should know."

Will said, "If it's a bloody nose you're angling for, Harry, I'm more than happy to—"

"Easy, brother. I just came over to ask you what the devil you thought you were doing, sending me this pointless swill?" He gestured with the whiskey, which spilled over the rim of the glass.

"Your absinthe habit seems to be getting a bit out of hand," Will said. "I'd rein it in if I were you."

"Ah, but you're not me. Nor are you my keeper. So I'll thank you to keep your nose out of things that are none of your concern."

"It's none of my concern if my brother has a steadily escalating habit that's been known to lead to full-blown psychosis?"

Harry smirked at the unfamiliar word. "If you're trying to dazzle me with arcane medical terms—"

"Lunacy," Will said. "Hallucinations, convulsions, violent outbursts. Absinthism has led to suicides, murders . . ."

"You're a fine one to lecture me on the subject of bad habits," Harry said. "What do you suppose I'd find if I went through the inside pockets of that handsome tailcoat of yours, eh? A hypodermic syringe, perchance? A little vial of morphine solution?"

"Which is precisely why I feel competent to deliver advice on the subject of bad habits," Will countered. "You've been an absinthe drinker for about half a year, yes? You'd do well to give it up while you've still got the mental rigor to do so."

"Mental rigor?" Harry snorted with laughter. "What on earth makes you think I've ever been burdened by such a malady?" Turning to Nell, he said, "That's *your* cross to bear, is it not, Miss Sweeney? If you've ever said or done an untoward thing—aside from that rather entertaining little spectacle in our opera box last winter—I was never there to witness it . . . until now."

She was about to ask what he meant by that when she realized that her mere presence in this den of sin, a drink in her hand, a man of William Hewitt's notoriety sitting across from her, would be more than enough to destroy any governess.

Harry puffed on his cigar, looking coolly amused. "What do you suppose my father would say if he knew I'd seen you here? He'd jump at the chance to be rid of you."

"Your mother prevented that once," she said. "She can do it again."

"How many reprieves do you think you'll get? Two? Four? Sooner or later, even Mother, resourceful though she is, will be powerless to save you from the chopping block."

"As long as we're speculating about ruined reputations," Will said, "how do you suppose Saint August would react if he found out how many bottles of *la fée verte* you consume in a given week? Or how much money you leave behind at places like this?"

"What makes you think I'm not winning tonight?"

"I've told you, Harry—they run a brace game here. Nobody wins."

Harry regarded his brother in surly silence for a moment. "You're a bastard, you know that, Will?"

"Yes, actually," Will replied through a haze of smoke. "I've known that for some time."

"Brother . . . Miss Sweeney . . ." Harry executed a stiff little bow in her direction. "I won't insult your intelligence by saying it's been a pleasure." He turned and left.

"Wasn't there something you needed to speak to him about?" Will asked.

Nell just sighed.

"Do you want me to call him back?"

She shook her head, raised her glass to her lips. "What would be the point?"

Chapter 9

"DINNERTIME!" Gracie called as she tossed chunks of bread into the water. "Come and get it!"

There arose a chorus of greedy quacks as half a dozen fat mallards paddled toward the little girl standing at the edge of the pond. They raced toward their afternoon snack, competing over the choicest bits as Gracie giggled and clapped.

Most afternoons in September, Boston's Public Gardens resembled a giant lawn party, with scores of young children frolicking together under the watchful eyes of their mothers and nannies. Today, however, it was nearly deserted, thanks to a cold leaden sky that prickled with impending rain. Nell had tried to talk Gracie into spending the afternoon at the library or the Natural History Museum, but the child wouldn't hear of it. Barely four and already a creature of habit, she tended to get out of sorts if she had to give up her daily walk and duck-feeding session.

"Can I have some more?" Gracie asked as she ran over to Nell, sitting on a nearby bench with a quarter-loaf of stale brioche wrapped in a napkin on her lap.

"Well, I suppose you *can*," Nell said. "But—"

"*May* I have some more?"

"Of course, since you've asked so nicely. But you need to break it into smaller pieces, like this." Peeling off her kid gloves, Nell tore off a hunk and shredded it into the child's cupped hands. "And don't throw it all in at once. Oh, and *do* try to stay clean," she added as she brushed crumbs off her own coat and Gracie's.

"Miseeney, why that man watching me?" Gracie asked.

"What man?" Nell's scalp tingled.

"That man wight over there," the child said, nodding over Nell's shoulder.

Nell turned to look behind her. A tall man in a low-crowned top hat, black frock coat, and fawn trousers stood about fifty yards away, leaning against the trunk of an enormous copper beech tree. He smiled and tipped his hat, then pushed off the tree and started toward them.

"Do you know him?" Gracie was watching Nell stare.

"I . . . yes, that's . . ." Nell looked from Will to his daughter, and back again. "That's a friend of mine." The statement came so easily. A friend. When, precisely, had she and the complicated, difficult, too-charming William Hewitt become friends?

His limp, as he walked toward them, was barely noticeable; he must have dosed himself with morphine very recently. By midnight last night, when he bid her good night at the front door of 148 Tremont, he'd been limping rather badly—but then, he'd probably gone over four hours at that point without an injection.

He'd insisted on escorting her home, despite the fact

that Patrick Nulty was waiting outside Poole's hell, as promised, to take her back in his hack. Will collected Nell's things and sent Mr. Nulty on his way with a quarter for his trouble, then took Nell's arm and walked her back to Colonnade Row. He asked her what she'd wanted to talk to Harry about, and she told him—about Bridie Sullivan's disappearance, her visit to Charlestown, and her abortive attempts to wring information out of Harry. She disclosed everything, even her visit to Duncan and the uninvited correspondence that had prompted it.

All Will really knew about Duncan was that Nell had been involved with him before Dr. Greaves, that he'd hurt her badly eight years ago, and that he was serving a thirty-year prison term for aggravated assault. That was essentially still all he knew. She hadn't told him everything about her life back then, nor did she intend to. It was one thing to trust him with information that could damage her; it was another to arm him with the ammunition to utterly destroy her.

It saddened her to have to cordon off parts of her past from this man with whom she'd forged, during their fiery association last winter, a grudging but very real bond of affection and trust. But then she reminded herself that she'd felt that same bond once with Duncan, and before that, with her brother Jamie, despite their being reprobates of the first order. Had her judgment improved so dramatically during the past few years? Like Duncan and Jamie, Will was an inebriate who lived outside the law. Perhaps he wasn't really that different. Perhaps he was just smarter, subtler, better at disguising his true nature.

And therefore, potentially far more dangerous.

"Is he nice?" Gracie asked as she watched Will walking toward them, then answered the question herself while Nell was still ruminating over an answer. "Of course he's nice. Otherwise you wouldn't be fwiends with him—wight?"

"Wight. Um, right." More or less.

Will lifted his hat again and bowed when he joined them. "Ladies."

"Will." Nell's gaze connected with Will's for a brief, expressive moment; sensing his uncertainty at finally presenting himself to Gracie, she offered a smile of encouragement.

Gracie stared openly at Will as she cupped the bread crumbs carefully in the bowl of her chubby little hands.

Nell said, "May I present Miss Grace Elizabeth Lindleigh Hewitt. Gracie, this is . . ." She looked toward Will.

He hitched up his trousers and crouched down until he was eye level with Gracie. His smile touched something in Nell's chest. "Will Hewitt. I'm most pleased to make your acquaintance."

Gracie, in admirable command of her manners when it suited her, replied, "And I yours, Mr. Hewitt."

"Dr. Hewitt," Nell corrected.

"You're a doctor?" Gracie asked. "Like Dr. Dwummond?" Old Dr. Drummond had been treating the Hewitt family for the past three decades.

Will hesitated. "I used to be."

"Did you forget how?"

He scrubbed a hand over his chin. "No, but . . ."

"We have the same last name." Gracie's attention occasionally leap-frogged during a conversation.

Nell said, "That's because Dr. Hewitt is Nana and Papa's son."

"Like Uncle Martin and Uncle Hawy?"

"That's right."

Leaning toward Nell, Gracie whispered, "Then shouldn't I call him Uncle Will?"

Nell looked toward Will, who, still crouching, studied his hands for a moment. He nodded, smiled at Gracie. "That would be fine . . . at least for the time being."

Will reached out to straighten his daughter's hair ribbon, his fingers trailing lightly through her hair and along her big, downy cheek as he withdrew his hand.

Indicating her bread crumbs, Gracie said, "I've got to feed the ducks. I feed them evwy day after my nap. They get hungwy in the afternoon."

"Then you'd best get to it," he said as he straightened up.

She turned and sprinted to the edge of the pond, into which she sprinkled a few crumbs for the eagerly awaiting ducks.

Will watched her for a few moments, then turned to Nell and said, "You've done well with her."

"Thank you," she said, sincerely gratified.

"Does she know she's adopted?"

"She knows your parents aren't her real parents. Your mother told her she picked her out special because she'd always wanted a little girl just like her." It was actually close to the truth, if a simplified and honey-coated version of it. "That's as much as she can comprehend for now. Your mother intends to explain more when Gracie gets older, but she doesn't know whether she should tell her about you . . . and Annie." Annie McIntyre was the chambermaid whose one grief-fueled night in Will's bed during that Christmas furlough in '63 resulted in Gracie's birth nine months later.

Will looked thoughtful as he watched Gracie dispense the brioche a few crumbs at a time to the ducks.

"May I?" He gestured toward the unoccupied stretch of bench, on which she'd lain her large black umbrella and Gracie's smaller pink one.

"Please." Nell propped the umbrellas against the arm rest and scooted over a bit, gathering in her skirts, although there was plenty of room for him. She felt foolish to be rattled by his nearness, and embarrassed that he might realize it.

He seated himself a respectable distance from her, crossed his legs, and withdrew a handsome sharkskin cigarette case. "Do you mind?"

"I don't, but the Boston constabulary might."

"They tend to hunker down indoors on days like this with their bottles and their dice." He lit the cigarette, flicked out the match. "I went back to Poole's after I left you last night."

"Was your brother still there?" she asked, picking at the brioche as she kept an eye on Gracie.

Will nodded as he expelled a stream of smoke; it hung like fog in the sodden air. "Still hemorrhaging shiners at the faro tables. He'd lost over six hundred dollars by the time I got back."

The air left Nell's lungs. Six hundred dollars was a year's salary for her.

"He was down to his last two double eagles," Will said, "so it was no great challenge to talk him into going elsewhere. I suggested a little grog shop on Devonshire where one can play *vingt-et-un* on fair terms for low stakes. It's only a few blocks from Poole's, so we walked. I took him to task for dismissing you at the mill, and I explained that you'd wanted to ask him about this Bridie Sullivan—at the behest of Lady Viola, so he'd understand he was slighting her as well as you. He said a lady as savvy as our mother ought to know better than to enlist the likes of you for anything other than cooking and scrubbing, if that, and that he had no intention of encouraging your continued employment by cooperating in this—how did he put it?—'farcical attempt by one little high-reaching Irish drab to locate another.' "

Nell gritted her teeth against the insult; she'd heard worse. "Does it mean nothing to him that Bridie may have been kidnapped—or even killed?"

"I asked him that," Will said as he drew on his cigarette. From the corner of her eye, as she kept her gaze trained on Gracie, she saw him watching her. "He said the world was better off without the lesser breeds in general, and larcenous strumpets like Bridie in particular, and that if any harm had befallen her, it was almost certainly of her own making."

"Larcenous?" She turned to look at him. "Did you ask him what he meant by that?"

"I didn't have to. He was drunk as a lord by that point—he'd been swilling absinthe the whole time I was gone—and he tends toward verbosity when he's in his cups. He launched into a rather fervent soliloquy on the subject of Bridie Sullivan and her many defects of character, although she does apparently possess certain . . . amorous talents that made her acquaintance worth cultivating for a while."

"I'll bet." Cupping her hands to her mouth, Nell called out, "You're a bit too close to the water, Gracie. Back up a step." The child complied, albeit with a sigh and a dramatic rolling of the eyes.

"Bridie started at the mill in June," Will said, leaning forward to rest his elbows on his knees. "Harry noticed her the first day, as she was leaving work. The next morning, he summoned her to his office on some pretext. He said as soon as she walked in, he could tell by her smile that she knew exactly why she was there. He was quite eloquent on the subject of that initial encounter." He glanced at her, hesitated. "I'll spare you the details except to say that it was not remotely a seduction. She was no shy maiden he had to coax and romance—in fact, she took the reins herself rather early on."

"According to him." Painting Bridie as the aggressor would support Harry's image of himself as an object of desire to the females in his employ.

Will nodded to acknowledge her point. "In any event, she was his favorite all summer. At first, he just gave her the same sorts of little tokens he gave the others—lace stockings, hair combs . . . But she started demanding more lavish gifts—jewelry, bonnets, silk frocks. It rankled him—he felt manipulated—but by that point, he was utterly in her thrall. He told me he felt he'd finally met his match, in terms of . . . physical appetites, and he didn't want to lose her."

Having reduced the hunk of brioche to a pile of crumbs—more from nerves than industriousness—Nell gathered them up in the napkin and brought them to Gracie. The sky was darkening rapidly, the trees swaying. Had Will not joined them, she would have started back by now.

"Did he mention seeing Virgil kiss Bridie last Friday?" Nell asked as she returned to the bench.

"Mention it? He flew into a sputtering rage over it."

"Why? As you say, she was no innocent, and he knew that. Theirs was hardly an affair of the heart."

"To understand, you need to know that she'd informed him, not two weeks before, that she was . . . in an interesting condition."

"Oh, dear." Curiouser and curiouser, as Gracie would say. "By him?"

"She swore it had to be, that there'd been no one else all summer."

"Ah, yes. He didn't know about Virgil."

Will expelled a lengthy sigh. "He gave her forty dollars and the address of a French midwife who's apparently adept at, er, making such problems disappear."

Nell winced, one hand automatically coming to rest on her stomach. "It can't possibly cost so much to . . . avail oneself of such services."

"It's just a few dollars, from what I've been told," Will said as he ground out his cigarette. "The rest was . . . a bribe, if you will. Inducement for her to keep her mouth shut about her relationship with him."

A rather stingy bribe, Nell thought, considering how much Harry regularly threw away at the gaming tables. "Why did Harry make these arrangements himself? Your father always has Leo Thorpe take care of these things."

"It would appear that the old man's tolerance for Harry's antics is beginning to wane. He's started to fret about the family's reputation and standing. As far as Saint August is concerned, there are but two Hewitt sons—Martin and Harry. Now that Martin has settled on a religious vocation, that leaves Harry to take over the family enterprises and represent the Hewitts in Boston society. A couple of months ago, he called Harry into the Library and told him his days of carefree excess were over, that he was to start toeing the line or face the consequences."

"Consequences?"

"Disinheritance."

Nell turned to gape at Will. "He wouldn't."

"According to Harry, he was deadly serious. Threatened to have Leo cut him loose the very next time he got arrested, or knocked up a mill girl, or otherwise embarrassed the family."

Will gazed at his daughter as she strolled along the edge of the pond, sprinkling bread crumbs in front of a raucous parade of ducks. His sharply carved profile and marble pale complexion—the latter owing, most likely, to his morphine habit—called to mind what the mill girl Cora had said. *That fella had a face like on one of those Roman statues.* It was a dramatic face, a face that begged to be rendered in black, dense charcoal on paper that had a nice, rough tooth to it.

"Yes, well, threats or no," she said, "Harry doesn't exactly seem to have mended his ways."

"He did tell me he's trying to be more discreet," Will said. "He's limiting his carousing to indoor venues, at night, and he's having that vapid little valet of his act as procurer when he's in the mood for 'street trash,' as he calls it, rather than soliciting such trade himself."

"That's his idea of discretion?"

"As far as Harry is concerned, these are major accommodations. Believe me, he dreads the prospect of losing all those lovely privileges that come with being a Hewitt."

"So instead of running to Papa when Bridie got in trouble," Nell said, "he paid her off himself."

"And that was supposed to have been the end of it, which just goes to show how naïve Harry is, beneath his urbane exterior. Leo Thorpe would have given the girl much more money, sent someone with her to the midwife, and arranged for her to move somewhere quite far away, but Harry thought he could throw her a bone and get away with it. He let her stay on at the mill so that she could continue to pay him those diverting little visits up in his office.

He really hadn't thought the matter through at all."

"It's not so much naivete as deep self-involvement," Nell said, not even trying to keep the bitterness out of her voice. "Harry is so wrapped up in his own needs and desires that it never occurs to him that someone else, especially some lowly little Irish mill girl, might have needs and desires that conflict with his—and the cleverness to act on them."

"In any event, Bridie came back a week later and told him she'd had a change of heart. She'd decided to keep the baby, and would require regular and generous infusions of cash ad infinitum in order to rear it properly."

Nell let out a chuckle that sounded more like a groan. "I almost feel sorry for Harry. What did he say?"

"He balked at first, so she threatened to go to Saint August and tell him everything. His back was to the wall then, so he agreed to pay her a hundred dollars at the beginning of every month, once the baby was born, plus whatever other expenses she would require for the purposes of buying a house, educating the child, clothing him, and so forth."

Nell shook her head, impressed, in spite of herself, with Bridie's triumph over the loathsome Harry. "Quite a bonanza for someone like Bridie. She must have been ecstatic."

"Until Virgil Hines greeted her with that rather ill-timed kiss," Will said.

"No wonder Harry was so livid." And Bridie so furious with Virgil.

"Harry realized he'd been had. She was extorting money from him to support a child who might very well not be his. Of course, I didn't know that at the time. I was there, and I knew something had upset him, but he wouldn't talk to me about it, not then—didn't know how much he could trust me with, I suppose. It took a bellyful of absinthe to loosen his tongue."

"That kiss happened last Friday," Nell said, sorting through the chronology in her mind. "The next morning, Harry fired Bridie."

"That actually wasn't his intent when he fetched her up to his office. He told her he'd deny having fathered her child—after all, scores of people saw this Hines fellow kissing her. He'd claim he'd given her the forty dollars merely to avoid trouble, and he told her she could keep her job so long as she let the matter drop quietly. Unfortunately for Bridie, she called his bluff. Told him he could deal with her or with the old man—it was his choice. At that point, he was in no mood for ultimatums. He told her to collect her things and leave."

"Wasn't he worried that she *would* go to your father? Even if she couldn't prove her child was Harry's, she could prove he was still chasing mill girls."

"Harry did confess that he's breathed a bit more easily since she dropped out of sight."

"Yes," Nell said with a humorless little laugh. "I should imagine he has."

Will frowned at her tone. "Which doesn't mean he had anything to do with her disappearance."

Half touched and half disgusted by Will's fraternal allegiance, Nell said, "But it *was* rather convenient, no?"

He turned toward her, one arm draped across the back of the bench, his fingertips grazing the velvet collar of her coat. Quietly he said, "You're heading down the wrong path here, Nell—after all, Virgil Hines disappeared, too. Who's to say they *didn't* run off together? Or, if foul play was involved, that Hines wasn't responsible?"

Nell trained her gaze on Gracie, filled her lungs with

air, let it out. "I'm just taking a peek in Harry's direction, Will, not calling out the hounds."

He leaned a bit closer. "Look. I know Harry's a bit of a blighter—self-indulgent, immature. And I can't deny his moral compass is a bit out of whack . . ."

"He doesn't own a moral compass." Feigning a levity she didn't feel, Nell said, "Perhaps, as part of your campaign to rehabilitate him, you could buy one for him."

Will didn't smile. "He's not a monster, Nell."

Turning to face him, she said, very soberly, "That's what Father Beals said about Duncan. The problem is, not all monsters look like monsters. Those who hide their true nature the best are the most monstrous of all, because they ultimately do the most harm." Gentling her voice, in light of how painful this must be for him, she said, "Will, I know Harry is your brother, and that you feel a certain measure of fraternal loyalty toward him, but he simply has no conception of right and wrong. The rules the rest of us live by—they don't exist for him. He's selfish, demanding, vicious . . ."

"Vicious? Harry?" Will scoffed. "If the occasional drunken fistfight makes someone vicious, then you'll have to tar me with the same brush."

"Would you ever attack a woman?"

"No, and neither would Harry."

Nell looked at Will, sighed, looked away. "How I wish you were right."

"Whom is he supposed to have attacked? Bridie Sullivan?"

"No," Nell said. "Me."

Chapter 10

WILL stared at her. A bead of water quivered on the brim of his hat, fell onto the sleeve of his coat and dissolved into the fine black wool.

She looked up. The sky had grown dusky as twilight. Clouds hovered like smoke, roiling, swelling . . .

A droplet struck the corner of Nell's eye, slid down her cheek. She lowered her face to find Will tugging off his right-hand glove. He brushed his thumb across her cheek and then down along the raindrop's damp path, until it met the high collar of her coat.

Will reached around her. She flattened herself against the back of the bench as he lifted the umbrellas she'd leaned against the arm rest. He opened the large one with a whump and handed it to Nell, then sprinted over to Gracie with hers.

Nell closed her eyes, breathed in the saturated air, listened to the patter of rain on the drum-tight silk of the umbrella.

"Nell? Are you all right?"

She opened her eyes to find Will taking the umbrella from her and reaching for her hand.

"Yes, of course," she said as he helped her to her feet, his touch startlingly warm on her bare hand. "The air just feels so thick at the beginning of a rainstorm." She fumbled in her coat pocket for her gloves, tugged them back on.

"Uncle Will's going to walk us home," announced Gracie from beneath her dainty pink umbrella. "He says I can walk up ahead."

"So long as you stay in view," Nell cautioned.

Holding the umbrella over both of them, Will offered Nell his arm. She took it and let him escort her through the Public Gardens toward the adjacent Common, the most direct route to Colonnade Row. Gracie skipped along the path ahead of them, one hand outstretched to feel the raindrops.

"What happened?" asked Will, his expression grim. Nell felt the taut muscles of his forearm through the damp woolen coat sleeve.

She drew in a breath, but she still felt as if she couldn't really fill her lungs. It would hurt Will to learn the truth about his brother, but if she were in his place, she would want to know. "It was toward the end of May. Harry had been living in Jack's house on Commonwealth for about two months. He never came home for visits—because of me, he said. Because of how outrageous it was that I should 'eviscerate his character in public,' as he put it, and yet he'd still have to face me, holding down a position of responsibility, every time he walked into his own family's home."

"It was in public that you . . . ?"

"It was at the Tremont Temple, but in your family's private box. I'm quite sure they were the only ones who heard me. I felt awful for your mother afterward. She stuck her neck out for me, so I got to keep my job—and Gracie, which meant far more to me—but in doing so, she lost yet another son."

"Well . . . that may be overstating it a bit."

"Harry literally *never* came home, Will, and he didn't come to Falconwood for even a brief visit while we were there over the summer. As far as I know, your mother hasn't seen him once since he moved out."

"For which Harry, not you, is entirely to blame. You do realize that."

"In the abstract. But it pained me so much every time your mother would invite him to Sunday dinner and get no response. Needless to say, he was never in church. He'd only ever gone before because your father bullied him into it."

Will, an unbeliever who probably hadn't entered a church since *he* was last bullied into it in his youth, kept diplomatically mum.

The misty rain had intensified into a soft, steady shower, turning the surrounding parkland into a pastiche of greenish-gray smears, as if God had swiped His paintbrush haphazardly over soaking wet watercolor paper. Little Gracie was but a happily bobbing, pinkish-wet blur.

"I decided to initiate a truce," Nell said, "even if it meant humbling myself with further apologies. One evening around the middle of May, I asked Miss Parrish to feed Gracie her supper, and I walked over to Commonwealth. I'd wanted to catch Harry before he went out for the evening, and while he was still somewhat sober. He was home all right, but, well . . . He was eating his supper at one end of that huge Hepplewhite dining table—he's got all of Jack's old furniture, you know—but he was washing it down with absinthe . . ."

"MISS Sweeney," Harry said thickly, a glass in one hand, a knife in the other. "How oddly unexpected." He made no move to rise from his chair, merely waved away his man, Edwin Speck, who'd ushered Nell into the palatial formal dining room.

The room felt stuffy despite its size and the mildness of the evening because Harry had the windows shut, their oilcloth roller shades fully drawn beneath brocade-swagged net curtains. She was surprised to find that the Thorpes had left that monumental Venetian chandelier hanging from the lofty ceiling. Harry had the gas turned low, bathing the room in an eerie, crystallized half-light.

Dispensing with preliminaries, Nell said, "I've come to see if we can't bury the hatchet."

Harry thrust the knife into the half-eaten squab on his plate and swallowed down the contents of his glass. "Why?" Yanking the stopper out of a carafe containing a small amount of yellowish-green liqueur, he proceeded to refill the glass with a wobbly precision that betrayed how muddled he already was.

It wasn't a cut crystal wineglass he was recharging, as Nell had first thought, but one of those special absinthe glasses with a narrow reservoir at the bottom to mark off the dose. Pouring slowly, and with bleary concentration, Harry overfilled the reservoir by a deliberate half inch, then jammed the stopper back in the carafe so hard she almost expected it to crack.

In reflecting back on this evening later, she would regret not having turned and walked away right then. *He'll be easier to handle this way,* she thought at the time. *Slower, muzzier, more open to suggestion.*

More the fool she.

"You're breaking your mother's heart, estranging yourself from her like this," she told him.

"She might've thought of that before blackmailing the old man into letting you stay on." Harry balanced an absinthe spoon across the glass with exaggerated care before placing a sugar cube on its perforated bowl.

Nell stiffened her back along with her resolve. Before coming here, she'd changed into the blue merino suit she thought of as The Uniform because of its exotically martial Zouave jacket. Although fitted with hooks and loops all down the front, she wore it fastened at the neck only, to show off her favorite shirtwaist—white with little curlicues of black braid down the front. A stylishly mannish little bonnet completed the outfit, which always made her feel a bit more confident than usual, as if she were strapping on armor.

"Any responsibility for this state of affairs rests entirely with me," she said.

Harry appeared to contemplate that as he poured a slow stream of water from a pitcher over the sugar cube. As it dissolved, the mixture of absinthe and sugar water in the glass turned whitish and hazy.

"That would certainly appear to be the case, at first blush." He stood, his napkin falling to the floor, and held the glass up to the light, admiring the opalescent liquid, which really was quite wickedly beautiful. Even from her position at the foot of the table, Nell could smell the aromatic, anise-flavored liqueur. Harry had on a garishly striped vest and matching Dickens-style cravat, which he'd no doubt worn to the mill that day, but he'd replaced his business coat with a lounging jacket of amethyst velvet festooned with braids and tassels.

"You made an absurd accusation against me." He spoke slowly, pronouncing his words with care in an evident attempt to disguise the extent of his drunkenness. "Whas' worse, you made it in the presence of my family and half of Boston society. But!" He held up a finger to punctuate his point. "It was Mamá who kept Father from tossing you out on that pretty li'l rump, as you so well deserved." Harry raised the glass to his lips and drank half of it in one tilt.

Wavering slightly on his feet, he said, "She ought to've known better than to take your side against her own. It's a weakness of some of the more . . . tender-hearted among the better classes to assume that the lower orders share their sterling qualities deep down—that all that really separates us is filthy lucre. All that Unitarian bunkum Martin's been getting mixed up in. People like that—people like Martin and Mamá—they fall all over themselves making excuses when your kind show their true colors."

"My kind?" The words were out of her mouth before she could stop them. Dr. Greaves would have cautioned her to think before she spoke.

Harry drained his glass and reached for the carafe. "It's no secret why the Irish live as they do, crammed together in their squalid little wharfside burrows, preying on each other and any poor unfortunate who happens to get in their way. Yours is a primitive race—intellectually stunted, too shif'less to get regular work, too intemperate to keep it when you do, and all too readily—"

Nell let out a little gasp of outrage, her gaze homing in on the carafe, now empty, and the glass in his hand, which he'd just overfilled for the third—or possibly fourth or fifth time. "You're a fine one to talk about intemperance."

"Les' see, where was I? Ah, yes—and all too readily excited to anger." Harry directed an oily smile at her while struggling drunkenly to prop the spoon and sugar cube over the absinthe. "As you've just obligingly demonstrated. Look at you. You couldn't be any pinker if I'd slapped you. Nobody blushes like the Irish." Filling the glass with water, he added, in a cartoonishly bad brogue, "'Specially you creamy-skinned lasses with just a wee touch o' fire in your hair." He raised his glass in her direction, took a generous gulp.

Nell cursed the warmth in her cheeks, which only intensified as Harry stood there grinning at her. She unclenched her hands, took a calming breath. "I came here out of concern for your mother. Surely you care enough about her, despite the malice you bear me, to come to some kind of terms."

He sauntered toward her, swirling the remaining absinthe in its glass. In lieu of boots or shoes, he wore gold-embroidered slippers made out of the same amethyst velvet as his smoking jacket. "I must confess, thas' one thing I would've missed if Father'd managed to sack you—those red-hot blushes of yours. They give you away, you know. Every passion that inflames you—loathing, frustration . . . desire—it's all seared onto your cheeks like a brand."

Desire? "You're imagining things."

"Am I?" Harry paused a few feet away from her and bowed with mock gravity. "My apologies, dear lady, if your sensibilities have been offended." He straightened up, his gaze refocusing, with apparent difficulty, behind her. "Yes, Speck."

That obsequious little valet was standing in the wide doorway, one hand on each of a pair of ornately carved pocket doors, which he was in the process of pulling together. That Nell hadn't heard him doing so was a testament to well-oiled runners, a talent for stealth, or both.

"Shall I lay out your evening clothes, sir?" Speck asked.

"No, not tonight. But you can go down to the corner and get me another bottle of Pernod." Harry tossed back the rest of his absinthe and thunked the glass on the table. "It looks as if I'll be staying in tonight, seeing as I have such diverting company."

Nell said, "I'm leaving, actually," but Speck resumed pulling the doors closed as if he hadn't heard her. She said, "Excuse me, but I said I'm—"

"He'll only respond if he hears it from me," Harry said.

The doors met with a muted click. Nell took a step toward them, only to have Harry grab her arm. "Are you sure you want to leave so soon? What about burying the hatchet?"

Trying ineffectually to pull away from him, she said, "You've no intention of letting that happen."

"Oh, I don't know." He raked his gaze the length of her and back up again in audaciously frank appraisal. "We might be able to work something out."

"Let me go." She pried at his fingers, heart tripping, but he merely seized her other arm, his grip painfully tight, and backed her up against the table. *"Mr. Speck!"* she screamed, while straining to break free. *"Help me!"*

"You're turning quite red. Does it feel as warm as it looks?" Harry leaned close, his licorice-sweet breath hot on her face, forcing her to bend backward.

"Mr. Speck! Anyone!" Nell tried to writhe out of his grasp, but he was a good deal bigger than she, and surpris-

ingly strong for a man who'd never done a day of honest work in his life. She thought about Duncan, how effortlessly he'd overpowered her, how brutally he'd used her, and felt a paralyzing certainty that it was about to happen all over again.

Don't panic, or you're done for, Nell told herself. *Keep your head. Use your wits.*

"How I do love seeing the blood rise in your cheeks," Harry said, "seeing your own body betray you so cruelly . . . and all because I've managed to get you in a bit of a pucker—not all that hard to do. Your passions run close to the surface, don't thcy?—and hot as lava." He pressed closer, gripped her tighter, his fingers biting into her arms. "But you keep it all locked up tight, 'cause that's the way your man in Rome likes it, isn't that right?"

"You don't want to do this," she said, wishing to God her voice weren't so tremulous. "It's the absinthe . . ."

"Oh, I've wanted this since well before the absinthe." Gripping both her wrists with one hand, he unhooked her jacket and closed a hand over her snugly corseted bosom through her shirtwaist. "I've wanted it ever since Mamá first brought you back from the Cape."

"Well, *I* haven't wanted it. And I don't, so—"

"Come now, do you really want to go to your grave without knowing a man's touch, like some ugly little chit who never had a choice?" He flicked open the little buttons securing her shirt's high, starched collar. "I won't tell a soul, I swear, and then afterward, we can consider the hatchet well and truly buried, just as you wanted." Lowering his voice suggestively, he said, "Relax—I know how to take a maidenhead. And it'll be so much more pleasant if you cooperate."

"And if I don't?"

"Then it will be *un*pleasant. But then"—he showed his

teeth—"I sometimes like it that way." He yanked at the shirt, scratching her chest; fabric ripped, buttons popped.

"Somebody!" she cried out as she struggled against him. She tried to kick, but her spring-steel crinoline made that futile.

"You're wearing out your voice for naught," Harry said. "Speck is out buying me more absinthe, and even if he weren't, he's remarkably well-trained, as lapdogs go—hears only his master's voice. That leaves my cook, and she's deaf as a stump. Not that you shouldn't scream your heart out, if it pleases you. I know it pleases *me*."

He tried to tug her right hand toward that part of him that would presumably attest to this. Nell strained against him; he laughed.

She slammed her foot down on his, her boot's spool heel encountering little resistance from the velvet slipper. She felt a soft, stomach-turning crunch.

He bellowed.

She pushed him away.

He stumbled backward, swearing.

She ran to the door, reached for the pulls.

"Bitch!" Harry seized her from behind and wrestled her, thrashing and punching, back to the table. He bent her over it, facedown, kicked her feet apart. Tearing off her hat and the silk net that had secured her chignon, he fisted a hand in her hair, crushing her cheek against the slickly polished mahogany. She flailed at him with her fists, but because of her awkward position, the few punches that connected were too weak to even slow him down.

"This is your fault, damn you," he growled as he untied the sash of his lounging jacket. "You had to make this difficult. You couldn't just admit that you want this as much as I do."

"No!" Nell screamed when she felt him start to gather up her skirts.

Don't panic, don't panic. There must be something you can do, something you can use . . .

The absinthe glass. He'd set it down on the table, but she couldn't see it, so it must be behind her. Unable to turn her head, she groped blindly with her right hand.

"You'll thank me afterward," Harry rasped as he fumbled, one-handed, with the drawstring of her drawers.

Her fingertips brushed glass. She strained, reached . . . Luckily, he was too preoccupied—and too sotted—to notice.

"You'll beg me to do it again," he said. "I know your kind. I know what you need."

Nell hooked the stem of the glass with a finger, edged it toward her as she craned her neck to look at Harry—no easy task with him pushing her face into the table, and her crinoline bunched up around her hips. His expression was a study in frustration; he was having trouble with the drawstring.

Now. With her left hand, she seized his tie, wrapping it once around her fist; with her right, she smashed the glass against the table. It shattered, leaving the stem in her hand intact.

Harry looked more bewildered than anything; the absinthe had slowed his reactions. She yanked his head down until it was mere inches from her own and twisted toward him, pressing the makeshift weapon to his left eye—just firmly enough to get his attention without breaking the skin. The upper part of the bowl had splintered off, leaving the remnants of the narrow reservoir still clinging to the stem—a ring of jagged glass with a handle. Harry looked as if he were gaping through some sort of grotesque, nightmarish monocle.

She said, "I wouldn't move if I were you, except to let go of my hair."

Releasing her hair, he made a fist and drew back as if to punch her.

She jerked him back by his tie. The glass pierced his eyelid, not deeply—Nell eased up just in time—but blood ran from the little nick. "Didn't I tell you not to move?"

"Jesus Christ!" he exclaimed as crimson rivulets trickled down the stem of the glass and over Nell's hand. *"Jesus Christ!"*

"It's not quite as bad as all that," she said, relishing the sense of calm that came with knowing she could do some real damage if she needed to, or even if she just wanted to, no wonder men loved their weapons so. "Lacerations of the eyelid tend to bleed very liberally." She managed to turn and regain her feet—and the modesty of her skirts—without losing her grip on his tie or the broken glass.

Harry raved like a bedlamite, hoarse and wild-eyed, at one point calling her a truly repulsive name, something she'd never thought to hear uttered by a man of breeding. He concluded the rant with, "You goddamned lunatic, are you trying to blind me?"

"You'll only be partially blind if I gouge out the one eye, but you'll also be disfigured. My guess is that vanity actually trumps semi-blindness in your scheme of things."

His looked from her to the bloodied instrument in her hand, his visible eye narrowing, his own hands tensing.

"It's only fair to warn you," she said, tugging on his tie until he winced, "that if you make any move at all without my leave—be it to grab my hand, hit me, pull away from me, kick me, anything—I will scoop out your eye like a peach pit and make you eat it."

He gaped at her. "By Jove, you *are* mad."

"No, just Irish. You were right about one thing. We *are* rather readily excited to anger. Or at least, I am. And when I get angry, I'm capable of just about anything. So I wouldn't call my bluff if I were you. Now, you're going to pull out the chair at the end of the table, slowly. If you make a sudden move, even a small one, you lose the eye. Understand? Don't nod—just say yes."

His throat bobbed. "Yes."

After he'd pulled out the chair, Nell ordered him to give her the sash to his jacket, then sit with his hands clasped behind him. "Don't move a muscle." She released her hold on his tic, but exerted enough pressure with the gouger to force his head back slightly. The shield-shaped chair back had openwork carvings to which it was relatively easy, even one-handed, to lash his wrists. She double-knotted the sash and stepped back.

"That's scabbing over already," she said, indicating the little cut on his eyelid. "It'll leave a scar. You can tell people you got it saving a lady from being ravished by an absinthe fiend."

"Suppose I tell them that you attacked me without provocation?" He grinned smugly. "Suppose I tell my father?"

"Suppose I tell him that I was the lady being ravished and that you were the absinthe fiend?" Nell countered as she opened the pocket doors. "Suppose I tell all of Boston?"

"It would be your word against mine."

"Given your reputation, do you have any doubt as to whom they'd believe?" She smiled. "I can't wait to see the look on people's faces when they find out you were bested by a woman."

Now it was his face that reddened. She savored the sight as she turned and left.

Chapter 11

"YOU never told anyone," Will said. It wasn't a question.

They were standing together at the edge of Boston Common beneath Nell's umbrella, the rain rinsing off it in sheets. Across Tremont Street, the mansions of Colonnade Row blurred together until they looked like one great, sprawling castle in some European city. A few yards away, Gracie—thrilled to be permitted to frolic so freely in such weather—was practicing her newly acquired waltz pivots with her umbrella beneath the sheltering canopy of a giant pin oak.

Will had grown, during the course of Nell's account, even paler than before, his face leaching color until it resembled bleached bone in the silvery shade of the umbrella. He'd regarded her in grave silence as she spoke, except to press her, from time to time, to clarify something, usually one of the more indelicate details that she would have preferred to gloss over.

"No, no one knows," Nell said. "Whom would I have told?" Her threats to Harry notwithstanding, it had never been an option.

"The police? Not that I'm particularly eager to see my brother in prison—I do believe it was the absinthe that made him do what he did that day—but if I'd been you, I think I might have reported him."

Nell couldn't help laughing. "Your father would never have let that get very far, Will, you know that. Remember, this happened before his resolve to let Harry sink or swim. Leo Thorpe would have given the Chief of Police a nice, fat envelope, and that would have been that."

"What about that constable from Williams Court you're so friendly with? Big Irishman, giant head . . ."

"Colin Cook? He's not at the Williams Court station anymore. I ran into him at the Public Library right after I got back from Falconwood. He's been promoted to the Detective Bureau at City Hall. He thinks Chief Kurtz did it to ingratiate himself with the Irish." Cupping her hands to her mouth, Nell called out, "Stay where I can see you, Gracie."

"You might have gone to him," Will said. "It's possible he could have . . . I don't know . . ."

"Kept Alderman Thorpe from burying the truth beneath a pile of greenbacks? Let's say he managed to do that. What then?"

"Well, then I suppose Harry would have had to face the music for once."

"As would your mother. She would have been forced to acknowledge the fact that one of her sons—one of the two who still occupied her world—was capable of such brutality."

"Ah, yes—always thinking of Lady Viola."

"Because four years ago, she thought of me," Nell said with feeling. "She plucked me out of my humble existence on Cape Cod and brought me here and gave me the life I have now. To say I'm indebted to her would be an understatement."

Will looked away, his jaw set.

Gentling her tone, Nell said, "Will, I understand why you harbor such ill-will toward your mother, although I wish you could find it in your heart to forgive her. But for my part . . . she's been so good to me, so kind and giving. And she's seen so much heartache. If she had to face the truth about Harry, it would kill her."

He laughed shortly. "She's far tougher than that, I assure you."

"It wasn't just her I was thinking of," Nell confessed. "It was myself, too. If I'd brought charges against Harry, I would surely have lost my job."

"And Gracie."

Nell nodded, looked down. That Will had sired the child whom she had come to think of as her own seemed to bind them together in some curious alliance that had no name.

And no rules.

"So you just walked out of Harry's house that day," Will asked, "leaving him tied to a dining chair, and put the entire unpleasant episode out of your mind?"

She winced, remembering. "Oh, God, a man saw me leaving the house, all . . . undone, and with my hair loose and no hat."

"You left the house that way?" he asked through a gust of laughter.

"All I could think about was getting out of there. I forgot about my . . . my *state* until I was halfway down the front walk, and then I ducked back onto the front stoop to right myself. It was still somewhat light out. I was so embarrassed, thinking someone might have seen me, and sure enough, there was a man leaning against a tree on the esplanade that runs down the middle of Commonwealth, watching me button myself back up and tidy my hair."

"Oh, no," Will said, but he still looked pretty amused.

"He was some sort of laborer or workman or the like, judging from his clothes," she said. "You know—a leather cap, old reefer jacket, hemp trousers. God knows what he thought."

"He probably thought whoever lived in that house was a very lucky man."

Nell glanced at Will, wondering how he'd meant that—as a compliment? A tease? He reached into the coat pocket in which he kept his cigarettes, frowned distractedly, withdrew his hand without them. He must have decided the quarters were too tight, with the two of them huddled together in this intimate little refuge from the rain, for him to light up. Indeed, they stood as close as if they were dancing, her skirts rustling around his legs, their arms occasionally brushing.

It was as if they were surrounded by one of those glass domes, like the one that held a stuffed owl in Mr. Hewitt's library. Breathing in a heady fusion of Bay Rum, wet wool, and rainwater, Nell allowed herself to imagine that the world outside their little dome—except, of course, for Gracie—had simply dissolved away in the rain.

"This man who was watching you," Will said, "he didn't . . . say anything to you, or . . ."

"No, he was too far away, but I could tell from his expression that he thought he knew why I was so disheveled. Ever since that day, I've had this dread of being watched. I find myself thinking he's back, following me, lurking in the shadows."

"The same man?"

She shrugged. "It's just an absurd fancy, but yes, I suppose I think of him as being the same man. It's usually just some dark, anonymous figure I see out of the corner of my eye, some man about the same size. Perhaps I should ask Dr. Drummond for a nerve tonic."

"Given the way you turned the tables on Harry, I shouldn't think your nerves need bolstering. That was a remarkable accomplishment, Nell. You really showed your mettle."

She mumbled her thanks and looked away, heat blooming in her face until it felt like a box stove. Will followed her line of sight to Gracie, spinning and giggling. In her peripheral vision, Nell saw his expression soften as he gazed at this wondrous little creature who'd sprung so unexpectedly from one isolated act of comfort and need with a near stranger.

Her gaze still trained on Gracie, Nell saw Will turn to study her in that quietly intense way of his. He looked away, looked back, opened his mouth to say something, sighed. "I don't know what I would have . . ." He shook his head, a faint pink smudge streaking each cheekbone. "I mean, if Harry . . . if he'd managed to . . ."

"He didn't."

Will nodded in a preoccupied way. "I worry about . . . next time."

"There won't be a next time."

"I'd like to think so, but if his absinthe consumption continues at this pace—"

"No, I meant I won't give him another chance. I've no intention of ever being alone with him again. I must tell you, though—I'm not so sure it's the absinthe so much as, well, Harry himself."

"If I'd been through what you've been through, I'm sure I'd feel exactly as you do. In any event, it gives me some measure of comfort to know that you're so savvy, so adept at defending yourself."

"Savvy?" She shook her head. "If I were savvy, I wouldn't have *had* to defend myself. I would have seen what was coming long before Harry made his move, and gotten out of there before he'd had the chance to act. You'd think, after what happened with Duncan, I'd have learned to anticipate something like that."

"The signs aren't always so obvious," Will said. "Sometimes it's just a look, a comment, a hunch. Something seems out of place, something *smells* different, the little hairs at the nape of your neck start tickling. It's a matter of analyzing that which others don't even notice, not consciously, but as a matter of course. That way, if trouble is lurking just up ahead, you might be able to sidestep it before it trips you up."

"I suppose it was at Andersonville that you cultivated this instinct," she said.

"More so those places where the predators are a bit less obvious, but no less lethal. Certain quarters in Shanghai, Hong Kong, Paris, San Francisco, New York, New Orleans . . . Any place where there's gambling, money, and whiskey—or, of course, opium. One learns to be ever watchful for that flicker of steel in the dark."

"Are you telling me you can avoid trouble every single time if you're just vigilant enough?" she asked.

Will laughed. "If only that were possible. No, but I've learned how to deal with it when it arises."

"How to fight your way out of it, you mean?"

"How to keep a cool head so that I *can* fight my way out of it."

"Fisticuffs, or . . . ?" She thought about that little folding bistoury from his pocket surgery kit, the one with which he was presumed to have slashed Ernest Tulley's throat last winter.

Evidently sensing the direction of her thoughts, he said, "I rarely used the bistoury as a weapon—not that I didn't wave it about to good effect from time to time, but I've found that one or two well-aimed punches are generally quite sufficient, and a good deal tidier."

"Just one or two?" Nell teased. "I must say I'm disappointed, Dr. Hewitt. I wouldn't have thought you were the type to brag."

He grinned down at her. "And I wouldn't have thought you were the type to grace me with such a delightfully coquettish smile, Miss Sweeney—but I won't pretend to be disappointed."

Cheeks warming yet again—Will really knew how to get to her—Nell rolled her eyes and looked toward the big pin oak to check on Gracie, who was practicing her curtseys.

"There was a sort of unofficial boxing club at Oxford," Will said, "where I discovered that an eighty-four-inch reach tends to put one at something of an advantage."

"An eighty-four-inch . . . ?"

"Long arms—rather embarrassingly simian, actually. Makes me think Darwin is on to something. Over the past few years, I've found them to be as handy on the streets as in the ring."

Nell hated the image that materialized in her mind's eye: Will squaring off against a knife-wielding assailant in some dismal back alley halfway across the world. Redirecting the conversation, she said, "I utterly panicked, that day with Harry." All she could think about was what Duncan had done to her, and that it was about to happen all over again.

"You got hold of yourself in time," Will said.

"Only just. It was a narrow squeak."

"Best to take command of oneself right from the very beginning," he said. "When you're in danger, your heart starts racing. You tremble, perspire, grow breathless. The trick is in transcending your body's panic reflex, rising above it. Remove your mind from what's happening to you. Think outside of yourself—ideally, even before the threat is real."

"Think outside of yourself," she repeated dubiously.

"It's difficult to articulate, but that's how I think of it, almost as if I were an onlooker in the situation, rather than a participant. It helps me to think clearly, anticipate my opponent's moves, land the best punches."

"Yes, well, with any luck, I'll never find myself in such a situation again."

"If you rely on luck, you probably will."

"You know I don't intend to trust my fate to luck," she said. "I've told you I'm going to avoid being alone with Harry."

Will gazed off toward Gracie, rubbed the back of his neck. "I know what you think of him, but if you'd known him before the war, when he was just this young, carefree lad . . . He was high-spirited, yes, but not a bad sort, not really. He took Robbie's death hard. It changed him—made him not just self-involved, but self-destructive. The absinthe he keeps pouring down his throat, it may as well be arsenic, or a noose that he's slowly tightening . . ."

"If you're asking me to feel sorry for him after what he—"

"God, no! What he did to you was inexcusable."

"And yet," she said, "here you are making excuses."

Will stared at her as rain beat against the taut black silk overhead. He slowly smiled. "I meant it last night, when I said I'd missed you."

Did you miss me? Not wanting him to ask it again, because she didn't want to have to answer it, Nell said, "The entire world makes excuses for Harry. He'll never have to answer for his sins."

"I wouldn't put money on that if I were you." Before she could ask him what he meant by that, he said, "Harry's got his share of misdeeds under his belt, but I can't imagine he had anything to do with Bridie Sullivan's disappearance."

"Only because he's your brother." How, she wondered, could two men who'd sprung from the same womb be so vastly different? Will's loyalty was commendable but misplaced. What would it take for Will to accept Harry for what he was? "Bridie was blackmailing Harry, and she intended to keep doing so indefinitely. Once Harry found out about Virgil, he wasn't about to play along . . . but he wasn't about to let her tattle to your father, either, and end up disinherited."

"What is it you think Harry did to her?"

"I don't know that he did anything, but I can't simply ignore the possibility because he's your brother. I know you think he's just immature, or muddled by absinthe, but

I happen to believe that evil exists in this world, and that some people harbor it in their souls, and that one of those people is Harry. The fact that he's an absinthe fiend only makes it more likely that he's guilty. I'm sorry, Will, but I owe it to your mother, and to Bridie's mother—and to Bridie herself, for that matter—to sort this thing out."

"Curious," Will said, "that you feel you owe it to my mother to prove that her son was responsible for Bridie's disappearance, yet she mustn't find out that he tried to rape you."

Rape. There it was, the blunt, sordid word, spoken right out loud in this far too small refuge from the storm. Swamped with a sudden, bewildering rush of shame—unwarranted, perhaps, but no less real—Nell didn't know where to look, what to say.

Will cupped her chin to lift her face. "Nell . . ."

Her eyes stung at the tenderness in his voice, his touch. She shut them, swallowing hard against a spasm in her throat.

Softly he said, "It *is* inexcusable, what he did, and I know it was a nightmare for you—which makes it all the more impressive that you were able to get the upper hand."

She opened her eyes to find him leaning close. The rain had diminished to a whispery drizzle.

"Are you certain, though," he asked, "that your reason for suspecting Harry in the Bridie Sullivan thing has nothing to do with . . . what he tried to do to you?"

"You think I'm trying to punish him for one savage act by implicating him in another?"

"Not consciously, but perhaps—"

"No. No, Will. I suspect him because of who and what he is, not because of what he did to me. And as far as protecting your mother . . ." Nell drew a deep breath. "It's one thing to withhold the fact that her son gives such vent to his lechery, quite another to essentially cover up for . . . for whatever it was that happened to Bridie."

"Assuming she didn't just run off with—"

"Assuming she didn't just run off with Virgil Hines. Yes, it would break your mother's heart if she found out he'd done something to Bridie. But if he did, she deserves to know—and he deserves to be punished. There's only so far I'll go to spare her feelings. There's only so far she'd want me to go."

Will turned to look at Gracie, who had stepped out from beneath the huge, dripping oak to gaze upward at the sky. The rain had let up at last, and a gleam of late-afternoon sunshine was trying to insinuate itself between the clouds.

He lowered the umbrella, shook the rain off, folded it up. "If you mean to conduct a truly impartial inquiry into this matter, you should, by all rights, focus as keenly on Virgil Hines as on my brother."

Uncomfortably aware, with the umbrella gone, of how close they were standing, Nell took a step back. "I agree. Your brother has been, however, somewhat easier to locate."

His eyebrows quirked. "I wouldn't have thought you the type to take the lazy way out."

"If you knew how much work it is, looking after a four-year-old, you wouldn't even joke about that."

He said, "You *do* get a day off now and then."

"Of course. All day Saturday, and Sunday afternoons, after church."

"Don't tell me they make you go to King's Chapel with them."

"Do you honestly think I'm the type to be bullied into Protestantism against my will?" she asked through a chuckle. "No, I attend early Mass at St. Stephen's, then I watch Gracie while your parents and Nurse Parrish go to church, and then"—she shrugged—"I'm free to do as I please."

"St. Stephen's? Isn't that all the way in the North End? There must be something closer."

"Yes, but St. Stephen's is Irish. Brady worships there, too. He drives me."

"If you want to find Virgil Hines, and possibly Bridie Sullivan as well, I should think your first order of business would be to locate their weekend trysting place—that farm you told me about when we were walking home from Poole's."

"I mean to do that—or try—but it won't be easy. There must be dozens of farms south of Salem, probably hundreds."

"But it's not just any farm," he said. "It's one that's no longer in use."

"Am I to simply wander about looking for abandoned farms with white houses?"

Will smiled. "Still prone to galloping assumptions, I see." As she was digesting that, he said, "Tomorrow's Saturday. There's a livery barn at the Revere House where I can rent some sort of buggy for the day. I've been to Salem. Their City Hall is on Washington Street, I believe."

"City Hall?"

"That's where the Essex County land records will be housed, I would assume—although it may not be open on a Saturday, but there are ways around that. Salem is what—about two hours away if we get a decent pair of horses?"

We? "I . . . I suppose, but . . ."

"I'd rather not come calling for you at Palazzo Hewitt—the old man is presumably at home on Saturdays. What say we meet at the corner of Tremont and Winter at . . . eight in the morning? Is that too early?"

"No, I'm always up at dawn, but . . . I can't help but wonder why you want to be a part of this."

"I should think you'd welcome my involvement. I can act as your go-between with Harry. Of the two of us, I'm the only one he'll talk to—for the time being, at least."

"Yes, but that's not your real reason. Admit it—you think I'm so prejudiced against your brother that I need you along to keep me honest."

"Not so much honest as objective."

She bristled.

He smiled. "How I've missed your displays of cool indignation." Sobering, he said, "Look, Nell, I know you wouldn't unfairly target Harry—not deliberately. But you're only human. What he did to you, well that was *in*human, and you're justifiably incensed about it. I just worry that now, after having kept that anger under lock and key for four months, it may influence you more than you realize."

"You must think me very weak-minded indeed, if—"

"Weak-minded? You?" He laughed. "You have one of the sharpest, most capable brains I've ever had the pleasure of sparring with. Being human doesn't mean you're weak, it just means you're subject to the same little quirks and foibles as the rest of us—for which you should be grateful. If you were flawless, I wouldn't want to know you. Nothing's as dreary as perfection."

She smiled, shook her head. "Only you could make one's character defects smell like virtues."

He returned her smile. "Eight o'clock? Tremont and Winter?"

"I'll be there."

Chapter 12

THE "White House," as it turned out, wasn't white at all; nor, from the look of it, had it ever been. It was clear to Nell, even from her first distant glimpse of it as Will drove his rented buggy up the carriageway from the main road—really just wheel ruts through a forsaken apple orchard—that the old farmhouse had never once felt the swipe of a paintbrush. A classic saltbox with a sunken lean-to in back, it was sided in clapboards that had been scoured by four decades of New England winters to a dull, burnished gray. A dilapidated barn missing half its slats stood directly behind the house.

Upon their arrival in Salem that morning, Will had driven them straight to City Hall, a smallish but dignified granite-fronted edifice topped by a golden eagle. Unfortunately, he'd been right about it being closed for business; the only soul in the place was a grizzled old colored man scrubbing the floors. From him, they discovered that the

Registrar of Deeds, whose name was Ephraim Brown, lived on the corner of Putnam and Clement.

They found Mr. Brown on top of his roof replacing shingles in the harsh morning sun, his shirt and hair sodden, face and bald pate sizzling red. Short-tempered from the heat and determined to stay up there until the odious job was done, he refused Will's request to let them peruse the deed registers and plat books at City Hall, even after his visitor started pulling a series of five-dollar banknotes out of his pocket. It was only when Will shucked his coat and hat, rolled up his sleeves, and climbed up to the roof to help hammer in the remaining shingles that the clerk relented.

Will proved a surprisingly capable roofer; forty minutes later, Mr. Brown was cheerfully unlocking the records room, where after searching through a book of deeds, they learned that a man named Lawrence White had bought a nine-acre lot about two miles south of Salem on June 7th, 1829. The insurance company that held the most recent mortgage—it had been refinanced numerous times—foreclosed a year and a half ago, but apparently hadn't resold it yet.

"Do you smell that?" Nell asked as they rode up the path toward the house.

Will reined in the horses and turned his face to the warm breeze shuddering through the trees, bringing with it the fusty tang of fallen apples underscored by a breath of something more fetid than rotting fruit, and more ominous. The breeze was coming from the direction of an overgrown field on the east side of the orchard.

He said, "Opiates have ruined my sense of smell. What is it?"

"Death."

He looked at her. "Are you sure you're not—"

"I'm not imagining it," she said. "There's something dead nearby."

"Perhaps it's just an animal," he said as he flicked the reins.

"I hope so."

The smell diminished as they drove around to the front of the house, so Nell felt little hesitation in knocking on the door. It creaked open with the first strike of her fist, revealing a sizable but nearly bare front room, its windows uncurtained and patched with wood, its plank floor devoid of rugs. There was only a hint of that musty, old-house smell, the windows all being open to let in the fresh air. Dismal it may have been, and pitifully austere, but it had been swept and dusted by someone who clearly thought of himself—or herself, for this was Bridie's home away from home, too—as more than a mere squatter here.

The north wall was dominated by an immense stone fireplace in which the embers looked to have died down unattended. A cooking trivet—just the trivet, no pot—stood in the ashes. On the hearth sat a crock of bacon fat, a folded-up rag with scorch marks from lifting hot pans, and a big stone-china bowl. Sticking out of the bowl was a wooden spoon imbedded in a bit of congealed, gritty looking batter furred with mold.

Looking around for a place to set his hat, Will settled on the only real piece of furniture, such as it was—a battered old oak door that had been pressed into service as a table by being set atop a fruit crate, with a smaller fruit crate on one side and a step stool on the other to serve as chairs. Two place settings had been laid out, consisting of unmatched plates, forks, and fancily folded linen napkins. Between them, on an embroidered handkerchief, sat two apples, an oil lamp, and a blue Mason jar filled with wilted wildflowers in about an inch of murky water.

They found a small rear parlor behind that room, half-filled with junk, and two bedrooms upstairs, unfurnished except for a pallet in the back bedroom made up of a tidy arrangement of blankets and quilts.

Upon returning to the front room, Nell went to the makeshift table and lifted one of the forks, which was heavy, hallmarked sterling, albeit badly tarnished. Stolen, most likely. "They were obviously getting ready to eat," she said. "That batter bowl is almost empty, but where are the johnnycakes?"

"What the devil is a johnnycake?"

She grinned at his bemusement. "A griddlecake made of cornmeal. That's cornmeal batter in that bowl."

Will crossed to the north wall, on which there were a number of hooks. A pink and green flowered shawl and a bonnet adorned with green ribbon and pink silk peonies were hung on two of them, fireplace implements on a few, and one bore an enormous cast-iron skillet. He hefted the skillet, which was clearly heavy, glanced inside, sniffed. "Johnnycakes in bacon fat," he said, holding it up so that Nell could see the greasy residue on its cooking surface, in which she could make out six roughly circular shapes.

"I wonder why she put it away dirty," Nell said. "Bridie may have had her faults, but you could eat off the floor in here."

"As a matter of fact . . ." Crossing to the table, Will squatted down, reached beneath it, and came up with a johnnycake swarming with ants. He flung it out the front door, brushed his hands off. "She evidently made six of those things, which, by the way, don't look as if they'd be very appetizing even fresh off the griddle and sans wildlife. From the mold on the batter, I'd say they were cooked several days ago."

Nell said, "That kind of batter can grow mold in a day or two when it's left out. There's really no telling how long Bridie and Virgil have been gone."

"Or why they left as they did, having evidently tossed out their meal and put the skillet away without washing it." Taking hold of one end of the door-turned-tabletop, Will said, "Give me a hand putting this on the floor, would you? There's something underneath I'd like to take a look at. I saw it when I was down there."

Through the slats of the big fruit crate that had supported the door could be seen an old-fashioned gentleman's drawstring purse of age-stiffened leather and a polished wooden box that was about as large as a good-sized jewelry box.

Nell kneeled down to lift the box out of the crate; it was walnut, with brass banding and inlays.

Sitting back on his heels, Will opened the purse, extracted a roll of greenbacks, and fanned them with his thumb. "Twenty-eight dollars."

"You can tell that without counting it?"

"In my line of work, one learns to do that sort of thing without a lot of fuss. This must be what's left of the forty Harry gave Bridie."

"This box is locked." Feeling around in the crate, Nell said, "The key's not here. Virgil probably keeps it on him."

"Can you spare a hairpin?"

Nell slid one out and gave it to him. He jiggled it in the little brass lock, which sprang open.

"You have a great many shameful talents, don't you?" She took the box back.

He smiled at her. "You did miss me—admit it."

Nell pretended she hadn't heard him as she opened the box, which was divided into two rectangular, velvet-lined compartments. The larger one held good-quality ivory writing paper, while the smaller one was further partitioned for quill pens and pencils, an inkwell, sealing accoutrements, and a pen knife.

"Father Beals gave this box to Virgil when he was paroled, so he could write to him," Nell said.

"Has he?"

"Not yet." She lifted one of the quills, the nib of which was black with dried ink. "But it looks as if he's written to somebody."

"Would Beals have lied to you about that, do you think?" Will asked. "In order to protect Virgil, perhaps, in case Virgil had written something incriminating? You did say he was something of a crusader for prisoners and workingmen and so forth."

"I can't imagine it." She took the sheaf of paper out of its compartment and fanned it as Will had fanned the money, hoping to see writing; she didn't. "Father Beals struck me as a sincere and honest man. If Virgil was carrying on a correspondence with someone, I doubt it was him."

Setting the paper aside, she felt around in its compartment, and then all around the edge of the box.

"What are you looking for?" Will asked.

"A latch, a loose panel . . ."

"You think there might be a secret drawer?"

She nodded. "Dr. Greaves had a . . . well, it wasn't quite like this. It was more of a lap desk, but it opened up so you could keep your paper and pens and whatnot inside.

When the lid was up, if you looked carefully, you could see a slender little brass rod fitted into a groove on the top edge of the box. It looked like part of the decoration, but if you slid the rod along the groove, a drawer would pop open in the side."

"Did you discover this on your own?"

"If you're asking whether I snooped around in his things, the answer is no," Nell said as she continued to poke and prod in the box. "He showed me the drawer because he kept a thousand dollars in there, and he wanted me to have it should anything happen to him. His father had died young, of an apoplectic attack of the brain, and he was always afraid the same thing would happen to him."

Will fell silent. He lit a cigarette, then settled onto his side on the floor—the same reclining position in which he used to smoke opium. He knew that she'd been Dr. Greaves's mistress as well as his assistant, just as he knew that her relationship with Duncan had been no innocent courtship—not that she'd told him the full extent of it, but he knew enough. Sophisticated about such matters and gallant in spite of himself, Will had professed complete acceptance of her past. But now, watching him smoke his cigarette in brooding silence, Nell wondered how he really felt about the two men with whom she'd shared her bed—and especially about Dr. Greaves, for whom she still harbored a great deal of well-deserved, if platonic, affection.

Nell emptied the smaller compartment, all the sections of which were covered in velvet except for a little square nook made to fit a pewter inkwell of the same size and shape. Its sides were velvet-lined, but the bottom was bare wood. She tilted the writing box to compare the depth of the compartment that held the ink and writing implements with that of the box as a whole. There seemed to be about an inch unaccounted for at the bottom.

"Eureka." She laid the box on the floor.

"You found it?" Will sat up.

"I know where it is, and unless I'm very much mistaken . . ." She reached into the inkwell nook and pressed on its little wooden floor. Nothing happened. "Damn," she muttered.

Will chuckled as he crushed his cigarette out on one of the plates. "How I do love to hear vulgar language from those un-rouged lips of yours, Cornelia."

She glared at him as she pressed again, this time with more force. The floor sank inward, just slightly; she felt something give, heard a dull rasp of metal, and then a hinged panel sprang open along the bottom of the compartment.

"Ah, what a little righteous indignation won't do." Will leaned over, along with Nell, to peer into the inch-high niche that had been revealed. "Eureka, indeed."

The niche held a stack of envelopes, perhaps half a dozen. Nell pulled them out, finding them gratifyingly weighty. They weren't just empty envelopes, but letters, enclosed in coarse, brownish paper that she recognized immediately. Even before she saw the return address on the back, she knew they'd been sent from the Massachusetts State Prison in Charlestown.

"Virgil may or may not have written to Father Beals," Will said as he took the envelopes from her and flipped through them, finding them all identical, "but it would appear that Father Beals has written to him."

Nell shook her head, feeling starved for air, as if her stays had been suddenly yanked tight. In a voice that sounded small and distant even to her own ears, she said, "Those aren't from Father Beals."

Will looked at her, then down at the envelopes. "There's no name on the return address. What makes you think—"

"They're from Duncan. That's his handwriting."

Chapter 13

WILL opened the letter with the earliest postmark first. Nell read it over his shoulder.

May 15th 1868, Charlstn Chicken Coop.

Virge, you lazy dam bummer,

Its about time you wrote me, I was starting to think maybee you had 2nd thouts but you're smarter than that aint you. Im glad to see you came threw, youl be happy when I tell you wear to find them dimund braslits I bet.

"Diamond bracelets?" Will said.

"Remember me telling you that Duncan was in prison for beating and knifing a man during an armed robbery?"

"And mutilating him, as I recall."

"It was a jewelry shop he robbed, at gunpoint—Ripley's, in Newport. He locked the staff in the back room, and then he ordered old Mr. Ripley to unlock all the cases, but he refused." Nell took a deep, shaky breath. "So he, he tied him up and gagged him, and . . . he took out his knife, and . . ."

Will rubbed the bridge of his nose.

"Ripley was smart, though. He realized Duncan was fixing to basically torture him to death, so he started screaming about a pain in his chest, and slumped over. Duncan thought he really was dead, so he took off the mask he'd been wearing, and smashed the cases and snatched the best stuff. But the old man was still very much alive—cut up pretty badly, but alive—and he sent for the constables the second Duncan left. They didn't catch up with him til the next day, and by that time he'd hidden the stolen jewelry all over the upper Cape—a few pieces here, a few pieces there . . ."

"Did he tell you where he'd hidden them?" Will asked.

"God, no, he wouldn't have told me. He knew I'd be outraged when I found out what he'd done—which I was, of course. I told him I'd had enough. I tried to leave him. That's when he . . ."

Will nodded tightly; she'd told him last winter, in vague terms, about Duncan's having "hurt" her. Before he could say anything about that, because she couldn't take his pity right now, on top of everything else, she said, "After Duncan was arrested, he refused to tell them where he'd hidden the jewels. Because of that, and what he'd done to Mr. Ripley, he got the maximum sentence—not that he'll end up serving it. I told you what he said about getting out on 'hocus pocus.'"

"Surely there's something you can do to forestall that."

"If you get any brilliant ideas, don't keep them to yourself. In the meantime," she said as she returned her attention to the letter, "I'm more than a little curious as to what

Duncan and Virgil have been corresponding about for the past four months."

"Didn't Duncan say he hardly knew Virgil?" Will asked.

She sighed. "Duncan says a lot of things."

But like I told you before, Virge, you got to earn them braslits, I aint just giving them away cause you told me she lives across from Boston Commun and looks after a kid. I want the street she lives on and the number of the house. I want the name of the famly and the kid and evrybody else in that house and when she gets up in the morning and when she gos to bed at night and what she eats and drinks and if she stil gos to church on Sundays and what she tells the godam preist in confeshun. I want to know evrything.

"Oh, my God," Nell whispered.

Only when Will wrapped an arm around her shoulder, steadying her, did she realize how badly she was trembling. "Are you all right?"

She nodded yes, then shook her head. "No. Oh, God. I can't . . . all this time . . . oh, my God."

Will moved the letters out of her reach. "I'm going to read these and summarize them for you. In the meantime . . ." He withdrew from inside his coat a small silver flask, which he unscrewed and handed to her. "Brandy. I prescribe one good swallow every minute or so until the tremors have abated."

Twenty minutes later, Will said, "All right, this is it in a nutshell." He sat on the floor with all the letters—there were seven of them—spread out around him in a rectangle of sunlight from the east-facing window, for it was not quite noon yet. "Some time before Virgil Hines's parole, it came to Duncan's attention that Virgil wished he had enough money to buy this farm without having to serve time in a Cape May quarry. Duncan, having been fixated for quite a while on finding out what had become of you, entered into an arrangement with his chum Virgil, the nature of which you've already surmised. Virgil spies on you and reports back to Duncan, and in return, Duncan reveals to him the location of one of his caches of loot—eventually. He seems to be dragging his heels about it, to Virgil's frustration." He paused to light a cigarette. "How are you feeling, by the way?"

"Much calmer," said Nell, who was lying on her back with her hat and gloves off, admiring the way the sun sparkled in the cobwebs Bridie had missed when dusting the rafters.

Will took the flask out of her slack hand and shook it; it was still mostly full. "Doesn't take much for you, does it?"

"I'm not drunk, just . . ." Nell shook her head. "I should have suspected something like this. Duncan, he was always so . . ." She rubbed her face. "It doesn't matter. Go on."

Will took a puff on his cigarette, tapped the ash onto the plate, looked at her. "Virgil was the man leaning against that tree on Commonwealth, watching you button yourself back up after fleeing Harry's—"

She thought about it for a second, groaned. "Of course. Of course."

"That feeling you've had since then, that someone's been watching you? It hasn't been your imagination. It's been Virgil."

Nell closed her eyes, shook her head. She heard paper

rustling, felt vibrations in the floor beneath her as Will shifted his weight. When she opened her eyes, he was lying on his side again, stretched out next to her, the letters and the plate he was using as an ashtray in front of him.

"Duncan assumed, from Virgil's account, that you were having an affair with Harry," he said.

"When he said that about not trusting 'the son,' I thought he meant—"

"Not trusting the son? You didn't tell me this part. What did he say?"

I know he's the other one, the one you think you can trust. I know you're sweet on him . . .

"He, uh, he said I thought I knew you . . . well, I assumed he meant you, but he meant Harry."

"Ah, yes," he said through a stream of smoke, "those pesky assumptions of yours."

"He said, 'He's not what he seems. You think he's a gentleman because he's a Hewitt, but if you knew what he does when you're not around . . . ' " She shrugged.

"No wonder you thought it was me." Will's wry tone didn't completely mask a hint of something that might have been bitterness, or hurt, or a combination thereof. He stubbed out the cigarette and started sorting through the letters. "The reason he tried to warn you off Harry . . . ah, this is it. This one is dated July twenty-first, while you were at Falconwood—which he knew about through Virgil, of course. Thinking you were carrying on this torrid liaison with Harry, Duncan had instructed Virgil to keep tabs on him as well, from about mid-May on. That was how Bridie came to Virgil's attention. It would appear that he took one look at her, fell hard and fast, contrived to meet her, and before long, they were spending every weekend here. Of course, Virgil also had a job to do, so he dutifully told Duncan about Harry's Harem, the crown jewel of which happened to be his own lady love, Bridie Sullivan."

"Which led Duncan to conclude that Harry was two-timing me with Bridie," Nell said. "Hence his trying to warn me off him."

"He tried to warn Virgil off Bridie, too," Will said, scanning the letter in his hand. "Here it is. 'I seen plenty of her type, those painted-up tarts that'll raise their skirts for a pair of glass ear bobs. She's nothing but a whore that ain't honest enough to call herself a whore. She's using you, Virge, maybe for the farm, maybe for something else. She don't know any other way. You're crazy to get all moon-struck over a trashy piece like that. You're lucky if she aint given you the clap by now . . . ' And so forth and so on."

It didn't surprise Nell that Will chose to repeat Duncan's coarse language verbatim. Although restrained by the rigid decorum of his class from swearing casually in her presence, he'd never been under the illusion that such words would cause her to swoon from shock. Far from being insulted by this, she actually found it rather refreshing.

"It's a refrain that just gets more impassioned with every letter," Will said. "In the last one . . . Where is it? Ah. 'You think if you can talk her into ditching the husband and marrying you, she'll stop humping everything in trousers? It don't work like that with her type. You don't even know who got her in the club, if it was you or Hewitt or some guy she did once and never saw again.' " Will looked up. "In the club?"

"With child," Nell said.

"Hm. All right . . . 'You are one dum mudsill to think she don't have no interest in that farm just cause she's planning on squeezing that Hewitt bastard for money. Why settle for one pot of gold when she can have two? She'll use you up, Virge. She'll wait til you buy that place, and then she'll pick you clean and toss you out with the chicken bones. It's what my old lady did to my da, and then she tossed me out, too, which is a hell of a way to treat your own kid, which is why I'm telling you to cut her loose now, before she can finish what she started.' "

Looking up, Will said, "His mother kicked him out of the house?"

Nell nodded. "When he was nine."

"Nine?" Will whispered something under his breath, lit another cigarette, and continued reading. " 'If she won't go, make her go. Do whatever it takes, but get rid of her. If you're too much of a Nancy-boy to do it yourself, then I'll do it soon as I get out of here, on account of I hate to think of her getting her whorish hands on the farm you're buying with my hard-earned loot, but then you'll owe me, and I'll know you're as much of a puss as she is. Chew on that next time she comes home smelling of some other man's—' "

Will cut himself off, frowning at the page, an almost imperceptibly faint smudge of color rising on each cheekbone. "Yes . . . well . . ." He set the cigarette on the edge of the plate and gathered up the letters into a neat stack. "You get the idea."

Nell smiled to herself at the notion that Will had finally stumbled across a word too foul, even by his lax standards, to repeat in her presence.

"There's something I don't understand," Nell said. "From all accounts, Virgil was besotted with Bridie. Yet he knew she was at Harry's beck and call during work hours. Most men could never live with that."

Will shrugged as he brought his cigarette to his mouth. "It would appear he'd found a way to."

"It's just hard to imagine."

"Love is a curious malady. The symptoms vary widely among its sufferers."

Nell turned her head to look at him through a sun-washed haze of cigarette smoke as he lay next to her on this bare wooden floor. He met her eyes through the glittering veil, holding her gaze with an odd kind of stillness, until she looked away and sat up.

"We should look in that barn," she said as she dusted off the sleeves of her dress, "and the field between the house and the orchard, where that smell came from."

"You go ahead." Will gained his feet with some effort, favoring his bad leg, then held out his hand to help her up. "I'm going to put things right in here. I'd hate to leave it like this"—he gestured toward the disassembled table and emptied-out writing box—"when we found it so tidy. I'll meet you out there."

THE barn was much as Nell had expected. It reeked of sour straw, and was empty but for such detritus as a rusted-out wheelbarrow and a ladder missing half its rungs. There was a woodpile behind the barn that was half-split, and a chopping block with an axe stuck in it. Her most interesting discovery was the fact that Virgil Hines was evidently repairing the brick chimney on the north side of the house, crumbled sections having been replaced with new bricks, freshly mortared. He must have been pretty confident that Duncan's "dimund braslits" were forthcoming.

Nell reentered the house through the back door, which led into the junk-filled rear parlor. Upon opening the door into the front room, she found that Will had finished tidying up and was now seated on the small fruit crate in his shirtsleeves, the left sleeve rolled high above the elbow, thrusting a silver hypodermic syringe into his upper arm.

He looked toward her standing in the doorway, his fleeting expression of dismay swiftly replaced by that cool British stoicism he was so good at. There was a bleakness in his eyes, though, a hint of something close to shame. His arm bore clusters of needle marks and bruises.

Will thumbed the plunger home, injecting a dose of morphine into his left deltoid. A second passed. He let out a sigh, his eyes half closed, and withdrew the syringe.

She said, "You're better than this."

"If I were," he said as he unscrewed the needle, "I wouldn't be doing it, would I?"

Chapter 14

THE field beyond the orchard was a sprawling acre or so of dried grass and weeds dotted with the occasional tree. Given Nell's cumbersome skirts, she chose to inspect the section near the house and barn, where the grass wasn't quite so high, while Will directed his search toward the field's heavily treed eastern perimeter. She glanced up every now and then to see his black-clad form growing steadily smaller as he waded slowly through the swaying wheat-gold grass, his long strides relatively smooth and graceful.

Nell was thankful for the light breeze, which kept her from perspiring too badly despite the fierce midday sun. After a while, she unpinned her black straw bonnet and re-pinned it at a more front-tilted angle, the better to prevent her face from freckling, or worse, tanning. As she did so, she glanced toward Will to find him standing still near the trees at far the edge of the field, looking down at something she couldn't see.

He'd taken off his hat.

Lifting her skirts indecently high, Nell strode toward him as swiftly as she could through the crackling grass, the smell of decaying flesh growing stronger with every step. Will glanced up at her once as she neared, his expression grim. When she was about twenty feet away, the breeze lifted a few strands of something near his feet that fluttered above the level of the grass, glinting in the sunlight like spun copper.

My Bridie, she's got the prettiest red hair you ever seen—shines like heaven itself when the sun hits it just right.

Nell stopped walking, her breath harsh in her ears as she watched Will hike up his trouser legs and hunker down, laying his hat next to him. She waited a moment, preparing herself for both the smell and what she was about to face, before covering the remaining distance.

The first thing she saw was more of that striking red hair—great, serpentine masses of it, a few tendrils quivering in the breeze. She stopped short when she caught sight of Bridie herself lying supine in the grass, her hands clenched at her sides, her face turned toward Nell but obscured by matted hair. She wore a green-and-pink striped silk basque, gaping open to reveal her bosom and the top few inches of her corset, with a rust-colored scarf around her neck. Her pink skirt was pushed up to her thighs, along with a single petticoat; she wore no crinoline. Like her hair, her clothing had a slightly stiff, damped-down quality from having been rained on.

Nell was surprised, at first, to find Bridie so plump, except for that snugly corseted waist; her arms looked like sausages within the tightly stretched sleeves of her basque. But then Nell noticed her legs—thick and shapeless, with greenish-gray discoloration beneath shiny-taut skin—and she realized the body had merely become distended from a buildup of gasses.

A beetle scuttled out from beneath Bridie's skirts, crawled down her thigh, and paused to consume one of many little whitish grains scattered over her legs—seeds from the surrounding grasses, Nell thought, until she noticed them squirming.

Something brackish rose in her throat. It was only when Will asked if she was all right that she realized she'd made a sound.

"Yes," she said. "Yes, I'm . . . I'm fine."

"You *have* seen corpses before." He lifted Bridie's right arm, bent it at the elbow, lowered it; her hand remained fisted.

"Good Lord, yes." The earliest dead bodies she could recall had been those of the two sisters and three brothers she'd lost to various diseases during the first decade of her life; next had been her mother, of Asiatic cholera, after her husband's abandonment; and finally her last remaining sister, the baby—little Tess, with her winsome smile—of diptheria when it swept through the Barnstable County Poor House. Death had worn a different, bloodier face during the two years she'd been known as Cornelia Cutpurse. The knife fights, the savage beatings . . . And, then, of course, she'd spent four years as a nurse of sorts for Dr. Greaves, and all doctors, even doctors as capable as he, lost patients from time to time.

"I've been watching people die all my life," she told Will. "But I've never seen a body in . . . quite this condition before."

"I wish I could say the same thing." He started gathering up Bridie's hair to expose her face, his touch as careful as if she were alive. "During the war, the men who fell, on both sides, were often just left where they lay. I might pass the site of a battle that had ended hours, or days, or even weeks before, and find it strewn with corpses. If there was time, I would stop and take notes—how long they'd been dead, what kind of weather they'd been exposed to postmortem, their internal temperature, how decomposed they were, whether there was rigor mortis or livor mortis, what kind of insect activity was present . . ."

"Why, for pity's sake?"

"There are situations involving foul play, such as this one, I should think, where it can be helpful to know when death occurred—the better to identify and prosecute the killer. The legal applications of medicine had been a particular interest of my favorite medical professor at Edinburgh. When I found myself exposed to all those corpses whose time of death could be pinpointed within a few hours, I realized it was the perfect opportunity to do a little field work for him. My intent was to send him my notebook after the war, but of course the Rebs confiscated everything when they took me prisoner."

He peeled away the last hanks of hair to reveal Bridie's face—or what was left of it.

"Oh, God." Nell squeezed her eyes shut, but the image was emblazoned in her mind: the swollen, discolored face, the yawning mouth and milky eyes, but most of all the maggots, lazily roiling masses of them in every orifice.

Will touched her hand. "Why don't you go back to the house?" he suggested gently.

"No." She forced herself to open her eyes, to look, even as her stomach heaved. "I'm all right."

"Are you sure?" He gently straightened Bridie's head so that she was staring sightlessly into the sky; the right side of her face, where the blood had pooled after death, bore bluish-purple stains except on the spot where her cheek had been pressed against the grass. A whitish froth exuded from her mouth and nose, in addition to the maggots.

"You aren't going to faint on me," he said.

"I don't faint."

"Nell, I've *seen* you faint." He snapped a slender twig off a nearby plant.

"I don't faint often. What are you doing?" she asked as he scooped up one of the maggots on the tip of the twig and stood to scrutinize it.

"The life cycle of the blowfly follows a predictable pattern," he said as he took the tiny creature—a writhing grain of rice—onto the tip of a finger. "A body might be dead only minutes, seconds even, and they'll be right there laying their eggs. It takes about a day for the eggs to hatch into larvae, which feed off the host body with these rather sinister looking little mouth parts. See?" He held the maggot toward Nell. She took a step back, nodding mechanically.

He said, "The larva molts a couple of times and gets larger as it feeds, but then, after about a week or two, depending on the temperature and humidity, the mouth parts disappear and it shrinks again. Finally it develops a sort of hard, dark shell, and before the month is out, it's become a fly."

"You learned all this from observing dead soldiers during the war?" she asked.

"And at Andersonville. It was the deuce trying to keep the blowflies from doing this"—he gestured toward Bridie's grotesque face—"to those poor fellows in the hospital hut while they were still alive."

Nell shuddered.

"Unfortunately," Will said as he peered at the maggot, "the weather's been so erratic the past few days—cold and rainy one day, hot and sunny the next—that it's hard to say how long it might have taken these little buggers to get to this stage. All I can say with any confidence is that it was more than, say, a day and a half, but less than a week."

Warming to the subject, Nell asked, "What about those other indicators? Rigor mortis, decomposition . . ."

"There's no cadaveric rigidity except in the hands, and that's just spasm," he said, flicking the maggot away. "Rigor has already run its course, which means this poor girl died at least thirty-six hours ago—but, of course, we already knew that from the larvae. As for decomposition, that's also affected by weather and the like. In this case, it doesn't tell me much. I've no thermometer with which to take her internal temperature, but she's cool to the touch . . ."

Will might have been delivering a lecture to medical students, so quietly authoritative did he sound. Nell found this reminder of his former calling as a physician somewhat fascinating, but a little sad as well. Here was a man whom General Grant had once called the finest battle surgeon in the Union Army. Now those deft, well-trained hands that had saved so many lives performed no function more complex than shuffling a pack of cards.

"Livor mortis is present," Will continued, "as you can see on her face. If she were dead less than twelve hours or so, it would blanch when depressed, but it won't." He squatted down to press a finger against the purplish stain on her cheek, which, indeed, was unaffected. "She's definitely been dead a day and a half—probably longer, given the size of the larvae and the extent of decomposition, but again, there are so many variables where those are concerned."

"How do you suppose she died?" Nell asked.

"There are no superficial indications—she really ought to be autopsied—but I think it's safe to say she was murdered. Not by my brother, obviously."

"Why obviously?"

"Have you asked yourself where Virgil Hines has disappeared to? Mark my words, when we find him, we'll find the man who did this to Bridie."

"But he loved her."

"Would that love have survived Duncan's continued diatribes against her? He made quite a case for 'getting rid of her,' whatever that was supposed to mean, although I have my suspicions. What's more, he called Virgil's manhood into question if he didn't do it himself, and believe me, there are few men who are immune to that particular tactic."

Nell didn't pursue the subject. Either the truth would surface, or it wouldn't. There was nothing to be gained by entering into a protracted debate with Will. She studied Bridie's corpse, looking for anything that might help to explain what had happened to her.

"Her hands and feet are filthy." Crouching down, she stripped off her gloves, took tentative hold of Bridie's right hand, which felt a bit like India rubber, and pried her fingers open. The distended flesh was blackened as much by dirt as by post-mortem lividity, her palm scoured by irregular abrasions packed with grit and gravel. Some sort of vegetative matter—narrow leaves, or blades of grass—was tucked into the crease between her palm and fingers.

"Look at this," Nell said, running a fingertip along a

neatly seared stripe of flesh on Bridie's palm. She checked the other hand, which bore a similar mark.

Will said, "It looks as if she burned herself lifting that skillet without using the rag."

"Her own fingernails did this," said Nell, pointing to a series of nicks on the balls of the dead woman's hands. The tips of her fingers were scraped, several of the nails broken. Nell checked her feet, which were as badly abraded as her hands. "She didn't succumb easily. She struggled at the end."

"Yes. But not here." Will rubbed his thumb over Bridie's grimy palm. "This is dried mud. And there are bits of leaves and plant stems and such here and in her hair that aren't from this field." Rising to his feet, he looked around. "There looks to be a stream in this little patch of woods here."

The smell of death didn't dissipate as they made their way through the trees; if anything, it got stronger. The reason became clear when they arrived at the bank of a shallow, rocky stream flowing through a lush carpet of ferns and moss. Lying facedown in the water, his body floating on the surface, was a male corpse that was almost as distended as that of Bridie Sullivan, but not quite—probably because it was cooler here, in the shade, than out in that field.

The dead man wore a wool flannel shirt that was red on the exposed back and pinkish underwater, some of the dye having bled into the stream, and checked trousers with worn leather suspenders; no vest or shoes. He had dark brown, overgrown hair.

Will stared at the body for a long moment without looking in Nell's direction. "I'm going to turn him over." He took off his hat, coat, boots, and lisle stockings, then rolled up his sleeves and trousers and waded into the stream. Beneath the foot or so of crystalline water, the stream looked almost as if it were paved in cobblestones and gravel, but for various water weeds and the occasional boulder.

The unwieldy corpse proved difficult to budge from Will's position to one side of it. He tried to straddle it, one foot on each of a pair of relatively flat rocks, but he instantly lost his footing. Down he went, twisting to avoid landing on the body so that he hit the streambed on his right side, grunting with the impact.

"Will! Are you all right?" Nell asked as he sat up in the waist-high water, soaking wet.

"Yes, splendid," he said in a dryly baleful tone. "I quite like being humiliated in front of beautiful women. Improves the character."

"Oh, Will—your arm!" His sleeve was torn and muddied, and blood seeped through in several places, staining the snowy cambric a mottled crimson. "Here, let me help you." She lifted her skirts and prepared to cross to him via a series of rocks that formed a sort of stepping-stone bridge in his direction.

"No, Nell, don't. These rocks are all covered with moss. They're slick as wet ice. I'm fine, really." He rose onto his knees and, in that position, was able to heave the body over so that it rested faceup on the opposite bank.

The face was that of a young man with large, filmy eyes half-concealed by tendrils of hair. Even bloated and waterlogged as he was, and ruddy with livor mortis, Nell could tell that he'd been handsome before his demise.

"Would you mind moving the hair off his forehead?" Nell asked.

He glanced up at her quizzically.

"Virgil Hines has stars tattooed there."

"Served aboard the *Kearsage*, eh?" He pushed the hair back, revealing an area of bluish-red discoloration.

"Is that bruising or lividity?" Nell asked.

"Only an autopsy would tell for sure at this point." He leaned over to peer at the blemished skin.

"Are there stars? I'm too far away to see."

She could tell even before he spoke, because of his grimly resigned expression, what his answer would be. "Yes." He rose to his feet, dripping water and blood, unbuttoned his vest and wrung it out. "If you think this proves Harry did it—"

"It doesn't prove that," she said, "but it does narrow down the field of likely candidates." To one, but why belabor the obvious? Harry was Will's brother. This must be excruciating for him. "You should come here and let me look at that arm," she said, but he'd already turned and started wading downstream.

"Looks as if Virgil wanted some fish to disguise the taste of those johnnycakes." He pointed to something caught between two rocks. Nell had assumed it was a tree branch, but as she walked downstream, she saw that it was the bottom half of a fishing pole, split in the middle.

"What's that?" Nell asked, pointing. "There's something on that rock—behind you and upstream about a yard from where you are."

Will leaned over to peer at the tiny object on the rock's concave surface, looking like the last peppermint left in a candy dish. He picked it up and brought it over to Nell.

It was a little round button covered in pink silk, a few pink threads hanging from its frayed underside, as if it had been violently ripped from the garment to which it had been attached.

Stowing the button in her chatelaine, Nell said, "I'll tell

the Salem constabulary where we found this. We'll need to drive back into town and let them know what happened. Here—let me see that arm," she said as she pulled off her gloves. His sleeve was as red as Virgil's.

"It's fine," Will said as he sat down to put his boots and stockings back on. "Just a couple of scrapes."

"Scrapes don't bleed like that." Crouching down next to him, she reached for his sleeve.

He grabbed her wrist. "I said I'm fine."

"I've seen the marks already, remember?"

"They're uglier up close."

"I promise not to swoon from revulsion."

Looking exasperated even as he fought a smile, Will released her wrist and pushed the sleeve up. The needle marks *were* uglier up close, but she ignored them. There were two raw abrasions, but the real bleeder was a gash just below his elbow.

"That must have hurt." She unfolded a handkerchief—one of the set of prettily monogrammed ones Viola had given her as part of her birthday present last month, along with the pearl-tipped hair picks and a fancy new easel.

"Don't use that. You'll ruin it." Reaching into his pocket, he said, "Use one of mine."

"I'll use yours to clean it, but mine to bandage it," she said as she gently wiped bits of grit and gravel from the wound. "Mine is oversized. Hold still."

He watched her as she tied her handkerchief around his arm. "You've got a nice touch—gentle but not tentative."

"Thank you." She dipped his handkerchief in the stream to rinse off the dirt and tiny pepples. "Bridie had grit like this embedded in her hands, and the leaves she was clutching look like the ones on these plants. Then there's that button. But if she was killed here, what was she doing in that field? Do you suppose she was mortally injured but tried to crawl back to the house?"

"If so, why was she lying on her back with her arms at her sides?"

Nell shook her head as she squeezed out the handkerchief. "I'll be interested to see what theories the Salem Police come up with. For all that they call themselves a city, they're pretty provincial. I wonder if they've ever investigated a murder before."

On his feet now, Will said, "I don't see any need to offer up more than the basic information, do you? Certainly we can tell them who these people are and what we know about them, but not . . ." He raked both hands through his hair. "I mean, I know you have certain opinions about the matter, certain preconceived—"

"I won't point the finger at your brother, if that's what you're concerned about."

He met her gaze, looked away. "Thank you."

"But if they conduct anything more than the most cursory investigation, it'll lead them right to Harry—you do realize that. Everyone who works at that mill knew what was going on between him and Bridie. They all saw his reaction when Virgil kissed her. And those who didn't overhear them arguing about Bridie's blackmail scheme have surely heard about it by now. No one who gathers all the facts could fail to suspect him."

"*I* don't suspect him."

"You're his brother," she said gently.

"No, it's not just that," he said with a grimace of impatience. "You don't understand. Harry . . . yes, he's a blackguard, he's selfish and spoiled and lecherous and weak-willed and all the rest of it, but there are some lines even he wouldn't cross, no matter how much absinthe he'd poured down his throat. I know it in my heart. He may or may not be salvageable as a human being—I'm a bit doubtful of that myself now, knowing what he did to you—but that doesn't mean he deserves to be unfairly convicted of a murder he didn't commit. A double murder," he amended, looking toward Virgil's body lying amid the ferns on the opposite bank.

As Will was gathering up his things, Nell said, "You go ahead. I'll meet you at the buggy."

He looked confused. "I thought we were done here."

"I just . . . I feel it wouldn't be right to leave without saying something."

"A prayer, you mean?"

She looked away, blushing yet again, when it was he who should have been embarrassed, to be so godless. "You should go back. I'll be there in a few minutes."

"No, go ahead," he said after a brief pause. "I'll wait."

She turned toward Virgil and made the sign of the cross, almost wishing Will *had* gone back, because it felt so strangely intimate, doing this in front of him; she could see him out of the corner of her eye, watching her with solemn interest.

Closing her eyes to block him out, she clasped her hands and said, "Eternal rest grant unto him, O Lord, and let perpetual light shine upon him. May his soul and all the souls of the faithful departed rest in peace. Amen."

"Amen," Will said quietly.

NELL spoke different words over Bridie.

"Absolve, we beseech Thee, O Lord, the soul of thy servant Bridget Sullivan, that being dead to this world she may live to Thee, and whatever sins she may have committed in this life through human frailty, do Thou of Thy most merciful goodness forgive. Through our Lord Jesus Christ Thy Son who with Thee liveth and reigneth in the unity of the Holy Ghost, world without end. Amen." She crossed herself.

"Amen." Will put his hat back on, but slung his coat over his shoulder, hoping, no doubt, that his sodden, mud-stained clothing would dry in the sun, at least partially, on the way into Salem. "Poor Bridie," he said as he took in her ravaged remains. "Can you imagine her as a farmwife?"

Nell thought about it for a moment. "Yes."

Will looked at her, opened his mouth as if to say something, but seemed to reconsider it. Returning his gaze to Bridie, he murmured, "Take her up tenderly."

Nell looked at him.

"It's from a poem by Thomas Hood," he said. " 'The Bridge of Sighs.' " Removing the hat he'd just put on, he recited, in that drowsy-soft voice of his, "Take her up tenderly, lift her with care, fashioned so slenderly, young and so fair." He paused, as if trying to recall the words. "Touch her not scornfully, think of her mournfully, gently and humanly. Not of the stains of her, all that remains of her, now is pure womanly. Make no deep scrutiny, into her mutiny, rash and undutiful. Past all dishonor, death has left on her, only the beautiful."

"Amen," Nell whispered.

"Amen." He put his hat back on. "Come," he said as he turned. "Let's go fetch the constables."

"Could I just . . . I just don't want them to find her all . . . undone like this," she said, imagining the reaction of the constables as they gathered around Bridie. First, they'd be appalled, sickened. Then, as the reality of the sight sank in and they struggled on a subconscious level to deal with it, would come the snickering little asides, the vulgar jokes. Thus would Bridie Sullivan be transformed from a young woman tragically murdered to a *thing* lying out in a field to be dealt with. "Would it be all right, do you think, if I just tidied her up a bit?"

Will said, "We really should leave her as much as possible as we found her."

"You didn't leave Virgil as you found him."

"Point taken. Still . . ."

"We can tell them how we found her—how we found both of them. I could draw them a sketch."

Will smiled and shook his head. "You and your sketches. Yes, go ahead—tidy her up."

Kneeling, Nell pulled down Bridie's skirt and petticoat, smoothing the rain-stiffened silk. It pained her to think of Bridie lying here half-naked in yesterday's downpour. Nobody, regardless of her sins, deserved that kind of end.

She tried to rebutton Bridie's basque, but she was so badly bloated above her stays, and most of the buttons—to which the one they'd found at the stream was, of course, a perfect match—were missing, so it was a futile effort. To cover up the dead girl's bosom, Nell rearranged the long scarf tied around her neck, reflecting that rust was an odd color to have paired with this outfit. She thought back to the shawl and bonnet hanging in the house, which were decorated in precisely the same shades of pink and green as Bridie's dress; the hat had probably been custom made. Why go to all that trouble to have everything match, and then ruin it with a rust-colored scarf?

Nell spread the scarf over Bridie's chest, stilling when she noticed the monogram, embroidered in bronze-colored metallic thread: a pair of H's framed in a square of vines.

Behind her, Will whispered, "Bloody hell."

Chapter 15

"GOOD afternoon, Dr. Hewitt," greeted the doughy little desk clerk at the Revere House. "Ma'am," he added, with a nod in Nell's direction. He stole a look of dismay at Will's attire, still damp and mud-smeared some four hours after his fall into that stream.

"Had a bit too much absinthe and took a spill," Will explained. It was what he always said when he didn't care to launch into tedious explanations. "May I have my key?"

"Of course." The clerk smiled uncertainly as he fetched the key from a drawer, probably reflecting that the handsome, well-bred young surgeon who'd taken up residence in his hotel didn't seem the type for absinthe. With a glance at Nell, he asked, "Shall we hold a key here for Mrs. Hewitt as well?"

Nell looked from the clerk to Will and back again. "I'm—"

"Thank you, yes." Will curled an arm around Nell's

waist and led her toward the curved staircase in the corner of the lobby. "Come along, my pet. We don't want to be late for Reverend Beals."

On the way home from Salem, Will had brought up the subject of Duncan being paroled, suggesting they go directly to the man who'd first proposed it in the hope of talking sense to him. And, too, they had a few questions about Duncan's relationship with Virgil in prison, as well as his fixation on Nell. Therefore, their first stop upon returning to Boston had been Emmanuel Church on Newbury Street, where Adam Beals was formally assigned. Nell had introduced Will to Father Beals, but the priest was too preoccupied with church duties to talk to them right then, and arranged to meet them for supper in the Revere House dining room in an hour. Naturally, Will wanted to change first.

"I can't go to your room with you!" Nell protested as Will escorted her down a hallway lit with stained-glass sconces.

"No one will look askance. They think you're my wife."

"Do they? Or do they think I'm actually . . ."

"A harlot in sheep's clothing?" Will smiled as he guided her to a door labeled *2D*. "Does it really matter what they think, so long as you're treated with a modicum of respect?"

"How can you even ask that? Of course it matters."

He shook his head as he turned the key in the lock. "Poor, earnest Cornelia—whatever am I going to do with you?" Opening the door, he said, "Welcome to my humble diggings."

And quite humble they were, especially compared to

those of his parents, given that they occupied but a single bed-sitting room. It was a large room, though, flooded with sunlight and handsomely appointed in shades of sage and tobacco, with a bank of windows affording an excellent view of Bowdoin Square.

"It's actually quite nice," she said, starting when he closed the door behind them. Never, since coming to work for the Hewitts, had she been alone with a man in his bedroom; it was a challenge to keep her uneasiness from showing.

"Would you care for a drink before dinner?" Crossing to a desk in the corner, Will dropped his key onto a silver inkstand. He untied his cravat and tossed it onto the upholstered bench at the foot of his curtained bed, then shucked his coat and vest. "I've got a dry sherry you might like."

"No, thank you." Glancing around, she noticed, on one of the nightstands that flanked the bed, a vial of white powder, a syringe kit, a small apothecary's scale, a bottle of clear liquid labeled *Alcohol*, another that probably contained a solution of morphine, and a cotton roll.

"Some tea?" Taking a seat on the bench, he pulled off his boots and socks and started unbuttoning his shirt. "I've no means to make it here, but I can send up for some."

"N-no, I . . . I'm fine," she said as he stood and stripped off his shirt, then undid the top button of his trousers. "What are you doing?"

"Getting changed," he said, as if that were evident.

"Can't you do it"—she looked around and located the open door of a bathroom—"in the W.C.?"

"My clothes are here." He pointed to a black walnut wardrobe. "You're awfully bashful for a nurse. Besides, you've seen me naked before."

"I was never a real nurse, and as you—"

"Close enough." He flicked open another button.

"Stop that! And as you are very well aware, the only reason I saw you naked was that you ambushed me." It had happened last winter, in the bedroom of the colored actress Mathilde Cloutier, who'd been Will's sometime mistress before opium had rendered such fleshly pursuits a thing of the past. He'd arisen from bed in Nell's presence without a stitch on, for no better reason than to shock her.

"Every time I decide you're not quite as conventional as you'd like the world to believe," he said sadly, "you prove me quite wrong. Turn your back, then, if your modesty is so easily bruised."

Nell spun around to face the fireplace, her arms crossed. "You seem to delight in making me uncomfortable."

"You know why, don't you?"

She raised her gaze from the logs stacked on the grate, only to discover that she could see him reflected in the glass over the steel engraving hanging above the marble mantel. He was standing in his drawers, kicking his trousers off. The bandage tied around his upper forearm—her handkerchief—was brown with dried blood. She closed her eyes. "Why?"

"It's those blushes of yours. I can't get enough of them."

"That's what your brother said, right before he . . ." She sighed, shook her head.

A long moment passed.

She opened her eyes, glanced up at the picture. Will was rubbing the back of his neck, his jaw with that rigid thrust to it that betrayed him as thoroughly as Nell's blushes betrayed her.

He got dressed in silence.

* * *

"WELL." Father Beals—Adam, as he'd asked to be called—refolded the most recent of Duncan's letters, slipped it back in its envelope, and placed it atop the tidy stack next to his dessert plate. He'd ordered apple pie à la mode, but the ice cream had melted into a puddle around the untouched pie during the time it had taken him to work his way through the correspondence Will had presented to him as their dinner plates were being cleared.

Nell had been shocked to see Will withdraw the letters from within the black frock coat he'd changed into. He hadn't told her he'd taken them, no doubt because he knew she would be outraged at his absconding with evidence that ought to have been left at the scene for the Salem Police to find.

"I should inform you before you read these," Will had told Adam as he handed him the letters, "that Duncan is under some illusions regarding Nell and my brother Harry. Any suggestion of an illicit relationship between them is entirely without merit."

Adam had glanced at Nell, then at Will, and then he'd proceeded to work his way through the letters, not paying any mind when Nell engaged Will in a whispered debate over the ethics and wisdom of having taken them.

"They mention not just Harry, but you," he'd told her. "Do you really want people thinking you're having an affair with him?"

"I'll just explain that it isn't like that."

"Whom do you think they'd believe? A Hewitt or an Irish governess?"

"You didn't do it to protect me," she'd said. "You did it to protect Harry, but he's not worth it."

"Believe what you like, but I did it mostly for you. Letters or no letters, the police are bound to focus in on Harry straightaway—you made that point yourself. The letters make very little difference as to how he'll be perceived in all this, but a great deal as regards you."

She'd shaken her head. "I'm still not comfortable with it."

"I'm not asking you to be comfortable. I'm just asking you to kindly drop the subject so that I can enjoy my coffee while it's still hot . . ."

Adam stared at the stack of letters for a full minute after he finished reading the last one. "What can I say? Duncan . . . he's an extremely charismatic individual. His relationship with Virgil Hines, well, that was really more a matter of hero worship than real friendship. Virgil used to run errands for Duncan, do him little favors . . . roll his cigarettes, give him his bread at supper, that sort of thing."

"My brother Jamie used to roll Duncan's cigarettes," Nell said. "Duncan would do that—let someone with a weaker personality think they were the best of friends, when really Duncan was just using him."

Adam sighed. "Duncan wields a great deal of power among his fellow prisoners. He can get them to do anything. It just never occurred to me that he'd go so far as to enlist Virgil to act as his spy after he was paroled."

Adam lifted his coffee cup and gazed into it, paused, and put it back down. He pushed the cup and saucer to where the waiter had first placed them, then did the same with his dessert plate. "I've been so complacent, so smugly certain that they tell me everything—especially Virgil. Just goes to show you—we believe what we want to believe. I was proud of my rapport with the prisoners, but there's a reason pride is a sin."

"Don't be too hard on yourself," Nell said. "Duncan probably threatened to beat Virgil senseless if he talked about their arrangement."

Adam looked as if he wanted to say something. Instead, he picked up his coffee cup, took a careful sip.

"What is it?" Will asked.

"Nothing, just . . ." He set his cup down with a pained expression, turning it in its saucer so the handle was to the right. "This command Duncan exercises over the other inmates . . . He maintains it in part through, well, fear and coercion. He'll lie, threaten violence . . . And he *has* been known to use his fists to maintain his authority."

"You told me he'd changed," Nell said, "but he sounds like the same old Duncan to me."

"He *has* changed—in some very fundamental ways. He attends Bible study, he's learned how to read and write . . ."

Will said, "Those are superficial changes. If he's still prone to violence . . ."

"They're all prone to violence," Adam said, as if he were stating something ridiculously obvious. "That's why they're in prison, most of them. These aren't men who talk their differences out, Will. Sometimes bloodshed is all they understand. I've been working with Duncan, trying to teach him how to get a handle on that temper of his, how to think things through instead of lashing out."

"If he hasn't learned that lesson yet," Will said, "do you really think you ought to be recommending him for parole?"

Adam frowned into his coffee cup. "I put a lot of thought into that decision. My thinking was that I could help him get a real job and provide guidance and counsel to facilitate his reentrance into society. I must tell you, though, over this past summer, I've had reason to question the wisdom of my recommendation."

"Are you withdrawing it?" Nell asked hopefully.

"I'm thinking about postponing it, at least for another year or two, until he's had time to work some things out."

"What things?" Will asked.

Adam hesitated, looked at Nell, then back at Will. "I don't know if I should really—"

"Is it something to do with me?" she asked.

Adam patted his hair, nudged it out of his eyes. "Duncan's feelings in regard to you are . . . complicated. And those feelings absorb much of his thought and energy. He talks about you incessantly. On the one hand, he seems to care for you very deeply. Don't forget, he spent years learning to read and write just so he could correspond with you."

"He's obsessed with her," Will said shortly, "to an unhealthy degree. That's not the same as caring."

"I suppose one might call it obsession," Adam conceded, "but is it really unhealthy to care so deeply about—"

"It doesn't matter what it's called," Nell said. "Finish your point, if you would. Please," she added, modulating her tone. "On the one hand he cares for me. And on the other?"

Adam took his napkin off his lap, refolded it, and laid it to the left of his plateful of pie and liquefied ice cream. "My reason for rethinking the parole issue has to do with certain statements Duncan has made over the past few months. Actually, knowing what I know now about the information he's been receiving from Virgil all summer, I can understand the source of his . . ." He trailed off with a sigh.

"The source of his . . . ?" Nell prompted.

"Well, anger. He, uh, he's said some things that I've found . . . somewhat troubling. Not as a matter of course, just every once in a while, when he gets going on the subject of you and Harry Hewitt."

"Wait a minute," Nell said. "You *knew* about that? Before you read these letters?"

He nodded. "Duncan told me about it. I asked him how he'd found out, but he just said he had his ways. I didn't press him. If a prisoner starts to feel as if I'm prying into matters he considers private, he'll stop opening up to me—that's been my theory, at any rate."

"I take it he was upset about the situation," Will said as he lit a cigarette.

"Oh, he was beside himself—distraught, frustrated. There he was, locked up behind bars, and his rival was from one of the wealthiest, most influential families in Boston. He acted like a man facing the threat of a lifetime."

"Rival?" Will said through a burst of smoke. "He didn't understand that it was over between him and Nell? You'd think, after all these years . . . and, my God, after what he did to her . . ."

"He still feels she's his, body and soul." Turning to Nell, he added, "The idea that you'd betray him with Harry . . . well, he finds it infuriating."

Will sat forward, his elbows on the table. "Has he threatened to hurt her?"

Adam stared disconsolately at his neat arrangement of cup, plate, and napkin. "What you've got to try to understand is that his feelings stem from—"

"What I understand," Nell said tightly, "is that he's still trying to possess me, to control me, to *threaten* me from behind bars. What I *don't* understand is why you gave no hint of this when I was at the prison Wednesday afternoon. For that matter, neither did Duncan. You painted him as a man who'd found Jesus and resolved to change his ways, and that's exactly the role he played for me—fairly well, too. He almost had me convinced a couple of times. But then, he always could act. It was his greatest talent."

"It wasn't an act," Adam said. "He *is* trying to change. But change is a journey, and one that can take some time to complete. I told you what I told you—and left out what I left out—because I thought if he could only see you, talk to you, he could move beyond his anger and forgive you. And maybe you could forgive him, too. You and Duncan have a past together, Miss Sweeny. You've been through so much. For heaven's sake, you—"

"That was all over a long time ago." Nell caught Adam's eye and gave him a meaningful look, begging him without words not to say too much about her past with Duncan. "There's nothing to tie us together, not after what he did."

He held her gaze for a moment before looking away; she saw understanding dawn.

Nell heard Will's name spoken, and turned to see that desk clerk, the one who'd given Will his key, being directed to them by the headwaiter.

With a courtly little bow, the clerk said, "Good evening, Mrs. Hewitt, Dr. Hewitt . . ."

Adam looked at Nell. She cringed inside, knowing what he was thinking. Why would the hotel staff call her "Mrs. Hewitt" unless she were Will's wife . . . or his mistress.

"I'm sorry to interrupt your meal," the clerk said, "but there's a messenger at the front desk asking for you, Dr. Hewitt."

Will excused himself and exited to the lobby. Adam sipped his coffee without looking at her.

"It isn't like you think," she said. "Will and I—"

"Come now, I'm not naïve. I don't necessarily approve of these things, but I do understand how they happen. Believe me, I'd much rather you were honest with me and didn't pretend—"

"But it really isn't like that," she said. "You know I'm a governess for the Hewitts. I wouldn't jeopardize that by carrying on with a man."

He sat back, frowning with a severity she hadn't seen in him before. It was an expression that hinted at an undercurrent of grave intensity beneath his affable façade. "Secrets will eat you up like a cancer, Nell. Like this business about Duncan."

"That. Yes, well . . ."

"How much does Will know?"

"Only that I was with him. Not . . . how we lived, or anything else."

"Don't you think he has a right to know?" The query carried with it a whiff of judgment, reminding Nell that Adam Beals was, after all, an ordained minister.

She shook her head. "He knows too much about me as it is. He's a good man in many ways, but . . ." She paused, not wanting to compromise Will's privacy. "Men of his class have been known to be . . . intemperate from time to time. If he knew about . . . Duncan and all that, it might slip out sometime when he's been . . ."

"Drinking? He didn't even have wine with dinner."

She hesitated.

"It's not liquor, is it?" Adam asked.

"Please—I didn't mean to suggest—"

"You didn't. It's my business to dig beneath the surface, but there's a fine line between that and prying. I apologize if I've discomfited you."

"No, it's all right. I just don't want you to think poorly of Will. He really is a good man—despite his lack of faith."

Adam and Will had spent the soup course debating theological matters with a frankness that had Nell both laughing and cringing.

Adam smiled—a relief after such a serious interlude. "Most people are so intent on trying to act respectably around ministers that they can never really relax and be themselves. Will doesn't have that problem. He's excellent company, and that's not something I've had very much of since . . . well . . . since my wife passed away."

"Will likes you, too—I can tell."

"That's very gratifying. Speaking of the devil . . ." Adam said as the subject of their conversation came toward them holding an envelope.

"I'm sorry to cut things short," Will said as he signaled their waiter for the check without retaking his seat, "but my brother's being questioned by the Salem Police in connection with the murders at the White farm."

"That was quick," Nell said. The Salem constables must have talked to the mill workers this afternoon. How else would they have targeted Harry so soon? Neither she nor Will had mentioned his name.

"They're working with the Boston Detective Bureau, so they've got him at City Hall." The waiter came over, handed Will a gold-plated pencil, and flipped open a small leather folio. "He asked me to come right down," Will said as he signed for their meal.

"Do you think he did it?" Adam asked him.

The frankness of the question startled Nell, but Will merely slapped the folio shut and said, "No."

Adam looked toward Nell, wordlessly asking the same question as Will pulled her chair out for her. She said, "I hope for his mother's sake, and the sake of his immortal soul, that he's innocent."

Adam nodded solemnly as he stood, understanding, no doubt, that her answer meant *Probably*. "Have you considered leaving your brother to his own devices and trusting in God to sort things out?" he asked Will.

"My brother hasn't been on speaking terms with the Almighty for quite some time," Will replied. "I doubt God would trouble Himself."

"You might be surprised."

"I might be astounded. In the meantime, that leaves this humble mortal to do the sorting out. And, er . . . Nell, you might want to come with me. I believe my mother would expect it."

"Of course."

Adam took his leave after making arrangements with Will—at Will's instigation—to meet him in the Revere House barroom Tuesday evening to discuss "this parole business." Adam's willingness to postpone Duncan's parole for a year or two was hardly reassuring, given that he still intended to endorse it. She wasn't sure Will was likely to exercise any real influence, given Adam's strong feelings about the matter and the warden's support of it. Hopefully Duncan's recruitment of Virgil for spying purposes would work against him; perhaps not. Limited though his chances of success were, Nell was touched that Will was making the effort.

"He's a little sweet on you, I think," Will said as they walked from the dining room to the hotel lobby.

"Who? Adam? Don't be silly."

"He avoids looking at you. It's a sure sign."

"He's an Episcopal clergyman and I'm Irish Catholic."

"If you think that would keep him from admiring you, you don't know very much about men and women."

"Besides," she said, as casually as she could, "he thinks I'm your mistress."

"He does?" Will grinned. "I'm flattered."

"What's in the envelope?" she asked, wishing she didn't find his reaction so gratifying.

Will withdrew a sheet of notepaper, unfolded it, and handed it to Nell. "This is what the messenger brought. He was instructed to hand it to no one but me."

Will,

You're just about the last person I want to see, after last night, but . . .

"What happened last night?" Nell asked. She'd last seen Will around dusk at the edge of Boston Common as she'd escorted Gracie across the street for dinner.

"Just read." He led her with a hand on her back to the front desk, where he asked the clerk to retrieve his bag from the safe.

. . . but you're the only one I can ask for help without it getting back to Father. I'm at City Hall, in the office of some detective. They seem to think, "they" meaning two coppers from Salem and the Boston cops who seem to be walking them through this, that I might have had something to do with the death of Bridie and that jailbird she was screwing, which is preposterous, obviously. They told me you found the bodies, but I'll be damned if I know how you got mixed up in this.

This matter must be nipped in the bud here and now, before they take it into their heads to arrest me. I cannot, I mean I absolutely CANNOT let the slightest whiff of this get back to the old man, or I'll be cut off without a fip, and I'm not sure I could survive that.

If you would be so kind as to bring me $1,000 cash (the Salem cops want National banknotes in large denominations) AS SOON AS POSSIBLE so that I can get out of this shit hole and figure out how to come up with the rest without the old man finding out (because $1,000 is just a down payment on what it will take to make this go away) I would be most humbly appreciative.

Will, I know how you feel toward me right now, but they're telling me I might hang. I am prepared to repay the $1,000, with interest if you so require, but for God's sake bring it.

H.

Nell refolded the note without comment, but her face must have reflected her thoughts, because Will said, "He has no one else to turn to, Nell. You know my father means to disinherit him the next time he gets in trouble."

"Do you realize you'll be just one more person helping Harry Hewitt to buy his way out of his problems?"

"Do *you* realize how my mother will take it if yet another son is arrested for murder and threatened with hanging? Thank you," he said as the clerk handed him a fat, one-handled satchel made of alligator leather.

"That's a doctor's bag," she said as he guided her across the lobby to a secluded corner.

"Don't read anything into that." He set the bag on a tea table, retrieved a key ring from inside his coat and unlocked it.

Nell sucked in a breath when she saw the banknotes—stacks and stacks of them, bound with ribbon and string—stuffed into the yawning satchel amid little sacks bulging with coins that looked large enough to be double eagles.

She said, "Your gambling swag, I take it."

"That's right." Will slipped two stacks of bills inside his coat and returned the case to the clerk.

"I didn't realize you were quite so lucky," she said as he ushered her out the front door.

"It's not about luck. It's about mathematics—and common sense. Anyone who can add and subtract—and knows enough to steer clear of the skin shops—can win just a little bit more often than he loses. And in the long run, that's all it takes."

They went out to the sidewalk to search for hacks among the private carriages and horse cars rattling in and out of Bowdoin Square. It was getting dark; most of the carriages had their lanterns lit.

"You must harbor *some* doubts about Harry," Nell said. "Do you intend to just help him to squirm out of this predicament and then completely forget the possibility that he may have murdered two people in cold blood?"

"Do you think I could do that?"

"No."

Will looked at her for second, seemingly gratified by her answer. "Thank you." He stepped into the street, arm raised. A little maroon cabriolet pulled over. "I mean to satisfy myself as to his guilt or innocence. In the meantime, I see no reason my mother should have to find out that he's being questioned about these murders. City Hall," he told the driver.

"You do care about her," Nell said as he helped her into the open carriage. "I realized it last April, after Jack's funeral, when you told your father he should put in an elevator for her."

"I should have known he'd react as he did." Will settled in across from her as the driver guided the little cab into the street. "He loathes new inventions—except for those that increase his profit margin."

"He's making inquiries, actually, about the elevator."

"You're joking."

Nell shook her head. "An engineer came to the house a few weeks ago and drew up plans. I think your father might actually put one in."

"The steam kind?"

"No, it has a sort of pulley system, like a big dumbwaiter."

"Still . . ."

Nell smiled. "Yes, still . . ."

Chapter 16

"WHAT the devil is *she* doing here?" greeted Harry as Nell and Will entered Detective Colin Cook's office at the Boston City Hall.

It was a much finer office than the cluttered little cranny Cook had occupied at the station house on Williams Court. There were papers and books strewn about, to be sure, and the walls were papered with Wanted notices and crime scene pictures, as at Williams Court, but the room was twice as large and had windows on two sides, open to let the cool night air dispel the smoke from Harry's cigar.

Harry sat—or rather, lounged—behind Cook's desk, a glass and a bottle of whiskey in front of him, staring in disgust at Nell. Nell stared back, startled to find his nose heavily bandaged and an eye blackened. Two middle-aged men—immediately recognizable as constables despite their civilian sack suits—occupied the two chairs facing the desk, while Cook himself sat perched on the edge of a big filing chest, a dainty tea cup cradled in his massive bear's paw of a hand.

Big Irishman . . . giant head. That was Colin Cook.

All the men except Harry rose to their feet when Nell joined them; Harry just glared and puffed on his cigar.

The detective bowed toward her. "Miss Sweeney," he said in his faded but dense-chested brogue. "Always a pleasure. And Dr. Hewitt . . . Let's see, last time I saw you, you were in a holding cell, covered in blood and filth."

"I've had a change of clothes since then."

"They suit you."

"Christ, Will." Harry gestured with his cigar toward Nell. "Did you have to bring along that goddamn—"

"You'll watch your mouth in front of the lady," warned Cook, "or I'll give you a shiner to match the one you got. I don't care what your name is."

Nell expected Will to ask Cook if his men were responsible for Harry's injuries. He didn't, merely tossed the two packs of bills on the desk in front of his brother.

Harry picked them up and handed one to each of the Salem cops without even looking at them. Bracing himself to rise, he said, "I take it I'm free to go?"

They told him they were done with him for now, thanked Detective Cook for the cooperation of the Boston Police, and took their leave. Harry crushed out his cigar and stood. As he was reaching for his homburg and scarf on the coat tree in the corner, Will said quietly, "I'd like a word with you before you go."

"Look . . ." Harry lowered his voice to a whisper. "I'll pay you back as soon as the cards start falling my—"

"It's not about the money." Glancing toward Nell and Cook, Will said, "I wonder if you'd mind . . . ?"

"Not at all." Cook escorted Nell out into the central,

high-ceilinged clerical area and shut the door, the upper half of which was glass hung with open blinds, like the door of Harry's office at the mill; she couldn't hear the two men inside the office, but she could see them. Harry sat down and poured himself another whiskey with a here-we-go-again expression. He offered some to Will, who shook his head. Will said something; his brother smirked.

"He's a bad egg, that one," Cook said.

"What happened to his face?" Nell asked.

"I know what you're thinking, but I'll have you know he came to us that way. Even those Salem yokels aren't dumb enough to start whalin' away on a Hewitt. What he told us was, he had a little too much absinthe and took a spill."

"Did he, now."

"That's a lot of green that just changed hands in there," Cook said. "I wouldn't have expected a right-thinking, churchgoing lass like yourself to be a party to such shenanigans."

"I'm more of a grudging witness than a party."

Will was leaning over his brother, both arms braced on the desk, speaking intently, while Harry stared straight ahead, his whiskey untouched.

"Then we're in the same boat, me and you," Cook said. "I'm supposed to be showin' them jackanapes the ropes, on account of neither one of them's ever investigated a murder before. Only they don't want my advice, they just want an office where they can conduct such business as you and me just bore witness to in there."

Nell said, "Please, Detective, don't try to pretend that you're above taking graft. I know better, remember?"

Cook shrugged, swallowed the last of his tea. "And what would you do, Miss Sweeney, if they paid you peanuts, but there's folks throwin' money at you from all angles, and you've got a sweet little wife who deserves to live someplace other than a Fort Hill hovel and cook up something a little better than dried peas and potatoes once in a while? Yeah, a few stray shinplasters end up in my pockets now and then, but, see, there's so much of it here in Boston that I can turn it down when I've a mind to. Them boys from Salem, they've *never* had nobody offer 'em the kind of cabbage Harry Hewitt's offerin', and they ain't about to say nay to it."

"You turn it down sometimes?" she asked skeptically.

"Some of these miscreants"—he glanced through the door at Harry—"they're just begging to get what's coming to 'em." He shook his head. "Two young folks like that, layin' out there dead for God knows how long, the girl strangled and . . . who knows what else. But . . ." He lifted his thick shoulders. "It's not my case. Not even my jurisdiction."

He swallowed the last of his tea and gestured with the empty cup. "Would you care for some? I drink gallons every night. Only thing that keeps me going til my shift's over."

"No, thanks—I just had two cups of coffee. Is this your regular shift?"

He nodded as he refilled his cup from a pot sitting on top of a little stove. "Four to midnight, later if there's anything afoot. Many's the shift I've eaten breakfast at my desk. Low man on the totem pole, don't you know, and a mick to boot, so I'll probably be the night man til the Second Coming. The weekend man, too, 'cause they've got me workin' Saturdays and Sundays."

"You must get days off, though."

"Mondays and Tuesdays, but it's not the same."

The office door slammed open. Harry stalked out without a word, his battered face darkly flushed, his expression that of a surly adolescent who's been forced to sit through a dressing-down.

Will stood in the doorway rubbing the back of his neck as he watched his brother leave. "Were you there the whole time they were questioning my brother?" he asked Cook.

The detective nodded. "Strictly as an observer. Nobody was much interested in what I had to say."

"Do you mind if I ask you a few questions?"

"Not at all." Cook invited them back into his office and gestured them into the chairs facing his desk. "Hitchcock!" he called.

A young uniformed cop appeared at the door. "Detective?"

Cook held out the whiskey bottle and glass. "Take these back to where you got 'em. Can't stand the smell of the stuff, not since I gave it up. And close the door on your way out, would you?" When they were alone, he asked Will, "What is it you want to know, then?"

"Did they actually interrogate him, or was it a complete farce?"

"Well, they started out pretty serious—had to put the fear of God in him, don't you know—but after about five minutes of that, your brother started making offers. Once they agreed on a price, they treated him like the Prince of Wales."

"Did they ask him about the scarf?"

"First thing. He told 'em it went missing from his office recently—he's not sure when, 'cause he didn't notice it right away. Said he assumed Bridie Sullivan stole it, on account of she'd always admired it."

Pretty convenient, Nell thought.

"They asked him about his comings and goings over the past week or so," Cook said. "Not that it matters much, seeing as how nobody knows when those two were done in. That was about it, I guess. Not much in the way of an interrogation."

Nell asked, "Are they allowed to just stop investigating a case without solving it?"

"They're calling it a murder-suicide," Cook said. "The official story's gonna be that Virgil Hines strangled her out of jealousy over Harry Hewitt, then realized what he done and drowned himself."

"Drowned himself," Will said.

"In a foot of water?" Nell asked.

Cook shrugged. "I seen a drunk drown in a rain puddle."

"Because he passed out," Nell said. "A man can't commit suicide by lying facedown in a shallow stream."

"Won't there be a coroner's inquest?" Will asked.

"Nah. Why would they want the coroner involved, and post-mortems, and folks asking all kinds of prickly questions?"

"It isn't routine in suspicious cases?" Nell asked.

"It is in Boston," Cook said. "And probably in Salem, too, unless the right palms are greased. All's they have to say is that it's an open and shut case and autopsies would just prove what they already know. Saves the city of Salem the cost of hiring a surgeon to cut those two open."

Will scrubbed his hands over his face, muttering something under his breath.

Detective Cook sat back and folded his arms, his chair squealing rustily as it swiveled back and forth. "You're a curious family, you Hewitts. First you get pinched for murder, and your old man moves heaven and earth to make sure you swing. Now it's your brother that's facing a murder charge—*two* murder charges—and he buys his way out of that mess, with your help, mind you, only to have you boo-hooin' 'cause he's getting off."

"Dr. Hewitt doesn't think his brother did it," Nell said. "He thinks Harry just paid off those cops to avoid trouble with his father, and that an autopsy might help to prove that it wasn't him."

"How so?" Cook asked.

Will said, "The scarf around Bridie's neck was knotted rather than twisted, and it didn't leave much of a ligature mark. Also, if you were of a mind to murder somebody, would you do it with a weapon that was undeniably yours, and leave it around the victim's throat for the police to find? It's too obvious, absurdly so."

"You think he was set up?" Cook asked.

"I think it's a possibility, and if that's the case, I want to clear my brother's name for real."

And, Nell suspected, Will also wanted to know in his heart that Harry wasn't guilty of such a heinous crime. But William Hewitt was hardly the type to so casually bare his soul.

"I wouldn't draw too many conclusions about that scarf being left behind," Cook said. "You'd be surprised, the bone-headed things some criminals do, especially the amateurs—and especially when they're under the influence. Your brother's absinthe habit is no secret in this town, Dr. Hewitt. As for the ligature, they don't always leave obvious external marks."

"I know," Will said, "but an autopsy would show signs of strangulation. Or it might reveal how she was really killed."

"What if it helps to point the finger at your brother?" Cook asked. "What then?"

"I suppose I'll have to address that problem when it arises—but I don't think it will."

Cook scratched his great jutting boulder of a chin. "Do you share Dr. Hewitt's opinions on the matter, Miss Sweeney?"

"I'm as eager as he is to uncover the truth," she said, diplomatically omitting the fact that her working theory—Harry strangling Bridie and killing Virgil when he tried to intervene—wasn't quite the same as Will's.

Detective Cook twirled back and forth for a minute as he sipped his tea. "Like I said, those Salem cops nixed the idea of autopsies when they took that money from your brother. But before they knew how it was gonna play out, they went to the trouble of asking the families to sign letters of consent for post-mortems."

Will sat up straighter in his chair. "Did they sign them?"

"Virgil Hines's folks did—anything to clear their son of the murder-suicide stigma, even posthumously. But the Fallons—the dead girl's folks?—they were another story. Didn't want their daughter's body cut up just to prove that Hines was the no-good, vicious brute they always thought he was."

"Just hypothetically," Will began, "what if the families insisted on autopsies? What if they both signed the consent letters and provided their own surgeon?"

Cook sipped his tea thoughtfully. "Surgeons don't come cheap."

Will said, "What if one volunteered his services? What would he have to do to get access to the bodies?"

Nell turned to look at Will.

Detective Cook smiled slowly. "They're at a private mortuary in Salem. You'd—the surgeon—he'd have to bring the letters of consent, and then they'd let him at it, I suppose."

"These letters," Nell said. "How are they worded?"

"You mean could you write them up yourselves?" Cook shook his head. "Sorry. They've got to be issued by the City of Salem, in the right clerk's handwriting, with the city seal on the bottom. And signed by the next of kin, of course. No mortuary employee would settle for anything else."

Will slumped back in his chair, cursing under his breath.

"And the thing is," Cook said, "when those Salem cops worked their deal with your brother, they threw out them letters, figuring they wouldn't need them anymore." He raised his teacup to his mouth and drained it in a leisurely but thorough manner.

Nell and Will both looked toward the wastepaper basket next to the detective's desk, a few inches from Will's feet.

"Course, it'd be worth my job to let such documents fall into the hands of mere civilians—and I like my job. Oh, lookit this." Cook tilted his cup to show them its empty interior. "Time for another refill. Can I bring some back for either of you?" he asked as he rose and circled his desk.

"Er, no," Will answered. "We've got to be on our way fairly soon."

"I'll just be a minute, then." Cook paused a moment to shut the blinds on his door before leaving.

The moment the door clicked shut, Will dragged the wastebasket toward him and started rummaging through it. "Here, open these." He dropped a handful of crumpled papers in Nell's lap and emptied the rest onto his own. They worked swiftly, flattening out paper after paper until at last Nell saw the glimmer of a gold seal imprinted with the words SALEM, MASSACHUSETTS. "Will—I think this is it."

It was two sheets crushed up together, both neatly inked on engraved vellum bearing the heading *Consent for Post-mortem Examination of Human Remains*. The letter granting permission for Virgil's autopsy was signed *Clement Hines*. That for Bridie was unsigned.

The doorknob rattled.

Nell folded up the letters and stuffed them in her chatelaine as Will returned the wastebasket to its former position. They both stood as Colin Cook reentered the room.

"Setting off now, are you?" the detective asked.

"Yes, you've been most helpful," Will said as he held out his hand. "If there's ever anything I can do for you, you mustn't hesitate to ask."

"Just let me know how it all turns out," Cook said. "I hope you're right about your brother's innocence—for your sake, not his. My gut tells me nothing's gonna save that one in the long run."

"It won't be because I didn't try," Will said.

"WHAT happened to Harry's face?" Nell asked Will as they stood beneath a streetlamp in front of City Hall trying to hail another hack.

"He said it was a mishap resulting from an overindulgence in absinthe." Will stepped off the curb to scrutinize the approaching vehicles.

"Because that's what you told him to say. You did that to him. You went to see him last night and . . . Was it an actual fistfight, or . . . ?"

He sighed, his back to her. "Not a fair one, I suppose. Harry's not very good at that sort of thing. Another gap in his tutelage for which I am ultimately responsible."

She waited.

Presently he turned to face her, his expression grave. "Some lessons need to be seared in place with pain. It's the only way some people can learn."

"You were punishing him for what he did to me?"

"How could I not?" He looked down, rubbed his neck, met her gaze. "I, uh, I told him I'd break both his arms if he ever touched you again. A compound fracture of each radius. Not too much effort on my part if I had a good club or mallet or some such, but the experience would be memorable, I should think."

"Yes, I should think it would."

He spied a hack then, and flagged it down. Nell smiled all the way home.

Chapter 17

"FINALLY," Nell muttered when the steeple bells started pealing, signaling the end of Mass. She and Will had been killing time on the front steps of Charlestown's Immaculate Conception Church for over half an hour, waiting for Bridie Sullivan's parents, who worshipped here, to step outside.

This was the first time since Nell had come to work for the Hewitts that she'd had the middle of a Sunday morning to herself. Her usual practice was to attend the six o'clock Mass at St. Stephen's, then watch Gracie while Nurse Parrish went to King's Chapel with the Hewitts, after which she was left to her own devices. But last night, after returning home from City Hall, she'd asked Viola for the entire day off, explaining that she had the opportunity to uncover new information about the death of Bridie Sullivan. Horrified by the double murder, and eager to provide Bridie's mother with any information she could, Viola—who knew nothing about Harry's possible involvement—had readily agreed.

Nell had attended early Mass as usual this morning, having arranged to meet Will afterward for their drive north through Charlestown to Salem. But as she was returning to her seat after receiving Communion, she noticed him sitting in the very last pew in his ubiquitous black coat and vest, his low-crowned stovepipe on his lap, quietly taking in the proceedings. He'd smiled at her, but she'd been too flustered by his presence there to smile back.

"Here they come," Will said as the front door of the modest brick church swung open. Parishioners filed out into the morning sunshine, all in their Sunday best, be it silk frocks and morning coats or patched calico and freshly boiled shirts. "You don't see them?" he asked as the procession started to thin; having met the Fallons, it was up to Nell to point them out.

She shook her head, wondering where they would be at this hour on a Sunday morning, if not at Mass—although it *had* been less than twenty-four hours since the discovery of their daughter's body.

"Perhaps," Nell said, "Mrs. Fallon was too distraught to come to . . ." A familiar face appeared among the departing congregants—*two* familiar faces, although they weren't those of the Fallons. They were young and flaxen-haired, the woman petite, the man big and slow-moving. "Evie?" Nell called out. What was the brother's name? Ah, yes . . . "Luther?"

Evie stared at Nell for a moment before recognition lit her eyes. She approached tentatively, her brother hovering over her like a pet bear. "You're the artist lady from the mill."

"That's right—Nell Sweeney." Nell introduced the siblings to Will, who lifted his hat and bowed to Evie while uttering some pleasantry.

"Are you kin to Mr. Harry?" Evie asked.

"I'm his brother," Will replied.

The girl nodded. "You're the one he was talkin' to in the courtyard the other day."

"That's right."

Luther stared at Will, slack-jawed. "You talk funny."

Will responded as cordially as if he were conducting small talk at a dinner party. "I was brought up in England."

"Is that near Boston?"

"Afraid not, no."

Nell said, "Evie, do you happcn to know what Mr. and Mrs. Fallon look like? Bridie Sullivan's parents," she added.

"I know who they are," Evie said. "The mother, she came to the mill after Bridie was fired, askin' about her. Terrible, what happened. Father Dunne told us at the beginning of Mass."

"Bridie's dead," Luther said.

"Hush, Luther," his sister murmured. "We all know that."

"She was a bad girl."

"I said hush," Evie repeated, a little more stridently. "Don't speak ill of the dead."

"Did you notice whether they were in church this morning?"

"Oh, sure. Mrs. Fallon, she's there every week. Mr. Fallon, too, usually. They both came today."

"Do you have any idea where they are now?" Nell asked.

"I seen 'em headin' into Father Dunne's office after Mass, with some fella. Someone said they was meeting with Father to plan the funeral, and that the other fella was Bridie's husband, but . . ."

"But what?"

"That can't be . . . can it? She never wore no wedding ring, and she was . . . She sure didn't act married."

"Good riddance . . ." Luther shook his big head like a horse trying to loosen its bit. "Bridie was bad."

Evie opened her mouth to chastise him, but before she could, Will asked, "Why do you say that, Luther?"

Luther looked at his sister, then at Will, and then he started scratching his big, unkempt head. "Couple reasons . . ."

"What's one?"

"She was tryin' to make Mr. Harry give her money."

"Evie told you about the blackmail?" Nell asked.

Evie said, "He don't know that word."

"It's like stealin', to make somebody give you money," Luther said.

"What was the other reason Bridie was bad?" Nell asked him.

He ducked his head. "I'm not s'posed to say."

Nell said, "Was it because of . . . what she did with men?"

"That's right," Evie said. "But he don't understand—"

"Not them others, just Mr. Harry," Luther said. "It's what she done with Mr. Harry, 'cause him an' Evie's fixin' to get hitched."

Evie blushed violently, her eyes like silver dollars. "Luther!" She slapped his arm. "Why would you say that?" She wouldn't meet Nell's gaze, or Will's. "He don't know what he's sayin'. He's simple. Been that way since—"

"Am not!" Luther exclaimed. "And I do so know what I'm sayin'. You said yourself you and him was gonna get—"

"I didn't mean it," Evie said, her chin quivering, her too-bright eyes flitting between Nell and Will. "Doggonnit, Luther . . ."

"You said 'good riddance' when Father said they found Bridie dead. You whispered it, but I heard you."

"I did not!" Evie gasped, her eyes shimmering.

"You did so. I know what that means, 'good riddance.' It means you're glad she's—"

"You just hush!" Evie grabbed a fistful of her brother's coat sleeve and started tugging him away. "We got to go. He don't know what he's sayin'. He makes stuff up sometimes."

They left quickly, little Evie hauling the big man behind her like a child walking some huge, lumbering pet, Luther whining all the while.

"An unrequited infatuation?" Will asked as he and Nell watched them disappear around the corner.

"Apparently. She gets teased about it at the mill. It upsets Luther. You wouldn't know from what you just saw, but he seems to be very protective of her. He almost killed a man last year for being rude to her."

"My word." Will's gaze shifted. "Nell . . . Is that them?"

Nell turned to see Mr. and Mrs. Fallon and a brawny young man with a shock of thick, sandy hair—Bridie's husband Jimmy Sullivan, presumably—coming down the church's front walk. "That's them." Except for Mrs. Fallon's hat—an old-fashioned black coal-scuttle bonnet—the couple appeared to be wearing the same clothes they'd worn for their audience with Viola last week, dyed black. Mrs. Fallon's eyes were glazed, her nose bright red. "This won't be easy," Nell murmured.

"You're good with people," Will said as he took her arm and walked her toward them.

"Good morning," Nell said.

Mrs. Fallon and the two men stopped walking. "Miss . . . Sweeney, is it?"

"That's right." She introduced Will; the Fallons introduced Jimmy Sullivan, who stood with his hands in his pockets, looking distracted, or perhaps just bored. He wasn't a tall man, but his arm muscles stretched the seams of his faded pea jacket. Although nominally handsome, his nose was bulky and dented, and he had a bruise over his right eye that was just starting to turn greenish; it was about five or six days old.

Nell said, "I can't tell you how sorry I am about your daughter. I was praying I'd find her alive. Please accept my most heartfelt condolences."

Mrs. Fallon sniffed, nodded. "You're a good girl. You tried. She's in the arms of the Lord now."

Not knowing how to broach the subject diplomatically, Nell said, "The reason we're here, Mrs. Fallon, is that . . . well . . ."

"Call me Moira—please."

"Moira . . . I know you were asked yesterday to approve a post-mortem examination of Bridie's remains. You chose not to sign the letter of consent, and whereas I understand that decision, I must ask you to reconsider."

"I . . . I don't know," she began. "My husband thinks—"

"We know who done it," Mr. Fallon said. "What's the point of butcherin' the poor girl like a side of beef?"

The poor girl? That was quite a turnaround from how he'd spoken of her just four days ago. *She was paintin' on the lip rouge when she was still in short skirts, that one. Weren't no better than she ought to be, right from the get-go.*

"An autopsy isn't like that, I promise you," Will said.

"It's a methodical operation, and one which can yield a great deal of useful information. And afterward, you won't even be able to tell that it was done."

Liam Fallon said, "You're talkin' like it's gonna happen, but we ain't signed that letter, and we ain't about to. There ain't no reason for it, that I can see."

"There's a good chance Virgil Hines wasn't the murderer," Nell said. "Wouldn't you like to find out what really happened?"

"Will it make her any less dead?" Mr. Fallon asked.

"If she were my daughter," Will said, "I'd want to know for sure how she died, and by whose hand. This is your one and only chance to find out. Once she's buried, the opportunity is lost."

"Oh, dear." Moira Fallon turned to her son-in-law. "You're her husband, Jimmy. What do you think?"

"He ain't got no say in this," Mr. Fallon protested. "He don't have no husbandly rights no more. He washed his hands of her last spring."

With a sneer at his father-in-law, Jimmy said, "I was gonna back you up, old man. Don't sit right with me, cutting her open and scoopin' out her insides. But you know what? You're right. It ain't none of my concern no more, so you can go ahead and make your stand on your own." Turning away, he said, "I got some fish to catch."

Moira rushed over and embraced him, murmuring things Nell couldn't quite hear. Clearly uncomfortable with this display, he patted her back once, then finally succeeded in squirming out of her arms. He turned and walked away, his hands still in his pockets.

"I don't know, Miss Sweeney . . ." Moira began.

"Nell—please."

"Nell . . . My poor Bridie, she's already been . . ." Her

voice caught. "She's been through so much. The idea of her being cut open like that . . ."

Nell said, "I promise you, Moira, it will be done with the utmost respect. Dr. Hewitt will do it himself, and I'll be there. I'll make sure Bridie is treated right."

"You'll be there?" she asked, her eyes lighting.

"Yes, I'll be assisting Dr. Hewitt. I've done this sort of thing before—I was trained as a nurse once. I'm a Catholic, too, you know. I'll say a proper prayer before we start."

"A prayer . . . I'd like that."

Her husband said, "Yeah, well, there won't be no prayer on account of there won't be no autopsy. The decision is made."

"By who?" demanded Moira, with a mulish thrust to her chin that Nell wouldn't have expected.

Mr. Fallon stared at her a moment in surprise, then stuck his chest out. "By her husband and her father, that's who."

"What was all that, then, about Jimmy not havin' any husbandly rights no more, eh? And you ain't her father at all, are you? You're her stepfather. You been makin' that plain enough all along. Seems to me the only one of us that's got any real rights in the matter is me." Turning to Nell, she asked, "Will you say a prayer afterward, too?"

"I'll be happy to."

Moira held out her hand. "Give me the letter, then."

Chapter 18

"ISN'T that Jimmy Sullivan walking up ahead?" Nell asked as Will steered their rented phaeton onto North Street.

"Mr. Sullivan," Will called as he reined in the horses. "Care for a lift? We've got room in back," he said, pointing to the groom's seat.

He shielded his eyes to look up at them. "Ain't that far. I'm just headin' home for my fishing tackle."

"Why walk when you can ride?" Nell asked.

He ruminated on it for a moment, shrugged, climbed up into the rear seat. "You turn right on Lynde."

Twisting around in her seat to face him, Nell said, "I'm sorry about your wife."

Jimmy trained his gaze on the passing houses. "I don't think of her that way no more."

"Still . . ."

His meaty shoulders twitched.

"Mrs. Fallon seems fond of you," she said conversationally.

He grunted, his expression unchanging but for a suggestion of something that might have been weariness, or even a hint of disgust.

"Perhaps I was misreading things," Nell said.

"Naw, she likes me, all right."

"You say that as if you wish she didn't."

He sniffed. "Is that tobacco I smell?"

Will took one hand off the reins to fetch a tin labeled *Arabi-Pascha* and a brass match safe from inside his jacket.

"These are them already rolled ones." Jimmy lit his cigarette, nodding as he expelled a stream of smoke. His hands didn't look as if they belonged on such a young man. They were cracked and leathery, the knuckles scabbed over. *He's got a short fuse, that Jimmy Sullivan, and he's a bruiser. Makes a pretty penny fightin' other bruisers bare-knuckled when he's in town.*

"Not bad." Jimmy handed the cigarettes and matches back to Will, picked a fleck of tobacco off his tongue. "Ma Fallon, she always thought me and Bridie could work it out, you know? I wanted to put an end to it, legal-like, but Ma said what God had put asunder and all that . . ."

"She was making it difficult for you?" Nell asked. Never mind that she herself was as passionately opposed to divorce, on religious grounds, as was Moira Fallon.

He nodded as he drew on his cigarette. "She talked Bridie into fightin' me on it. Said she wouldn't agree to a divorce on account of she didn't want to end up in Hell. I told her they already had a spit reserved in her name and a divorce wouldn't make no difference, but that didn't go over too good."

"It seems to me," Will said as he turned the buggy onto Lynde, "that she might have welcomed the idea, seeing as it would have accorded her . . . well, a certain measure of freedom to, er . . ."

Jimmy grunted. "Yeah, well, Bridie, she went ahead and 'accorded herself that freedom' long ago. Didn't need no divorce to do as she pleased. Me, I figure I'll be wantin' to get hitched again, to a good girl this time, a good Irish girl who'll bc there when I get home and have supper ready and the house fixed up nice. A girl who knows who's boss and don't run around on me or give me a lot of lip. Only, there ain't no good girls that'll have anything to do with me, on account of they all know I got a wife that won't let go. Or did."

"I can see why you were so frustrated," Will said. "And, to be frank, I *had* wondered why you were taking your wife's death so calmly."

"I'm a calm kind of a guy."

Nell said, "That's not what Liam Fallon says."

Jimmy stilled in the act of bringing the cigarette to his mouth. "What'd that bast—" He bit off the epithet with a grimace. "What'd he say about me? He thinks I had something to do with what happened to Bridie, don't he?"

Choosing her words with care, Nell said, "He didn't say it in so many words . . ."

"If that . . ." Jimmy swore under his breath and flung the cigarette onto the road, his hands clenching. "If he wants to make trouble for me, I can make trouble for him."

"I'm sorry I said anything," Nell lied.

"You know why he makes such a to-do about Bridie not bein' his real daughter, don't you?"

"No . . ." Nell said, although she was beginning to entertain some suspicions.

Jimmy looked away, grinding his jaw. "Let's just say I know some things he don't know I know."

"Things Bridie told you?"

He nodded distractedly. "That son of a . . ."

"Did he and Bridie . . . Were they . . . ?" Nell didn't know how to say it.

Jimmy emitted a kind of churlish sigh. "I wasn't never gonna say nothin'. Bridie, she made me promise." He rubbed his big, scarred hands on his denim pants, frowning at nothing.

"Would you like another cigarette?" Will asked.

"Um, yeah."

"Here," Will said as he handed back the tin. "Keep it."

"Yeah? Thanks." He turned it over in his hands, admiring it, before opening the lid.

"It seems to me," Nell said as he lit up, "that your promise not to talk about it died with Bridie. Of course, I suppose if the truth would end up compromising Mr. Fallon, perhaps you should—"

"The hell with him. I'll be damned if I'm gonna . . . Sorry," he muttered with a glance at Nell.

"Perfectly all right."

"If he wants to point the finger at me, I can point it right back. Him and Bridie, they . . ."

"Had relations?" Nell supplied.

"Yeah, lots of relations, when she was just fifteen. It went on about half a year. It was before I even met her, so I didn't get all het up about it, but she begged me not to tell, on account of him and Ma Fallon was married at the time."

"Do you know who broke it off?" Nell asked.

"Him. Father Dunne made him. She was the one that started it, though."

Will said, "You may think that, because of how you view her, but at that age—"

"No, she told me it was her. Said she got herself all tarted up one day and threw herself at him. Let me tell you, there was nothin' in long pants coulda said no to Bridie Sullivan when she put herself on display." He shook his head and whispered, "Damn," without seeming to remember that Nell was within earshot.

"Did she say why she did it?" Nell asked.

"She was in love with him. I asked her how she coulda been in love with her own father, and she said he wasn't her father. Her real father . . . all's I really know about him is on her eleventh birthday, he got stinkin' drunk and told her he wished she'd never been born, on account of now he was tied down with a wife and kid, and he couldn't stand the sight of either one of 'em. He went out that night and got hisself trampled to death by a horse car. Some birthday present, huh?"

Nell and Will exchanged a look.

"I suppose this is why Mr. Fallon dislikes Bridie so much," Nell said. "He feels guilty about having betrayed his wife with his own stepdaughter."

"If he does, that just goes to show what a jackass he is. Like I said, it was all Bridie's doin'. Not that she felt sorry for a second. She made like it was for her ma's sake that she wanted to keep it a secret, but I know it was so she'd have somethin' to hold over the old man's head if she was ever of a mind to. She'd get what she wanted any way she could, that Bridie. I heard about her tryin' to squeeze money out of Harry Hewitt."

"Did she ever try anything like that with you?" Nell asked.

"Naw," he said as he raised his cigarette to his mouth with his ravaged boxer's hand. "She woulda known better than that."

"YOU can put him back in the ice box now," Will told the mortuary aide after Nell concluded her post-autopsy prayer over the body of Virgil Hines. They hung up their soiled aprons and washed their hands, then retreated to an empty office to go over the notes she'd taken during the two back-to-back post-mortems.

It had been a revelation, watching William Hewitt wielding scalpels, bone saws, rib shears, dissecting forceps . . . all with such easy authority, although he hadn't practiced any form of surgery since removing that bullet from his leg four years ago. For that matter, it had been just as long since Nell had assisted at a post-mortem, but it had come back to her fairly readily. She'd felt an absurd surge of pride when Will had complimented her handling of the skull clamp.

In addition to providing an extra set of hands, Nell had recorded their observations in a little notebook she'd brought along for the purpose—no easy task, what with her hands coated with lard to help keep contagion out of accidental nicks and scratches.

"Let's start with Virgil," Will said as they seated themselves across a table from each other in a homey little room that was probably used for consultations with grieving relatives.

Nell flipped to the grease-stained page bearing the heading *Virgil Hines, Sept. 20, 1868*, followed by:

–24 yr. old male.
–5 ft. 11 in. in height, lean, muscular.
–Dark brown hair, blue eyes.
–All teeth present.
–Tattoo of stars on forehead, no other major scars.
–Skull: Outer table intact. Linear frontal fracture of inner table with extensive extravasation of blood between the bone and dura mater. Significant cerebral oedema with brown-green discoloration and softening of brain tissue near the site of the fracture.

"Virgil fell or was pushed into the stream," Will said, restating what they'd already concluded. "His head struck a rock, fracturing the interior of his skull, whereupon he suffered both an extradural hemorrhage and pronounced swelling of the brain."

He sat back in his chair, regarding Nell curiously. "If you had to hazard a guess, what would you say was the primary cause of death in this case—the hemorrhage, the swollen brain, or drowning?"

Nell twirled her steel pen as she thought it through. "With extradural hemorrhage, it can take hours for the pressure to become fatal, but cerebral edema as severe as Virgil's can kill very quickly. The edema's what did him in."

"Not drowning?"

"He definitely didn't drown—you know that as well as I do. There was no water in the stomach or the lungs, no bits of weeds or algae. The lungs weren't distended and spongy, the heart wasn't enlarged, there was no mucous froth in his airway, no hemorrhaging in the middle ear . . .

none of the indications we found with Bridie."

"Who definitely did drown."

"During or after a rape," Nell added, "and a rather brutal one, judging from those bruises."

They both fell silent for a minute. Bridie had been about three months pregnant when she died. Nell hadn't expected that discovery to break her heart. Yet it had.

"I need to find out who did this to her," Nell said.

Will nodded. "I know."

Chapter 19

"I'M sorry, miss," said the young waiter who blocked the doorway when Nell tried to enter the Revere House barroom Tuesday night. "It's gentlemen only."

"I'm just looking for someone. Dr. William Hewitt?"

He shrugged and shook his head.

"Tall, black hair . . ." Nell tried to peer around the waiter into the bar itself, but it was one of those darkly paneled, clubby establishments furnished with cozy little clusters of high-backed leather chairs. She couldn't make out a single patron. "He's with a minister wearing an Anglican collar."

"There's no minister here."

"Please, could you just look?" she begged, her voice shrill from strained nerves. "They must be here. I was with them when they arranged to—"

"Nell?" Will materialized out of the shadows. "Is everything all right?"

"Yes. No." Nell drew a steadying breath. "I need to talk to you." They hadn't seen each other since Sunday, when they'd performed those post-mortems. Will had had his "ultra high stakes poker game" to attend to yesterday. Nell herself had been unavailable today, having promised Viola she would accompany her and Gracie on an all-day excursion to the dressmaker, shoemaker, milliner, and furrier to place orders for their winter wardrobes.

"I explained to her that it's gentlemen only in here," the waiter told Will.

"But surely the occasional exception can be made." Will withdrew two little gold dollars out of his pocket.

"Perhaps," said the young man as he plucked the coins out of Will's palm, "if she sits where no one will see her . . ."

"Most accommodating of you. Oh, and if you wouldn't mind bringing the lady a sherry? She looks as if she could use one."

Will escorted Nell to a semicircle of four chairs facing a snapping fire, two of which were occupied—one by Adam, who rose and fingered his hair as she approached, and the other, to her dismay, by Harry, who merely gaped in outrage as Will seated her. "Not you," he growled thickly, obviously soused already. "Oh, Christ, now the evening is perfect."

Will said, "Harry, I understand, by now, that you can't help but blaspheme, but must you really do so in the presence of ladies and clergymen?"

Nell barely heard him, taken aback as she was by the condition of Harry's face. In addition to the broken nose and black eye he'd sported three days ago in Detective Cook's office, he now had several fresh facial contusions and abrasions—bad ones—as well as a split lip and a bandaged forehead. His left arm was in a sling, two fingers splinted. He glowered at Nell with raw loathing.

"What happened to you?" she asked.

"*You* happened to me, you—"

"Harry." Will said it softly, but with a subtly threatening nuance that seemed to do the trick. His brother slumped back in his chair, groaned, and clutched his midsection.

"Watch those ribs." Will crossed his legs and lifted his cigarette from the big marble ashtray on the table next to him. "It's the tenth, eleventh, and twelfth on the left side," he told Nell, as if chatting with a medical colleague. "I used his scarf to wrap them, which infuriated him, of course, because it might stretch the silk. He paid fifty dollars for it—can you believe that?"

Nell looked toward Will, silently asking the obvious question: *Did you do this?*

"Actually, no," he said through a stream of smoke. "It was someone else entirely this time."

"Who?" Nell asked.

"I don't know who," Harry said, "but I know why. It was 'cause of you." He raised his whiskey glass to his mouth, mewing pitifully when the alcohol came in contact with the cut on his lip.

Adam, who'd been watching the exchange as if it were a stage play, lifted his brandy snifter and took a sip, but not before Nell saw his mouth quirk. He set the snifter down, wiped a drip off the side with his napkin, then refolded it in a triangle and set it neatly to the side of the glass. He'd eschewed his clerical collar for a crisply knotted secular bow tie tonight, probably because he knew he'd be spending the evening in a drinking establishment.

"My brother showed up a couple of hours ago," Will

explained, "freshly trounced by some fellow he'd met in a dram shop on his way home from the mill."

"Some fellow you met in a dram shop?" Nell said. "How can that be construed as my fault?"

"He got me talking 'bout you," Harry slurred. "Sat down next to me at the bar an' asked what happened to my nose an' my eye. I tol' him my brother an' I got into a little set-to over some li'l Irish puss who wasn't worth—"

"Harry . . ." Will said in a warning tone.

Harry rolled his eyes. "Anyway, I'm a li'l muzzy on the details, but he ended up dragging me out back. Next thing I know, there's a fist coming at me."

The waiter placed a glass of sherry in front of Nell. She lifted it and brought it to her nose, savoring its nutty sweetness. "I don't suppose he gave a name?"

Harry shook his head, took a sip of whiskey, winced.

"Did he look Irish?" she asked. "Perhaps your calling me . . . what you called me . . ."

"I thought of that," Will said, "but all Harry remembers is that he was young—about his age, he thinks. He was wearing a cap, so he's not sure of the hair color. He had on an old sack coat."

"And a pair of those big, heavy brogans," Harry said, "all dirty an' scuffed up. I 'member thinking I'd rather die than be seen with crap like that on my feet." He looked down as his own footwear, a pair of glassily polished balmorals, with what could only be described as drunken reverence. "It was those brogans that did this," he said, patting his cracked ribs. "Bastard got me down on the ground and kicked me. Very unsportsmanlike."

Will crushed out his cigarette, looking as if he were fighting a smile. "Depends on what you consider sport."

Harry tossed down the remains of his whiskey, swearing heatedly as it stung his lip. He retrieved his homburg from beneath his chair and put it on, tilting it with inebriated care. "You'll 'scuse me if I'd rather not spend the rest of my evening in the company of a woman who's gotten me thrashed twice in one week."

He hauled himself to his feet, grimacing like a rheumatic old man, grabbed his walking stick, and shuffled out of the bar.

"Drink that," Will said, pointing to the glass of sherry in Nell's hand, which she'd forgotten all about.

She took a sip, felt her nerves quiver and then relax; took another sip and sat back, boneless. "Someone's following me."

Will frowned. "Someone new?"

"It must be, mustn't it? Virgil Hines is dead."

"Are you sure?" Adam asked. "This whole experience has been—"

"I'm not imagining it. I've been getting that feeling for days now, that feeling of being watched. Then, around dusk on Sunday, after we came back from Salem, I went for a walk by myself in the Public Gardens because it was so pleasant out, and after that mortuary . . . well, I just wanted to breathe some fresh air and think this whole thing through, sort it out in my mind. I saw him as I was walking. Every time I turned round, there he was, about a hundred yards behind me on the path."

"You didn't recognize him?" Adam asked.

"No, it was getting dark, and he was too far away. Sometimes he turned his back when I looked, other times he'd keep to the edge of the path and duck behind a tree. I cut my walk short and went back home. I tried to discount it—there are all kinds of strange men in a city this size. But today I saw him again, while your mother and Gracie and I were shopping. Or, I think I saw him. I saw *someone* dart into a doorway, and it could have been him."

She swallowed some more sherry. "I had to tell someone about it, get someone else's take on it, but if I tell your mother, she'll worry herself sick. I would have come here sooner, but I had to wait until Gracie was in bed. It's got me so rattled. Perhaps I really should ask Dr. Drummond for a nerve tonic."

"You don't need a nerve tonic," Will said in a tone that suggested he would brook no argument. "You need the police."

"I've got to agree with Will," Adam said. "Someone's out there. You don't have to know why he's spying on you to know that he could be dangerous. You should have police protection until it's sorted out."

"I'll bring you over to City Hall as soon as you're finished with your sherry," Will told Nell. "I feel certain Detective Cook will take this seriously. Perhaps we can talk him into assigning someone to keep an eye on you."

"He's not there on Tuesdays," she said.

"Tomorrow, then. When can you get away?"

"Not til around nine or nine-thirty at night. I'll have to wait for Gracie to go to sleep."

"Tomorrow night, then. I'll get a hack and meet you on the corner of Tremont and Winter at nine-thirty. In the meantime, try to stay in the house if you can."

"We're expecting rain tomorrow," she said. "I'll think up some indoor project to do with Gracie."

"Do the police actually do that sort of thing?" Adam asked. "Assign constables to guard people?"

"It's been my experience that the Boston police will do most anything, so long as one makes it worth their while."

As they were rising to go, Adam told Will, "We never did get to discuss this whole parole issue."

They agreed to dine together Thursday at Durgin-Park's, with Will promising to bring along a deck of cards so he could teach Adam how to play poker.

"Not that I intend to ever really play, mind you," Adam assured him. "Your profession notwithstanding, games of chance are a spiritual and moral menace."

"Spoken like a true shepherd to the black sheep," Will said wryly.

Adam shrugged, smiled. "But the prisoners talk about poker all the time, so I feel I really ought to know the rules, at the very least."

"And perhaps visit a gaming hell, just once, so as to fully understand the lure of it," Will said with a wink in Nell's direction.

"Gladly," Adam said. "If you agree to attend Sunday services at Emmanuel."

Will shook his head, chuckling. "If you think I can be so easily reformed . . ."

"Just once," Adam countered with a grin, "so as to fully understand the lure of it."

Chapter 20

DETECTIVE Cook swiveled back and forth, back and forth as he ruminated on Nell and Will's request, his chair's metallic squealing underscored by the steady drumming of rain against his office windows.

The skies had threatened all day, but the rain had held off until about five minutes ago, when it suddenly burst from the heavens, a full-blown downpour. Nell watched it sluice down the glass in sheets against an inky night sky. She wondered if she could capture the effect in paint—not just that exquisite, watery luminescence, but the purifying power of it, the way one good, pummeling deluge could wash away years' worth of grime and dirt.

The squealing abruptly ceased. Cook leaned back in his chair, arms crossed, and said, "All right, then, here's what I can do . . . and what I can't do. I can assign a man to one forty-eight Tremont starting tomorrow morning, and instruct him to accompany Miss Sweeney whenever she leaves the house. And I can have another man do the same at night. Put that away," he said as Will withdrew some bills from his coat. "If it was one of you Hewitts, I'd gladly accept your ill-gotten spoils, but it isn't. It's Miss Sweeney. Mrs. Cook would have my hide if she knew I'd let you pay me to watch after a girl from the old country."

They thanked him.

"So, that's what I can do." Cook rubbed his big jaw. "What I can't do is guarantee, with absolute certainty, that those men, or any men, will always be available. There's only so many constables to go round. If they're needed for more important business . . ."

"Of course," Nell said. "I appreciate anything you can do."

"You say you never got a good look at the fella who's following you around?" Cook asked as he sorted through drifts of papers heaped haphazardly on his desk.

"That's right."

"Nothin' about him looked familiar?"

"He was simply too far away."

"The reason I ask is . . . Ah, here we go." Cook pulled out a sheet of paper and skimmed it. "This came last week. It's a communiqué from the state prison in Charlestown. I didn't make the connection at the time . . . Well, maybe there is no connection. Probably not, but it's worth lookin' into, seeing as how this fella started shadowing you just a few days ago."

Nell said, "I'm sorry, Detective. I'm just not following you."

"There was a prison break last Wednesday—a week ago today. Fella by the name of Sweeney"—he squinted at the paper—"Duncan Sweeney . . ."

The air left Nell's lungs. She closed her eyes as Will sat forward in his chair. "Duncan *Sweeney?*" he said.

"That's right. Sweeney's a common enough name, which is why I didn't think much of it at the time. He escaped late at night Wednesday, September sixteenth. It was a moonless night, if you recall, black as pitch, which worked in his favor, but it seems he also had help from one of the guards. The guard admitted under questioning that the escapee had promised him part of his loot from . . . Miss Sweeney?"

Nell opened her eyes. The room tilted woozily. He escaped last Wednesday? That was the day she'd visited him. Why had Adam not said anything?

"You do know him," Cook said. "Who is he, your brother?"

Will was staring at her. She kept her gaze on Detective Cook. "Yes." The lie came out hoarse. She cleared her throat. "Yes. He's my brother."

"You think he might be the one who's been tailin' you?"

She nodded numbly. "Yes. Maybe. I . . ." She shook her head. "I don't know."

She stood. Her umbrella, which had been lying across her lap, fell to the floor. Will picked it up and stood to hand it to her. She took it without meeting his eyes.

"Thank you, Detective," she said. "I'm sorry, but I have to go now."

"DAMN it, damn it, damn it," Nell muttered as she strove to open her umbrella beneath the columned portico over the front entrance of Boston's stately, Parisian-style City Hall. The rain fell in a rumbling sheet between her and the front walk. All she could see beyond it were two watery glimmers, one being the lamp atop a stone gatepost; the other had to be a carriage lamp, but it wasn't moving. If it was a hack and she could commandeer it before it pulled away . . .

"Open, damn you," she muttered as she struggled with the umbrella, only to have it snatched from her hands. She turned to find Will unfolding it with a single thrust. Holding it over them, he wrapped an arm around her, guiding her swiftly down the stairs and front walk toward School Street.

A hack was, indeed, sitting at the curb, its driver hunkered down in his box with his macintosh over his head. Will opened the door and handed her in, then had a brief exchange with the driver that she couldn't hear.

He's sending me home alone, she thought. But then he collapsed the umbrella and ducked into the carriage, an old single brougham. He settled in next to her on the cracked leather seat and crossed his legs. With the dripping, folded-up umbrella held upright between himself and Nell, like a walking stick, and his hat on his lap, he laid his head back on the seat and closed his eyes.

Nell expected the vehicle to start moving. It didn't. "Why isn't—"

"He's waiting for the rain to lighten up," Will said without opening his eyes.

She nodded, although he couldn't see her, and stared out the front window as it began to grow hazy.

"Were you ever going to tell me?" He said it so quietly that she wasn't sure he'd really spoken until she turned and saw him looking at her, his head still resting on the seat-back. The amber glow of the lamps on the front corners of the hack, filtered through the rain-dappled windows, bathed his face in bubbly golden light. Only his eyes were in shadow.

She looked down at her hands. "I don't know. No. I . . . I was afraid to."

"I thought . . ." He turned away from her, his jaw thrust out. "Never mind."

"Will—"

"No. I thought you and I . . . I thought you trusted me. I thought you knew me. I thought we . . . were friends."

"I was afraid," she repeated miserably.

"That I would tell all of Boston that *Miss* Nell Sweeney, the oh-so-proper little Irish governess, actually has a husband in prison? You *are* still married, I take it. You never got divorced?"

She shook her head. "Divorce isn't recognized by the Church."

"But you were afraid if you told me, that I'd blab it to all of—"

"No, not . . ." She looked away, shook her head.

"Not what?"

"Not if you were sober."

There came a pause as he digested that. "I haven't been drunk on opium—or anything else—since last winter. I only take enough morphine to maintain a state of normality. You know that."

"Yes."

"But you don't really believe it. You expect me to slip back into my old habits any day now."

"No, I—"

"It's all right, perhaps I shall. I've been feeling a bit restless lately. Perhaps it's opium I'm starved for."

"Will, don't say that."

He made no response, simply closed his eyes again. The rain continued to fall, not quite as heavily as at first, but at a steady rate, its reverberations making the small coach feel even smaller. The windows grew steamy, the air sultry; there were none of the usual street sounds from without, just the incessant rain.

Will lay so still that she might have thought he'd fallen asleep, except that he continued to hold that umbrella upright between them, his long fingers curved gracefully over the porcelain knob.

"You're his wife."

Nell turned to find his eyes open, although he still lay back against the seat.

"That's why he's still as possessive as he is," Will said, "why he wrote you those letters, why he was so outraged when he thought you and Harry . . ." He shook his head. "Why he's been following you round, because I'd bet my last nickel it's him."

"It's him," she said with certainty. "The height, the way he moved . . . I suppose I just hadn't considered the possibility before because I thought he was locked up behind bars."

"He's still trying to keep you under his thumb. You're married. In his eyes, why shouldn't he?"

"We may be married," she said, relieved that he was talking to her, if only about this, "but I haven't been under his thumb since I was eighteen."

"Did you marry that young?" he asked, then waved a dismissive hand. "No, forget it—it's not important."

"It is to me. And perhaps if you understood how it came about, how he and I—"

"All I care to understand right now is how to eliminate the problem of Duncan Sweeney so that I can get on with my life as it was before."

He may as well have said *the problem of Nell Sweeney,* because that was surely what he meant. His ultra high stakes poker game was over; he was eager to be moving on. It was as if the glass dome that enveloped them had shattered, instantly dispelling their fragile rapport, that unacknowledged aura of familiarity and understanding, that aching sweetness that she'd come to treasure without even realizing it.

"Let's look at this thing logically," Will said as he sat upright. "Duncan—well, he's unhinged, obviously."

"I . . . suppose so," Nell said.

"Think about it—he escaped from prison. He could have fled the country, started a new life somewhere far away, where he'd never be caught. Instead, he came here, where he must know they're actively looking for him, so that he could monitor your every move—possibly with the aim of doing you great harm. Your Detective Cook does intend to catch him, by the way. He told me he's going to alert the entire Boston police force to be on the lookout for him."

Nell shook her head. "Duncan *must* be daft, to be taking such a risk."

"Have you considered the possibility that he's responsible for what happened to Bridie and Virgil?"

She looked at him.

"He escaped a week ago today," Will said. "That would fall within the period in which the murders must have taken place. We know from his letters to Virgil that he loathed Bridie sight unseen, and he was furious with Harry for stealing you away from him. He could kill Bridie and frame Harry for it, thus destroying his rival, and then concentrate his attention on you. He knew about Bridie's blackmail scheme, and he also knew that Bridie was two-timing Harry with Virgil—both credible motives for murder. He got hold of Harry's scarf—"

"How?"

Will lifted his shoulders. "Stole it from Harry's office at the mill, got someone else to steal it . . . Who knows? Maybe Bridie really did take it, and Virgil told Duncan about it in one of his letters. Your visit to Duncan inspired him to put his plan into action immediately—that, and possibly the lack of a moon that night. He went to the White farm the next day and found Bridie—"

"The next day? Thursday? That would have been"—Nell counted it out on her fingers—"five days since she'd been fired."

"Which was the last anyone in Charlestown saw of either one of them. I'm thinking they ran away together to set up housekeeping at the farm."

"Bridie's mother told me she would never just pick up and leave like that, not without telling her. She was convinced of it."

"Mothers always are. In any event, Duncan went to the farm and found Bridie alone in the house, cooking."

"Virgil was down at the stream," said Nell, letting it unfold in her mind, "trying to catch something to go with those johnnycakes."

Rubbing his chin in a preoccupied way, Will said "Duncan accosted Bridie, who tried to defend herself with the skillet. Perhaps she got a lick in, perhaps not. Perhaps he took it away from her and tried to use it against her. She did manage to get out of the house and run to the stream, probably screaming for Virgil."

"She must have been a fast runner," Nell said, thinking of Duncan's long, sinewy legs. She saw it all clearly in her mind's eye—the field of golden, crackling grass, the distant woods, Bridie sprinting with raised skirts, heart pounding, as Duncan gained on her.

"Women are often surprisingly fleet, especially barefooted, as Bridie was. Virgil would have been confused to find Duncan out of prison and attacking Bridie, but my guess is he would have tried to defend her—probably with the fishing pole, but it broke."

Nell said, "Virgil would have been no match for Duncan no matter how many stone-cutting muscles he'd acquired. And a fishing pole? I've seen Duncan, completely unarmed, take on two men with knives, and leave them bleeding in the dirt. It would have been over between him and Virgil in seconds."

"Assuming Duncan didn't balk at dispatching an old friend. Do you suppose Virgil simply slipped on those mossy rocks?"

"Either way, it was ultimately Duncan's doing." She took a deep breath. "And then he turned to Bridie."

Nell shuddered, remembering those awful bruises between Bridie's legs—the same kind she'd been left with herself after Duncan's final savage attack on her. She thought about Bridie thrashing wildly, clutching at weeds and gravel and mud with her burned hands as Duncan held her head beneath the surface of that deceptively placid little stream.

Will's face, in the dim amber light, was grim. "When he was done with her, he dragged her into the field and went back to the house. He hung the skillet back on its hook, gathered up the johnnycakes that were strewn about—except that one under the table, which he didn't notice—and tossed them outside for the birds to finish off."

"Cleaning up?" she said with a dubious little quirk of the eyebrows. "That would have been a first for Duncan."

Will appeared to think about it. "I suppose he didn't

want to leave evidence of an altercation in the house. Perhaps he felt it would draw attention away from the scene he was trying to stage out in the field—that of Bridie being strangled with Harry's scarf. Or perhaps he thought the skillet business would simply complicate matters. In any event, he grabbed the scarf off its hook—"

"Unless he already had it with him."

"Right. And he went back out to the field and tied it round Bridie's neck. He pushed her skirts up to make it look as if the rape and murder had taken place right there."

"Or maybe just to compound her degradation," said Nell, who was glad, after all, that she'd tidied Bridie up before the constables came. "And then he came to Boston and turned his attention to me."

Will looked away, his fingers tightening on the porcelain knob.

"I'll bet it was Duncan who beat up Harry," she said.

"A little prelude to the murder charge?"

Nell nodded. "It wouldn't have been enough, just getting him arrested—or even seeing him hang, if it came to that. That's too remote, too civilized. I know him. He would have had to get his fists bloody to feel any real satisfaction."

Will turned toward her for the first time. "You do know him. What do you think? Why is he shadowing you? Does he want to win you back or . . . ?"

"Or do to me what he did to Bridie?" She shrugged. "Even if he just wants me back, he must know I won't return to him voluntarily."

"He could be following you around looking for an opportunity to abduct you."

"Or kill me." She shivered despite how humid it was inside the little coach. "He could have followed us here. He could be out there somewhere, watching us even now."

"Yes, but we're on to him now," Will said. "Every constable in Boston will be looking for him—and sticking close to you. In a day or two, this will all be over."

Had they had this conversation an hour ago—before the revelation about her marriage—Nell felt sure Will would have offered her something more in the way of comfort and reassurance, touched her hand . . . but no such gestures were forthcoming. To be treated by him with such cool civility stung more than it ought to have.

From outside came the clopping of hooves and rattling of wheels over the wet granite-block pavement as a carriage—another hack, Nell saw when she wiped the vapor off the window—pulled up to the curb in front of them. Will opened the window on his side, letting in a rush of cool, clean-washed night air. The rain had lessened considerably, a fact evidently not lost on their driver, who could be heard readjusting his macintosh and fiddling with his reins.

A man carrying a black umbrella—the passenger from the hack in front of them—headed up the rain-shimmered front walk of City Hall at a swift trot. There was something familiar about they way he moved . . . that slight awkwardness . . .

"Adam!" Will called through the open window.

Adam turned, paused, jogged toward them. "Will . . . Nell." He called to the driver of his hack, who was about to pull away, to wait for him, then came up close to the window, his face shadowed by the umbrella. "I went to the Revere House, but you weren't there, and then I remembered you'd planned to meet with that detective tonight."

"Is something wrong?" Nell asked.

"It's Duncan. I was at the prison today—I'm there on Wednesdays, you know—and they told me he escaped. I wanted you to know as soon as possible."

"Detective Cook told us," Will said. "We think Duncan is the man who's been following Nell. Cook is assigning some men to guard her, and the constables will be on the lookout for him."

Adam nodded, slightly winded. "If only I'd known sooner. I didn't see him Sunday, but I often don't, so I didn't think anything of it. When he didn't show up for Bible study this afternoon, I thought he might be sick. I asked around and found out he's been gone for a week—ever since the day you visited him, Nell. He bribed one of the guards to get him out of the building."

"Did you talk to him that day," she asked over Will's shoulder, "after I left?"

"Oh, yes. He stayed after Bible study. He was beside himself, kept talking about you and Harry. He kept quoting Leviticus and Deuteronomy on the subject of adultery, saying you deserved to . . . Oh." He looked at Nell, wincing because he'd spilled the beans about her marriage to Duncan.

"Will knows," she assured him, to his obvious relief.

"Deuteronomy . . ." Will said. "That would be chapter twenty-two."

Adam blinked at him. "Yes," he said, clearly surprised, as was Nell, that Will knew this.

" 'If a man be found lying with a woman married to a husband,' " Will quoted, " 'then they shall both of them die, both the man that lay with the woman, and the woman. So shalt thou put away evil from Israel.' "

Nell and Adam gaped at him.

"Is that what Duncan means to do, then?" Will asked. "Carry out his misguided interpretation of the Old Testament?"

Adam looked pained. "I've no idea. I don't know how things ever came to this pass. It never occurred to me that he would become this desperate, this bereft of reason, but it should have. It's my job to look into the hearts of men. I feel as if I've failed him—and you, Nell."

"It isn't your fault," she said. "And I'm sure the police will have Duncan in custody soon."

"I hope, for his sake as well as yours, that they get to him soon. Well . . ." Adam lowered his umbrella, the rain having finally ceased, and folded it up. "You've obviously got things in hand for the time being. I'll see you tomorrow night, then, Will? Durgin-Park's?"

"Hm? Oh, yes," Will said distractedly. "Say, do me a favor, old man, and drop Nell off at one forty-eight Tremont, would you? I've got someplace I've got to be."

Nell looked at Will. He didn't so much as glance in her direction.

"Oh. All right," Adam said. "Of course. More than happy to."

Will got out of the hack, held the door open for Nell, and handed her down. "Good night, then." He didn't smile, barely met her eyes.

"Good night." She took her umbrella from him and accompanied Adam to the other hack as he climbed back into his.

Adam opened the door and held out his hand. As she reached for it, she heard an anguished wail, footsteps on the wet pavement . . .

She turned, along with Adam, to find a man sprinting

out of the darkness—hatless, wet—his arm outstretched, his eyes wild.

"Duncan," she whispered. *Oh, God, no.*

"Viper!" he screamed. "Deceiver!"

He raised his hand; metal glinted in the lamplight—a gun.

"Duncan, no!" Adam grabbed Nell.

Will leapt on Duncan like some great black hawk, coat-tails flapping. He struck, flat-handed, at Duncan's fore-arm—a blur of movement.

Duncan cried out. The gun clattered to the ground. Will kicked it away.

They grappled. Nell couldn't see much in the dark, but she could hear the scuffle of feet, the grunts of pain as punches found their mark. It wouldn't last long; Duncan's fights never did.

She crossed herself, thinking, *Please, God, don't let Duncan kill him.* But when the decisive blow came, it was Duncan who hit the ground, twisting from the impact of Will's fist so that he landed facedown. His head struck the pavement with a thud Nell felt in her bones.

He blinked, tried to rise, then slumped back down, un-moving.

Will knelt over him, took his carotid pulse. "He'll be all right." He looked toward Nell, his hair hanging over his forehead, blood trickling from his nose, one cheekbone badly abraded, and then toward Adam. "Would you be so kind as to go inside and fetch Detective Cook?"

It took the dazed priest a moment to respond. "Oh. Yes. Of course." He sprinted up the walk.

Will wiped his bloodied nose with the back of his hand, dragged his fingers through his hair.

"H-here." Nell rushed forward with her handkerchief. "Let me—"

"I've got my own." Standing, he pulled out his handkerchief and dabbed his nose with it.

"Will, I . . ." What did one say when one's life had just been saved?

"Don't mention it," he said without looking at her.

Chapter 21

"I can't let you see him, Miss Sweeney," Detective Cook told Nell the following evening when she tried to visit Duncan in the City Hall holding cell where he'd been detained since the previous night.

"I must. I need to speak to him, explain some things." Like the fact that she had no relationship with Harry—but nor did she, anymore, with Duncan. In the eyes of the Church, they were man and wife and always would be, but in her eyes their marriage had ended eight years ago. She had to put that in plain words, make him come to terms with it.

"Your brother didn't come to til around noon today," Cook said, "and when he finally grasped where he was, he started raving, sobbing . . ."

Sobbing?

"The guards couldn't take it," Cook said. "They gagged him and put him in a straight waistcoat."

Nell just stared at him.

"The prison chaplain from Charlestown came to see him, and he had a conniption. He kicked and thrashed, hurled himself against the bars . . . Split his forehead open and just kept at it."

"My God."

"The Black Maria's coming to take him back to Charlestown in about an hour. Maybe in a day or two, if he's got his wits about him, you can visit him there. Right now you'd best go home and try to put him out of your mind."

Nell walked back to Colonnade Row in a desolate trance, her shawl drawn snugly around her to ward off the chill of the evening, remembering how Duncan had looked ten years ago, the first time Jamie had brought him around—so tall and golden, with those eyes that saw right through her and that boyish grin. She tried to reconcile that Duncan in her mind with the one who raved and sobbed and threw himself against the bars of his cage. The pain and confusion of it rose in her throat and squeezed, made her eyes prick with tears.

Don't cry, she commanded herself. *Not here on the street, for pity's sake.*

Nell rarely cried; there was little to be gained from surrendering to despair. Yet sometimes, as now, despair was a force of nature that would not be denied.

She would close the door of her room as soon as she got home, she decided, and bury her face in a pillow and soak it with tears, then rinse her face at the wash stand and get on with things. But no sooner had she walked through the front door of the house than Mrs. Mott materialized in the entrance hall. "There's a gentleman waiting for you in the music room. A Reverend Beals."

"Oh."

"Mrs. Hewitt is in the solarium with the child. She thinks she can teach her to paint. She instructed me to tell you that you may have the rest of the evening to yourself, if you wish."

"Thank you," Nell said, but the housekeeper had turned and was already walking away.

She found Adam sitting on the piano bench, laconically picking out a tune on the big, darkly polished Steinway—a dirge, from the mournful sound of it.

"I waited for Will at Durgin-Park's for about forty-five minutes," Adam said as he handed her down from the hack that had just let them off in front of the Revere House. "When he didn't show up, I came here. I knocked, but he wouldn't let me in—told me he was busy—but I knew what he was doing. I could smell it right through the door."

"You know what opium smells like?" she asked as he paid the driver.

"My ministry takes me to all sorts of places." He escorted her across the hotel's marble-floored lobby toward the front desk. "I knew about the morphine—Harry brought it up Tuesday night. Will told me it was just for pain relief, and to keep himself from going into withdrawal. He said, 'If I ever get hooked on gong again, do me a favor and put a bullet in my brain. It's quicker.' "

"My key, please," Nell told the fleshy little desk clerk with as much nonchalance as she could summon.

"Here you go. Have a lovely evening, Mrs. Hewitt . . . Reverend."

Adam didn't look at her as they climbed the stairs to the

second floor. "I know what you're thinking," she said as they walked down the hall to Will's room. "But I never asked them to leave a key at my disposal, nor to call me—"

"Don't. Please," he said, exasperation creeping into his tone, as if he wished she would just stop lying to him.

"But—"

"This is it," he said as they drew up in front of Room 2D. He'd been right; she could smell that distinctive scorched-treacle odor right through the door.

She slid the key into the lock, then hesitated and knocked. "Will?"

Silence. She turned the key and opened the door.

"Oh, Christ, not both of you," he muttered.

It took her a moment to locate him in the dim, smoke-hazed room. Although the sun had yet to set, he had the curtains closed. Aside from a waning fire on the hearth, the only real source of light was a little spirit lamp on a lacquered Chinese tray laid out with opium paraphernalia. The tray sat on a low table in front of the couch on which Will reclined in a collarless shirt and trousers, braces dangling, hair uncombed, a cigarette hanging limply in his hand. Ugly abrasions marred his left cheekbone and unshaven chin, and dried blood was crusted in a nostril. Nell suspected he hadn't washed or changed since last night.

"Will, why are you doing this?" Nell asked.

"I'm a hop fiend, Cornelia. It's what we do." His eyes were heavy-lidded, glassy, and his voice had that drowsy-thick quality that it only got when he'd been "rolling the log" for hours.

"How many bowls have you smoked?" she asked.

"Not nearly enough." Will took a final puff on his cigarette and stubbed it out, then lifted a little penknife and a bamboo smoking pistol from the tray and proceeded to scrape bits of opium dross off the pipe's egg-shaped ceramic bowl. "Adam, if you've got any business at all wearing that collar, you'll get her the hell out of here."

Adam unfastened his clerical collar and tossed it onto a chair.

"We came to talk sense to you," Nell said. "We care about you. We hate to see—"

"Oh, Christ," Will growled as he scraped. "Well-meaning friends who care what becomes of me. The bane of my bloody existence. Go away, Miss Sweeney. You, too, Father."

"We're not leaving," Adam said.

"Then I shall." Will snapped the pen knife shut and hauled himself to a sitting position with some effort. "I shall go back to Deng Bao's, where they let me smoke my gong in peace."

"Here, Nell, give me that." Adam took the key from her and used it to lock the door from the inside, then slipped the key in his vest pocket.

Will's gaze cut to the desk in the corner. Adam noticed, and fetched Will's key as well.

"Suit yourself." Will stretched out on his side on the couch, which was upholstered in leather, but with spiral-carved wooden arms fitted with padded armrests. He lay his head on the armrest and used a spindle to scoop a little daub of opium paste from a wooden box. Holding the opium just above the flame of the lamp, he twirled it until it bubbled and seethed, then kneaded it upon the roof of the pipe bowl.

"Just two days ago," Adam reminded him, "you asked me to kill you if you ever took up this habit again."

"I won't hold you to that." Will rolled the opium into a little nugget on the end of the spindle, seated it in the bowl's small aperture, and leaned over the spirit lamp. Keeping the opium in place with the spindle, he watched it vaporize while inhaling its fumes in one long draw.

Smoke fluttered from his mouth; his eyes drifted shut. The pipe rolled out of his hand and onto the tray as he went utterly limp on the couch—a six-foot-plus rag doll.

Nell said, "I'd like to take everything on that tray and burn it—whatever's burnable—and throw the rest into Boston Harbor."

"He'll be furious."

"Because we didn't put a bullet in his brain instead?" she asked as she bent over the tray, sorting the flammable from the nonflammable. "It takes him up to twenty minutes to rouse from an opium stupor. That's how much time I've got to destroy this—or as much as I can—because once he's awake again, he can be remarkably alert."

"What about that?" Adam pointed to Will's morphine and related accoutrement on the nightstand.

She shook her head. "He'll suffer from withdrawal sickness without that, and he needs it for pain—although he might try cutting down his dosage."

"If he had any real backbone, he'd go without it altogether. I used to take it for my leg—I injected myself, just as Will does—but I gave it up when I realized I was becoming dependent on it."

"The circumstances that led to Will's addiction were extraordinary," Nell said. "He escaped from Andersonville with a terrible bullet wound, and it took nine months for him to make his way north through enemy territory. I . . . well, of course I have no idea what's wrong with your leg. I'm sure it's quite painful, but—"

"Syphilis."

It took a second for Nell to realize that she was staring

with her mouth open. "Oh. Oh, I'm . . . so sorry." And so astounded that he'd just come out with it, to a female, calling it "syphilis," no less, rather than the somewhat more delicate "blood-poison" or "French pox."

"I've shocked you," he said. "I thought, since you were a sort of nurse—"

"Yes, of course. I'm not shocked, just, um . . ." She couldn't keep from glancing down at his bad leg.

"It's just started to affect the bones and joints, and my vision isn't what it used to be. I had a seizure a few months ago, and I get the most god-awful headaches. Of course, you're familiar with the late-stage symptoms."

"To some extent." Enough to know that dementia, blindness, and paralysis were what Adam had to look forward to unless the disease was brought under control. "Can't they do anything for it?"

"I had four years' worth of mercury treatments. I ate mercury, I had it rubbed onto me, cooked into me . . . They put me in a cabinet with my head sticking out and lit a fire under it so the mercury inside would vaporize—pounds of it, literally. I can't begin to tell you how hellish that was."

"Oh, Adam." Nell felt feverish just thinking about it; her forehead actually grew damp. "Did it do any good at all?"

He shook his head. "Came back every time. The doctors want to try potassium iodide, but if it's half as grueling as the mercury . . ."

"It isn't," she said. Nor was it as toxic as mercury, which could cause the very symptoms it was enlisted to cure. "And it works. You should let them try it."

Will stirred, rolling onto his back, one arm thrown over his head.

"Perhaps," Adam said, "God means for me to suffer. Perhaps it's my penance."

"Penance for what?"

"For disobeying His commandment."

"Ah." *Thou shalt not commit adultery.* "You mean, for . . . having contracted syphilis in the first place?"

He regarded her in obvious bewilderment for a moment before shaking his head. "No. No, you have the wrong idea. I'm not the one who . . . That is . . . my wife gave it to me."

She gaped at him for a moment before finding her tongue. "Oh . . . oh, I . . ."

"It was early in our marriage. She was . . . not the person I thought she was." He looked away, his expression hardening. "Not remotely."

Nell couldn't, for the life of her, think what to say to that. Lifting the tray with hands that felt, for some reason, just ever so tremulous, she said, "I think the pipe and the sponge will burn. And the box the opium came in." She carried the tray to the fireplace and set it on the mantel. "I don't know about the opium itself. If I put it in the fire, do you suppose the smoke will do that to us?" She nodded toward Will, shifting groggily on the couch.

"There should be a washout closet in the W.C.," Adam said. "I'll get rid of it there." He took the little box and the spindle into the bathroom and turned the gas jets up high.

The glass over the steel engraving was as reflective as a mirror in this light. In it, Nell could see the room behind her in minute detail, including the brightly lit bathroom, visible through its wide-open door. Adam was leaning over the toilet, using the spindle to scoop opium paste out of the wooden box.

Nell tossed the sea sponge, used for cooling off the hot pipe, into the fire. It was damp, so it steamed and popped, but presently it caught around the edges. She watched it smolder with a curious detachment. It was almost as if she were watching herself from without—as if she were looking down on herself standing in front of the fireplace in her dove-gray dress and smart little hat, utterly absorbed in watching a sponge catch fire.

The smoking pistol came next. It was slow to catch, as well. The clay bowl would be left intact, she realized, unless the heat cracked it—unlikely, since it had presumably been fired in a kiln.

Curious, that she should think of that. She wasn't usually so analytical. She raised her gaze to the tray on the mantle. Everything else—spirit lamp, horn-handled penknife, wick scissors, china bowl, stone ashtray—couldn't be burned.

Nell picked up the knife and unfolded it, only to discover that it wasn't a penknife at all, but a slim little folding lancet. It looked brand new. She wondered if Will had purchased it just that day.

A glimmer of movement caught her attention. She looked up at the engraving to see Adam standing in front of the toilet glass over the bathroom sink, running his fingers through his hair with an unaccountably grim expression.

He looked toward Nell, clearly unaware that she could see him. His expression didn't change, but that wasn't what took her aback. He'd pushed his hair aside rather haphazardly, revealing his forehead and the mark thereon.

Must be a birthmark, Nell thought, one of those big, livid port wine stains. But its contours were too precise, as if someone had taken a good detail brush loaded with alizarin crimson and painstakingly painted a crescent moon—the convex edge especially dark and crisp, the convex a bit more shaded. Port wine stains tended to be irregular.

It looked like a burn, and a fairly bad one—like those on Bridie's palms from the handle of the hot skillet.

Perhaps she got a lick in, Will had said, *perhaps not . . .*

Nell's heart batted against her stays like a bird in a box. The lancet trembled in her hand.

"Think outside of yourself," she whispered.

"I beg your pardon?" Adam came up behind her, smoothing his hair over his forehead, still oblivious to the fact that she could see him in the glass.

"Oh, it was . . . just a little prayer." Her back still to him, she slipped the lancet into her right-hand glove, sliding it along her palm and the underside of her index finger. The steel was just visible through the black crochet, and her finger stood straight out, as if splinted; she would have to have to be aware of how she held her hands. "I was asking God to help Will."

"Here." Adam handed her the box. "I got out as much of the opium as I could."

She turned to take it with her left hand, and added it to the fire. The residue of opium inside began to sizzle almost immediately, its odor thick and sweet.

"I thought you might be asking me what I meant about penance," he said. "I never explained that, did I?"

He was standing just a little too close for propriety.

Nell edged away a bit. "You said something about disobeying a commandment."

He frowned into the fire as the flames licked at the box. "It's a challenge sometimes, interpreting God's laws, figuring out what to do and what not to do. The commandments might say one thing, scripture another . . . Thou shalt not kill, for example. Did you know the Old Testament statutes *require* punishment by death for certain offenses? Will knows this. He quoted Deuteronomy on the subject of adultery just last night."

"I'm still in," Will muttered groggily, possibly in reaction to hearing his name. "I'll see you an' raise you five hun'red."

"Deuteronomy, Leviticus, Proverbs . . ." Adam continued, as if he hadn't even heard Will. "All state that adulterers must be destroyed."

It might just have been the dim light, but Adam's eyes, which she'd thought so darkly expressive when she'd first met him, looked as flat and soulless as if they'd been painted on a statue.

"So therein lies my problem," he said. "The Old Testament scriptures dictate—*demand*—a certain course of action, which the commandments appear to denounce. I can't obey both. I've got to choose one—and I've done so—but the fact that it was a difficult choice doesn't absolve me from penance for having disobeyed the word of God. Do you understand?" he asked, as if it were important to him that she did.

"Er, yes. Yes, I . . . believe I do." She backed away a step, feeling the lancet slide against her sweat-dampened palm as she nervously smoothed her skirts. With feigned composure, she said, "Will seems to be coming to. I think I'll try to take him outside so he can walk this off."

Adam smiled, but it was the smile of someone whose child was trying to get away with something absurd.

"May I have the key so I can open the door?" She went to hold out her right hand, remembered the lancet, and held out her left.

He shook his head, the cold-eyed smile still in place, as if to say, *I'm on to you. We're on to each other.*

Steeling herself, Nell walked right up to him so that he stood between her and the fireplace, her hands clasped in a supplicating manner so that that he wouldn't see her pushing the lancet through the fingertip of her glove. The blade was keen; it sliced with ease through the delicate crochet. Through an effort of will, she envisioned the two of them as if from above, he with his back against the marble mantle, she with a weapon.

You can do this, she told herself. *You got the better of Harry, didn't you? This is no different.*

In a softly inveigling tone, she said, "It doesn't have to be this way." He stared at her unblinkingly as she stepped closer, reaching up to caress his face. "Just give me the keys," she murmured as she slid her left hand into his hair and closed it around a thick fistful, while at the same time pressing the tip of the little knife to his Adam's apple. "Both of them. And then stand over there by that bedpost." To which she would tie him so that he'd still be there when she returned with the police.

His smile changed as he stared at her; he was, it seemed, grudgingly impressed. "You're full of surprises, aren't you?" The smile faded; his eyes betrayed a glimmer of that sweet melancholy she'd seen in them in the beginning. "If only you weren't what you are," he said as he retrieved the keys from his vest pocket . . .

And dropped them into the fire.

Nell gasped and pushed him aside, thinking only of retrieving the keys—a fatal mistake, she realized when she saw him hauling back to strike her.

This will hurt, she thought as he backhanded her, hard, into the marble mantel.

It did hurt—her world bloomed with bright white pain. It detonated again as her head struck the slate hearth, then sputtered away into blackness.

Chapter 22

"LEVITICUS, chapter twenty, verse ten. 'And the man that commiteth adultery with another man's wife . . .' "

Coaxed awake by the sing-songy cadence of Adam's voice, Nell opened her eyes to find her head pulsing with pain, but cradled in downy pillows.

" ' . . . the adulterer and the adulteress shall surely be put to death.' "

It took mere seconds for it all to come back to her—Will and his opium, Adam and his delusions . . . *Syphilis . . . Mercury . . . I ate it, I had it rubbed onto me, cooked into me* . . . the keys, the lancet, Adam hurling her into that mantel . . .

Nell lay half sitting up against a mound of pillows on a bed—Will's bed—fully clothed but for her gloves and hat, although her hair had been unpinned. She felt a sticky film on the left side of her face that she knew to be blood trickling from a gash on her forehead. When she tried to rise, she discovered herself to be tethered to the green-painted iron headboard by rope tied around her wrists and neck. There was just enough slack on the neck rope for her to sit up; her hands were bound tightly to the rails.

Someone groaned; Will.

Nell looked toward the couch on the opposite wall, craning her neck to see beyond the damask bed curtains gathered with silken tiebacks to the bottom bedposts. The little spirit lamp was on the nightstand now, casting its meager, wavering light over about half the room. Things seemed to be shifting, as they had that time she'd shared a whole bottle of cognac with Viola, so it took her a moment to make out what was happening. Adam was tying Will's hands to one arm of the couch, having already tied his feet to the other. Will was clearly still insensible, but coming to. He pulled blearily at the restraints, muttering something under his breath.

Adam, a coil of rope in his hand—had he brought it with him?—looked toward Nell. "You're awake, I see. Do you think he heard any of that?" He slapped Will's face; Will flinched, blinked his eyes open. Leaning over him, Adam recited loudly, as if to a someone who was hard of hearing, " 'And the man that committeth adultery with another man's wife, even he that committeth adultery with his neighbor's wife, the adulterer and the adulteress shall surely be put to death.' Do you know what that means? Do you?"

Will looked at Adam with an expression of utter incomprehension. When he tried to sit up and discovered he couldn't, he yanked in bewilderment at his fetters.

"Will . . ." Nell began.

Adam wheeled around, screaming, *"Did I say you could speak?"*

"Nell?" Will met her gaze, his eyes widening in shock when he saw her tied up and bleeding. "Jesus! Nell, are you all—"

"Do you know what that means?" Adam repeated.

"What the hell *is* this?" Will demanded, straining against the ropes. "What did you do to her?"

"Do you know what that means?"

"If you've done anything to her, so help me God—"

" 'And the man that committeth adultery with another man's wife'—that would be you, Will—'shall surely be put to death.' A man who lies with a married woman is just as guilty of adultery as she is. He doesn't have to be married to be guilty of adultery in the eyes of the Lord. That's the law as handed down by God, Will. It's right out of the Bible."

Will look toward Nell as if to ask, *Is he serious?*

She nodded balefully.

"You're daft," Will said. "Untie us both right now."

"Deuteronomy, chapter twenty-two, verse twenty-two. You know this one. 'If a man be found lying with a woman married to a husband, then they shall both of them die.' *Both* of them, Will. They're equally guilty."

"You bloody lunatic, neither one of us is guilty. It's . . . it's not like that between us."

"Don't lie to me!" Adam screamed, the rope shaking in his hand.

"I'm not—"

"*Stop lying to me!* Do I look like a fool?"

"Adam," Will said in a quiet, strained voice, "just listen to me."

"No, you listen to me. You need to understand why I'm doing this. You need to accept that it's God's will."

"All right," Will said softly. "All right, Adam. I'll listen as long as you like, and I'll understand and accept, and then you can do what you please—to me. But you must let Nell go."

"Will . . ." Nell pulled at her ropes.

Adam barked with laughter. "Let her *go?*"

"She's blameless, Adam. I'm the guilty one. I've been guilty all my life, of one thing or another. Ask anyone who knows me. Keep me here, punish me as you will, but let her leave."

"A surprisingly gallant gesture, but I'm not quite that easily misled. If either one of you is more to blame, it's her." Pointing to Nell, his face a mask of contempt, he said, "Women like you, you snare men in your net just because you can. You snared Duncan, and now look at him. I went to see him at City Hall today. I saw what you did to him, what you turned him into. Are you proud of yourself? You took a harmless, good-natured man and destroyed him."

"Harmless?" Nell said. "You told us yourself he gets what he wants through fear and coercion and violence. He threatened my life!"

Will muttered something under his breath. "How much of what you told us about him is true?" He asked.

Adam thought for a moment. "Virgil did roll his cigarettes."

"Oh, dear God," Nell whispered.

"He rushed at Nell with a gun!" Will said.

"He was rushing at *me* with that gun," Adam replied, as if to a simpleton. "It was almost certainly a misguided attempt to protect Nell. I'd tried to explain things to him last week, after Nell visited him, in a way he could grasp. I tried to make him understand that Nell is unworthy of him, and that he'll be free of her soon, but he . . . became agitated. And, of course, that night, he escaped. When I found out he was in Boston, and trying to keep me from carrying out God's will, I had no choice but to try to discredit him in case he was caught."

Duncan did it for *her*, Nell realized. He escaped from prison and risked being caught to save her. She closed her eyes, as close to tears as she'd been after her trip to City Hall today. *Don't fall apart now. Keep your wits about you.*

Quietly Will said, "I think I understand now, Adam. I do. You're right, adultery is a sin. By your definition—"

"It's God's definition."

"By God's definition, I'm an adulterer, because I've had relations with married women. But I beg you to believe me when I say that Nell wasn't one of them."

"Enough!" Adam whipped a handkerchief out of his pocket as he strode toward Will, who thrashed furiously as it was stuffed in his mouth. Using the rest of his rope, Adam secured the gag. "I *told* you to stop lying to me."

Adam, looking weary, dropped into a leather chair facing the fireplace. He gazed into the low flames for several minutes before speaking. "Twelve years ago, when I started breaking out in sores, and I realized what my wife had done, what she'd turned me into, I agonized over how to deal with it. I tried to forgive her. For four years I tried. I'd sit for hours at a time in that damned box, steeped in mercury, sweating and weeping while I imagined my wife, my sweet little Clarissa, moaning in the arms of another man. It became unendurable. I turned to the Bible, looking for answers, for a path—and I found it. Finally it became clear to me the course God wanted me to follow, and I've been following it ever since."

"Your wife's boating accident . . ." Nell said.

He turned to look at her. "God's will. I was only his instrument."

"And Bridie and Virgil . . . ?"

"Yes, of course, and others in between—although I must confess, I almost weakened when it came to Virgil, but in the end I did what had to be done. My only regret was that I was naïve enough to think I could leave Harry's fate in the hands of the commonwealth. Oh, how he needed to dangle at the end of a noose."

He stood, sighed, walked over to the nightstand, lifted the bottle of morphine solution and shook it. "They'll find you in bed, naked," he told her, "with Will by your side, both of you dead from morphine overdoses. In case you were wondering."

"Adam . . ." Nell began.

"Shh." He held a finger to his mouth. "It's pointless now."

Nell met Will's anguished gaze across the room as Adam uncorked the vial of morphine powder, emptied it into the solution and shook it, thus greatly augmenting its potency.

"It's a fitting death," Adam said as he screwed a needle onto the syringe and filled it from the bottle. "It will be clear to all that you were brought down by your own sin. And, given the dose, it should be relatively quick. Respiratory and cardiac failure, isn't that right, Doctor?" he asked with a glance at Will. "Your lungs will simply shut down, then your heart, in short order. Not the best death, but not the worst. And then the world will know what you both are, which is only right and just."

He laid the full syringe on the nightstand and turned to Nell. His gaze crawled down the length of her. "You need to get out of those things."

She shrank back against the pillows as he sat on the edge of the bed, facing her. He pulled her pendant watch over her head and set it on the nightstand, then started unbuttoning the front of her dress. Across the room, Will writhed against his bindings, straining to get free.

Her dress undone, he spread it open to reveal her muslin corset cover. He paused, then retrieved a folding knife from inside his coat and opened it.

"Oh, God, don't," Nell pleaded as he sliced the left sleeve of her dress from shoulder to wrist, and then the right, scratching her in the process. He pulled off the dress, petticoat and crinoline in one unwieldy mass, then stood at the side of the bed looking down at her.

Despite her layers of underpinnings—shimmy, stays, corset cover, knee-length drawers, stockings and boots—she felt naked beneath his gaze. No man, except for Duncan and Dr. Greaves, had ever seen her in such a state of undress. And even they had never looked at her quite the way Adam was looking at her.

He sat down again, studying her as if trying to decide what to remove next. He fingered the ruffled frill at the hem of her drawers, stroked the lace that edged the neckline of her corset cover, then stilled, his hand resting over her breast.

Will thrashed frenziedly, his gag muffling his cries of rage and distress.

Nell squeezed her eyes shut. *God, help me to get out of this . . . Show me what to do . . .*

"You like to do this to men, don't you?" Adam said. "You like to incite their lust, make them forget themselves. Bridie was like that."

Nell pictured those awful bruises they'd found on Bridie, and shivered.

Adam stood, shucked off his coat and vest, shrugged off his braces, his gaze never leaving her.

"You can never get enough, your kind. You're always asking for it . . . begging for it. It's in your eyes, the way you move, the depraved thoughts you make us think, the things you make us do . . ."

I know your kind, Harry had said. *I know what you need.* She'd turned the tables on Harry. She could do the same to Adam. She could. *Think outside of yourself.* She just had to keep a grip, keep thinking . . .

"Not in front of Will—please," she begged. "Can't we go somewhere else?"

"You'd like that. You're clever. You'd find a way to get free." He shook his head as he popped open the top few buttons of his shirt. "We're staying right where we are. Although, if you prefer," he added with that dead smile of his, "I can dispatch Will now rather than later, so he doesn't have to watch. You see? I can be reasonable."

"How can you do this?" she asked, desperate to get through to him, to the good, rational man he must have been before syphilis and mercury poisoning ravaged his mind. "This is rape. You must know this is wrong."

"It's only rape if the woman doesn't want it, but your kind always wants it."

"No, Adam, you're—"

"Liar!" He slapped her across the face, reigniting the pain in her head. She cried out.

Will flailed and kicked, screaming through his gag.

"You lying bitch," Adam growled, "don't you dare try to play the innocent with me. And don't bother struggling," he said as he untucked his shirt, "because we both know what a farce that would be."

"At least . . . at least let me undress myself," Nell said, trying to dismiss the pain from her mind so that she could think. "You hurt me with that knife." She looked at the scratches on her arms. "Untie me so I can—"

"*Untie* you?" His laughter had a frantic edge. "Are you joking?"

"Just my hands, then, so I can get my clothes off."

He nodded as if working something out in his mind. "If you like. And I'll even close the bed curtains so Will doesn't have to watch. But in return, you have to cooperate—completely. At the first sign of resistance, I'll truss you up and open the curtains. And then, when it's time for Will to get his dose, I'll give him just enough to make it slow and agonizing. Otherwise it'll be almost instantaneous. It's your choice."

She looked toward Will, his eyes bleak and desperate as he continued to wrestle with his bonds, the couch creaking from his efforts.

"Close the curtains," she said.

Adam pulled the curtains shut, plunging them into semidarkness, released her hands, and sat on the bed to watch her undress. She plucked open the tiny shell buttons of her corset cover, thinking, *Be calm. Remove your mind from what's happening to you.*

She slipped off the corset cover, leaving her in her stays of quilted sateen over a cap-sleeved shimmy. The corset's front busk was secured by means of a row of hooks and loops. Nell allowed her hands to tremble just slightly as she fumbled with the top hook, shaking her head in a display of exasperation. "I can't . . . It's my hands, they won't . . ."

"Here." Leaning over her to see the tiny hooks in the dim light, Adam pried open first one, and then another, as Nell reached toward the nightstand. Slowly, quietly, so he wouldn't notice, she felt around until she came upon the syringe.

Adam popped open a third hook.

Nell grabbed the syringe with one hand, a fistful of his shirt with the other.

"Shit!" Adam seized her wrist just as she was about to jab the needle into his arm. "Bitch. You think you're pretty smart, don't you?"

She cried out as he gave her wrist a sharp twist, causing the syringe to drop from her hand. He grabbed it and aimed it at her own arm.

"I'm losing my patience with you," he said, his eyes like black buttons in the dark. "Perhaps what you need is a little of what's in here," he said with a nod at the syringe. "Just a little. Just enough to take the fight out of you."

She reached up, took hold of his little finger—the easiest to break, if you used a sideways motion—and yanked as hard as she could.

Bone snapped. Adam howled.

The syringe dropped into the mound of pillows and disappeared. He aimed a fist at her face; she rolled aside to avoid it, felt a sting as the needle pricked her, rolled away.

She slammed the heel of her hand into his nose; he roared. They grappled furiously. She punched and kicked, cursing the rope around her neck, which hindered her enough for him to swiftly gain the upper hand. He pinioned her body with his own and wrapped his hands around her throat, his grip surprisingly strong despite his broken finger.

He squeezed, pressing his thumbs into her trachea, his

fingernails biting into her flesh. Her lungs spasmed as she tried to draw a breath and found she couldn't. She tugged at his hands, beat on them, clawed them. He pressed harder, quivering with the effort, his face blood-flushed, a vein snaking through the burn scar on his forehead. "Whore," he rasped. "Adulteress. You asked for this."

From beyond the curtain came Will's stifled cries and the furious groaning and creaking of wood as he strove to free himself. Nell's heart pounded; her head pounded; her vision grew murky.

"I can't tell you how it excites me to see the panic in your eyes," Adam panted, "to see you turn blue and gasp for air . . ."

The trick is in transcending your body's panic reflex, rising above it.

Rise above it . . .

It was like floating, like rising out of her body and hovering over the two of them, locked in a fight to the death within this curtained-off bower.

Something glinted in the dark, an almost imperceptible spark of light.

Was it real, or just a fancy of her oxygen-starved brain? Struggling to keep her wits as her lungs burned and heaved, she looked to where she'd seen the spark.

Nothing.

But there *was* something there, hidden among the pillows right in that spot. She knew it. She'd felt it only moments before.

Nell hooked a leg around Adam, grabbed him by the hair. Summoning all of her remaining strength in one great burst, she rolled him faceup onto the spot where the syringe was lodged between two pillows. He flinched and swore rawly as the needle pierced his back, but he kept his grip on her neck.

She pressed her hands to his chest and pushed as hard as she could to force the plunger in.

He grimaced, stilled, looked up at her with an expression of surprise. His hands dropped from her neck.

His back arched; his eyes rolled up. He jerked as if yanked by a string, mouth wide open as if begging for air.

That part of it lasted mere seconds. He stopped struggling and met Nell's gaze, his expression slightly confused, his eyes as sweetly soulful as the first time she'd seen him.

Those eyes lost their focus as the air sighed from his lungs. He went utterly lax, his complexion taking on the waxy pallor of death almost instantly, a phenomenon she'd seen before.

He hadn't made a sound from the moment the morphine entered his bloodstream.

Nell checked his carotid; nothing, of course.

The air left her own lungs. "Jesus," she whispered, and crossed herself. "Thank you."

She untied the rope from around her neck with palsied hands, becoming aware as she did of dull thumping sounds from the direction of the couch, along with muted grunts of effort from Will. He had no idea what had just transpired. He would have heard Adam gloating as he throttled her, then the sounds of a struggle. Did he think she was dead?

There came an explosive splintering of wood as she threw open the bed curtain and stepped out into the room.

Will, still wearing his gag, looked up from trying to free his bloodied hands from their ropes—having already freed his feet by kicking that arm off the couch—and met Nell's gaze. He stared at her for one long, breathless moment, eyes wide, face sheened with sweat, then closed his eyes and slumped over, a ragged groan rising from his throat.

She went to him, not caring that she was in her underwear, her corset half undone, hair tangled down her back, bloodied and shivering like a rabbit. His folding lancet was on the table next to him, along with her gloves and hat. Using the lancet, she cut away his gag and the ropes that bound his hands.

"Nell, on God . . ." He wrapped her in his arms, pulled her onto the couch, held her so tight she could barely draw a breath. His eyes shone wetly; he was shaking from head to toe. "Thank God. Thank God . . ."

He buried his hands in her hair, rubbed his beard-roughened check against hers, both their faces damp with tears. It was quite some time before they drew apart.

Chapter 23

"HE had me completely hoodwinked," said Duncan, sitting across the visiting room table from Nell the following afternoon. His face was heavily bruised, his forehead marred by a dreadful, scabbed-over gash and livid contusions. The gag and straight waistcoat were gone, however, replaced by a striped prison uniform.

"Adam had us all hoodwinked," she replied. "Himself included."

"I never woulda told him all the stuff I told him, about you and me and what we used to do and all that . . ."

"I know."

"I thought he could maybe help me win you back. Give me advice, and all. That's why I got Virgil to find out where you were livin' and what your life was like. I thought after I got paroled, maybe you and me . . ."

She looked at her gloved hands on the table. "We've

gone on two different paths, Duncan. They don't meet up."

He looked away, a muscle in his jaw flinching. "Yeah, well, it don't matter no more, anyway, 'cause I'm in for the full thirty now. Warden says I can kiss that hocus-pocus goodbye."

"You knew that when you broke out of here," she said. "You knew if you got caught it would ruin your chances for parole, but you did it anyway, for me. I . . . I can't believe you did that."

He shrugged his big shoulders. "I'm your husband, Nell. I'm supposed to take care of you. And I figure I owe it to you, after . . . you know."

She didn't know what to say to that.

"Look." He leaned forward on the table, imploring her with his eyes—those painfully beautiful eyes—to look at him. "I know we can't be together again, not for real. But in the eyes of the Church, and in my eyes, we're still man and wife. Nothing can ever change that."

How could she argue with that? "Thank you, Duncan, for what you did. It was a very great sacrifice."

He shook his head. "What an ass I am. I never shoulda told Father Beals all that, about Virgil and that Bridie girl, and that farm, and you and Harry Hewitt—"

"You know he and I aren't really . . ."

"Yeah, I know that now. But Virgil and that girl are dead, and they wouldn't be if I'd of been able to see through that loony priest. And then, after you left that day, the things he was sayin' to me . . . like how you'd get your comeuppance real soon, and Harry Hewitt, too. He said I'd be free of you once and for all. He said you'd come to a bad end, just like Bridie and Virgil, which didn't make no sense to me, 'cause I didn't know at the time that they were already . . ." He trailed off, shaking his head. "Poor ol' Virgil."

"That was enough for you to break out of here and try to save me?" she asked.

"Nah, I started getting a funny feeling about things, and askin' questions he didn't want to answer. I think he started feelin' like he shouldn't of told me nothing. He said somethin' about how Harry Hewitt was gonna end up hanging, so I got to thinking maybe he knew something. Maybe he knew Hewitt was planning to do you in, 'cause he said I'd be free of you, and how else would I ever be free of you unless you died? It's a Catholic marriage. There ain't no divorce. And I'm thinking for some reason Father Beals knows what Hewitt's fixin' to do, but he ain't gonna stop it."

"You didn't suspect him?"

"Not at first, not really. He *is* a priest, you know. Was."

"Are you the one who beat up Harry Hewitt?"

Duncan whooped and slapped the table. "Damn, that was fun. Been eight long years since I'd bloodied my knuckles."

"Did you do it because you thought he and I . . . ?"

"Nah, I knew from talking to him there wasn't nothin' like that goin' on. But he told me what he tried with you, and you can't let a thing like that go by without drawin' a little blood. Not if it's your own wife."

Harry's account of that dram shop conversation, Nell reflected, had excluded some pertinent details. Either he really had been too woolly from absinthe to recall them, or he'd deliberately omitted them out of embarrassment.

"The more I thought about it," Duncan said, "the more I started thinking maybe it was Father Beals himself who was aimin' to do you in. Problem was, I couldn't hardly go to the cops, what with them on the lookout for me, so I tried to keep an eye on you—and keep an eye out for Beals."

"That's why you were at City Hall that night."

He nodded. "I hid behind a gatepost to watch you. When I saw you leavin' with Beals, I knew I had to stop it. Only I didn't count on that fella with those big fists on the end of them long arms."

"William Hewitt," she said. "Harry's brother. A much more worthy person."

Duncan studied her for a moment, hesitated, then said, "He's the other one, ain't he? The one you can talk to, the one you trust."

Thinking Duncan had earned the truth, Nell said, "Yes."

He looked down, nodded, ran his hand over his jaw. "Are you and him . . . ?"

"No."

He looked up, begging her with those translucent blue eyes to tell him the truth.

"No," she said. "I can't . . . I couldn't . . ."

"Because of me?" He looked hopeful.

"I *am* a married woman," she said carefully. "My employers may not know that, but I do. And as a governess, there are certain standards I'm expected to live by. If I were to enter into a . . . romantic relationship with a man, there could be no future in it, and I could never acknowledge it openly." Of course, that had been the case with Dr. Greaves, yet she'd been his willing mistress for four years. Was it really unthinkable that she might be coaxed down the same path again?

Eager to redirect the conversation, she said, "I've been talking to Warden Whitcomb. It turns out he sent Adam a note about your escape the day after it happened. Adam assumed you'd flee the country. That's what he would have wanted, because he knew you were on to him. But in case you *were* caught, he needed to plant the idea that you were violent, and a liar, and that you'd threatened to kill me. That way, no one would believe you if you told them what Adam himself was up to."

"Piscopal bastard," Duncan muttered.

"Naturally, he couldn't tell us you'd escaped," Nell said, "because then we'd try to find you, seeing as how you'd supposedly threatened me. But then Tuesday, when he found out I was being followed, he realized it must be you. So he told us about the escape the next day, as if he'd just heard about it, along with some tale about you spouting Leviticus and Deuteronomy."

"It was him that used to get all worked up about adultery and all that," Duncan said. "I ain't the guy he made me out to be."

"I know that. The warden told us you've never given him any real trouble."

"I gave you plenty, though. If it wasn't for me, Beals woulda never latched on to you."

"You made up for it," she said.

"You don't have to worry about any more letters from me. I'll leave you alone from now on, but don't ever think I've forgotten about you. It'll always give me comfort, knowing my darlin' Nell's still mine and mine alone."

WILL was waiting for her in the prison courtyard in his new black phaeton, purchased, along with a pair of fine horses, just that morning. She'd teased him about it's being the quintessential doctor's buggy, and wondered out loud what it meant that he'd chosen to own rather than rent his means of transportation in and around Boston. He'd just lit a cigarette and changed the subject.

"How did it go?" he asked her as he helped her up into the carriage.

"I felt more kindly disposed toward him than I have since we first met. He says he's going to leave me alone, but he also considers me very much his wife, for all time."

Will frowned as he gathered the reins.

"Are you ill?" she asked. "You look even worse than when you first picked me up."

"I didn't sleep well last night." He flicked the reins and drove the carriage through the front gate; with any luck, Nell would never have reason to come here again.

"So," he asked when they were on their way, "how old *were* you when you married him?"

He was taking up where they'd left off in the hack the night before last, pursuing the subject he hadn't wanted to pursue then, in the wake of the revelation of her marriage.

"I was sixteen," she said. "I've told you how we met, I think. My brother Jamie introduced us when I was still at the county poorhouse in Barnstable."

"Yes, I recall you telling me that."

"Duncan captivated me completely, right from the beginning. I'd never known a man like him. He was a firebrand, but with the most boyish smile. I knew he was just a small-time crook, like Jamie, but he told me he wanted to go straight, maybe build boats. He said he knew a shipbuilder in Wareham who'd hire him. Within a month, we were married."

Now for the rest of it. She drew in a breath, let it out. "He taught me how to pick pockets."

Will looked at her; she focused on the road ahead of them.

"I got good at it," she said. "I had to—Duncan didn't bring home that much from the jobs he pulled. I kept trying to get him to go to Wareham and talk to that shipbuilder. Finally he had enough of that, and he just exploded. It was the first time he hit me."

Will's hand tightened on the reins.

"Usually it happened when he was drunk, which got to be pretty often. He hated me picking pockets, even though he was the one who got me doing it, because I usually did it by bumping into men on the street. He didn't like the way they looked at me, the things they sometimes said. He'd start fuming if he saw any man talking to me, even one of our own friends. He didn't even like me being with the women we knew, because most of them were whores or as good as, and he thought they were a bad influence. He laid it all out—who I could talk to, when I had to be home, what I could wear, how I could act . . . Anything could set him off. He kept me so nervous I couldn't eat. I was thin as a rail that second year with him, and I usually had at least one bruise somewhere."

"Why didn't you leave him?"

How could she explain it? Even she didn't fully understand the person she was then, the person Duncan was. "He was always so contrite afterward. He said it wasn't really me, it was because he felt like less than a man, letting his wife essentially support him. Of course, by then I knew not to bring up the shipbuilding. He said he needed one big job, something with a really good haul."

"The jewelry shop."

"I only found out about it the next day, when the cops were on his tail and he was frantically hiding the loot. I asked him where the blood on his shirt had come from, and he told me what he'd done to Mr. Ripley. I told him we were through, which was a big mistake. I should have just slipped away quietly after the cops got him, because I knew they'd catch up to him sooner or later. Telling him then . . ." She shook her head. "He just snapped. Once he started in on me, I knew he didn't have it in him to hold back. I told him I was pregnant and I was afraid he'd hurt the baby. He thought I was just making it up to get him to stop."

Will turned to face her, hesitated a moment as it sank in. "You weren't?"

Nell tried to say, "No," but her throat contracted around the word. She swallowed. "No, I'd just found out. But he thought I was lying to him, and that made him even madder. He kicked me. He used a knife on me. He . . . forced himself on me. He wanted it to hurt, and it did. I don't know whether it was that, or being kicked in the stomach, but when I came to on the floor, he was gone—he was already in custody, as it turned out—and I was . . . I'd already started miscarrying."

Will rasped something under his breath.

"It was an incomplete miscarriage," she said, "but I didn't realize it til days later, and by then I was half-dead from infection. My landlady took me to Dr. Greaves. He . . . performed the necessary procedures, and with a great deal of skill. I'm not sure just any doctor could have saved me at that point. But I was left . . ." This was the worst part, that for which she would never forgive Duncan. "I won't ever be able to have children."

There came a weighty silence. "How can you be sure? These situations aren't always so cut and dried."

"I know. All Dr. Greaves told me at the time was that I *might* end up barren. But I must be, because . . ." She hesitated. "You know that I stayed with Dr. Greaves, and that we became . . ."

"Yes."

"We were intimate for three years, and I never conceived."

"Surely you . . . took precautions. He was a doctor. He must have known about the various devices."

"I wouldn't have anything to do with them."

"For religious reasons."

"Yes."

"You do realize the Church's rules were written not by God, but by men professing to speak for Him."

"It's the faith I was born into," she said, "the faith of my fathers. I'm not about to start picking and choosing which rules to apply to myself. You may scoff, but it became important to me, after . . . Duncan, and picking pockets and all that, to put my old life behind me. To let God—or God's representatives on earth—govern how I live, instead of someone like Duncan."

"Is it so important to be told how to live?" he asked. "Have you so little faith in your own judgment of things?"

"After marrying Duncan? Oh, yes."

"That's why Gracie is so important to you," he said. "Because you don't think you'll ever have any children of your own."

"In my mind, she *is* mine. If I were to lose her . . . well, I can't imagine it. I'd literally rather die."

He fell silent for a while. "It threw me, when I found out you were married, not just because . . . Well, mainly because you'd kept it from me. I think of us as being . . . Of you as being a confidante, someone with whom I needn't hold back. Knowing you'd withheld something so important . . ."

"I know. I'm sorry."

"Don't be. I was an ass. I was thinking of my own

bruised feelings, not of you and your . . . well, your *life*. As you say, Gracie is the only child you'll ever have. In a choice between jeopardizing that and telling me all, there was only one sensible option."

"I appreciate that, Will. Thank you."

They drove in silence for miles. Lulled into drowsiness by the motion of the carriage and the comfortable seat, Nell was almost asleep when Will said, "Couldn't you get an annulment?"

She looked at him. He kept his gaze on the road. He was dreadfully pallid.

"I petitioned the Church years ago," she said. "Dr. Greaves helped me. They wouldn't grant it."

"Divorce is utterly out of the question?"

"The only reason to do it would be to remarry, and if I did that, I'd be excommunicated. Anyway, your mother expects me to remain unmarried until Gracie is old enough not to need me about so much."

He sighed and wiped his damp forehead with a tremulous hand.

"Did you miss a dose of morphine?" she asked.

He hesitated, then said, "I haven't had any at all today."

She waited for him to explain.

"I should have been able to defend you yesterday," he said. "Instead, I lay there in an opium haze and left you to fend off a murderous madman by yourself. Of all the shameful things I've done in my life, that one ranks right up there at the top of the list."

"So you're . . . Are you giving it up altogether?"

"That's right. As of this morning."

Nell knew, from what he'd gone through last winter, that the most hellish aspects of his withdrawal would begin in a few hours. "Let me help you," she said. "Tomorrow's

Saturday. I'm free all day, and all night if you need me. And then Sunday, after church. Or perhaps I can even get Sunday morning off—your mother will understand. I can see you through the worst of it."

He shook his head. "I don't want you to see me like that, raving and vomiting . . ."

"I *have* seen you like that, Will—last winter."

"Yes, well, things have changed since then."

"Have they?"

"I should bloody well hope so."

It was almost midnight when Nell approached the desk clerk at the Revere House and asked for her key.

"Certainly, Mrs. Hewitt. Sleep well, then."

Sleep? If she'd been able to sleep, she wouldn't be here.

Unsurprisingly, there was no answer when she knocked on the door to Room 2*D*. She twisted the key in the lock, eased the door open.

The only light came from the fireplace. Will was curled up on top of his still-made bed in an open shirt and trousers, shuddering and sweating. He raised his head to look at her as she closed the door.

"Oh, Nell . . ." His head sank back onto the bed. "Why did you come?"

She fetched a bowl of water and a washcloth from the bathroom, set them on the nightstand, and sat on the edge of the bed. "There's something I've been meaning to tell you."

"What?" he asked.

She dipped the cloth in the water, wrung it out, and stroked it gently over his face. "I missed you, too."

KATE KINGSBURY

THE MANOR HOUSE MYSTERY SERIES

In WWII England, the quiet village of Sitting Marsh is faced with food rations and fear for loved ones. But Elizabeth Hartleigh Compton, lady of the Manor House, stubbornly insists that life must go on. Sitting Marsh residents depend on Elizabeth to make sure things go smoothly. Which means everything from sorting out gossip to solving the occasional murder.

A Bicycle Built for Murder
0-425-17856-0

Death is in the Air
0-425-18094-8

For Whom Death Tolls
0-425-18386-6

Dig Deep for Murder
0-425-18886-8

Paint by Murder
0-425-19490-6